CRAZY GIRL CHRONICLES:

A VANISHED HOPE

Asianna "Imani Fé" Joyce

This is a work of fiction. Although its form is that of an autobiography, it is not
one. Space and time have been rearranged to suit the convenience of the book,
and with the exception of public figures, any resemblance to persons living or
dead is coincidental. The opinions expressed are those of the characters and
should not be confused with the author's.

Positive You Transformation Enterprises Inc
633 W 5th Street, Floor 28, Suite 2844
Los Angeles, CA 90071

Ordering Information:

Quantity sales. Special discounts are available on quantity purchases by
corporations, associations, and others. For details, contact the publisher at the
address above.

Orders by U.S. trade bookstores and wholesalers. Please contact Positive You
Transformation Enterprises: Tel: (213) 223-2061; or visit
www.pytpublising.com; Email: info@pytglobal.com.

Event Information:

Positive You Transformation Enterprises Inc can bring authors to your live
event. For more information or to book an event, contact Positive You
Transformation Enterprises Inc at info@pytglobal.com, or visit our website at
www.pytpublishing.com.

Back cover artwork by Big Mama.

Manufactured in the United States of America | First Release: January 23, 2023

First Printing, January 2023. Revision, February 2023.

V1: ISBN: 979-8-9876485-0-6 (paperback) | ISBN: 979-8-9876485-1-3 (hardback)

V2: ISBN: 979-8-9876485-8-2 (paperback) | ISBN: 979-8-9876485-2-0 (eBook)

ISBN: 979-8-9876485-5-1 (hardback)

DEDICATION

I dedicate my book to my loved ones:

My beautiful mother who embodies strength and love like none other. My loving father who inspired me to do big things in a small world. My amazing mentor, Ms. Dana, who shows me how to expand my horizons. My beautiful grandmother, Grammy, who taught me about beauty and grace. My gorgeous great-grandmother, Mama, who teaches me to dance between the raindrops. My great-grandmother, Nana, who taught me elegance and class. My second dad, Hershey Bone, who always uplifts my spirit. My stepmom, Princess, who always showed me love. My brothers and sisters who are my constant motivators to keep going. My grandfather, Stoney, who shows me how to allow my heart time to grow strong. My cousin/big sister, Shy, who teaches me to cry with my head up. Nylah Wylah the Warrior Princess, who showed us angels do exist on earth. Uncle Jermaine who always has an ear to listen and a shoulder to lean on, never failing to encourage me. My grandparents, uncles, aunts, cousins (who are more like siblings), nephews, and nieces, who show unconditional love. My friends, who continue to inspire me. I value and love you all to the moon and back. There is no me without you.

To those who opened their homes and/or helped us during our homelessness - Grammy, Uncle Louie, Aunt Tonya, Aunt Tina, Aunt Earlene, Ms. Dana, Ms. V, Ms. J, Grandpa Leonard, Uncle Bobby, Aunt Michelle, the news station staff, and everyone else who gave a hand - thank you for being there for us during our time of need.

To Bishop, thank you for your spiritual guidance and leadership.

To my angels - DaddyO, Grammy, Nylah Wylah, Princess, Nana, Grandma Louella, Pru Little, Daddy, Big Damo, Laronda, Ms. Wyjean, Uncle Louie, and more - I love and miss you all so much… this is for you.

A Special Thanks to my mom, sisters, and Bree for encouraging me to get this book done. I love and appreciate you all so much. This is happening!

Best of all, all glory be to Heavenly Father who never once gave up on us and guided me on what to write in this novel. For an untold story cannot change the world.

God is GOD-ING!

Love,
Asia

Jesus looked at them and said, "With man this is impossible, but with God all things are possible." Matthew 19:26 (NIV)

TABLE OF CONTENTS

PROLOGUE

THERE IS A white space filled with a blinding light. A woman walks as water drenches from her curled and coiled hair. Her blood-stained white dress flows behind her, swiping against her sweaty skin. She rubs her eyes with her scarred wrists, attempting to glean past the white light. The sound of a childlike giggle fills the atmosphere. She turns, searching for the root of the laughter. Her face twisted and puzzled, she grows more confused and curious of whom else could be there.

This woman is me: Imani Fé Holley.

In pain from interior wounds now made manifest into exterior ones, I bear the pain of greater curiosity about who this could be. For I have yet to see their face. Therefore, I turn right around a 90-degree cornered hallway very similar to a maze. Picking up the pace - one, two, three, four - counting quicker and quicker as I walk, peeking around each bend. Corner after corner, turn after turn, I still cannot identify who is giggling.

As I turn around, a little girl - seems about seven-years-old - zooms by on a bicycle, missing my toes as she crosses in front of me. Taken aback by the sudden movement, I am turned around by the swift, forced air from the bicycle.

"Wee!" the little girl exclaims.

I turn, only to see the little girl's braid floating past the bend of the corner. Excited to catch up, I follow her for what feels like miles of adventure; finding joy in the childlike experience of run and hide. She stops past the angled wall. I approach her, slowing my heart rate at the thought of getting an answer. I swivel my body around the wall, hoping to get a closer look. She giggles and disappears into a room. The door closes behind her as her laughter echoes throughout the white space.

Filled with a mix of curiosity, excitement, and plain ole irritation, I rush toward the door, pressing my ear against its wooden barrier. There is no sound or laughter. I take a deep breath, pursuing to turn a supposed locked knob.

I knock twice. Nothing happens.

"Hello?" I ask.

I knock on the door again. The door creaks open.

"Hello?" I repeat, peeking around the cracked door.

I open the door, revealing a dark, dust-filled room that resembles an old psychiatrist's office. There is antique furniture, a patterned brown love seat with green stripes, and a desk and chair positioned in front of the only window. The door closes behind me as I walk through it. The little girl is gone.

I look under tables in search of her. As I get closer to the window, sunlight abruptly illuminates through a set of torn blinds and old wool curtains. Blinded by the light, I cover my eyes with my hand as the sun's rays shine on my arms, warming the scars on my wrist.

Silence lays upon the room, causing my thoughts to scatter, and provoking me to scare myself with my mind's own pondering. Still curious about the young girl, I realize I have not checked the desk chair yet. More hesitant than before, I approach the desk. The floor creaks as I tip-toe closer and closer to make sense of what lies behind it. I notice a woman with a high-bun hairstyle sitting facing the wall.

Clearing my throat, I ask, "Excuse me?"

Stopping a few inches from the desk, I stand there, awaiting an answer. The silence stiffens; so stiff that one could cut it with a knife. So, I take a deep breath, and then take two more steps toward the person: right foot, left foot. Still dripping with water and spotted with blood, I reach for a paper towel positioned in the center of the Traditional Mahogany desk. As I attempt to pick it up, I notice a charm bracelet lying behind the napkin. The charms hold pictures of my grandmother, Sylvia, as well as butterflies and roses. Puzzled by the unearthing, I decide to pick up the charm bracelet instead.

"You found it," says the woman in the chair.

I jump back, dropping the bracelet to the floor. The woman pivots in her chair to face me.

"You found the bracelet," says the woman.

At a loss for words, I stumble backwards, falling to my face.

"Do not run, Imani. You are destined for greatness," says the woman.

Still facing the floor, gasping for air, I look to the chair; only to find a mere silhouette of this mysterious woman.

"Who are you? How do you know my name?" I say, sitting up.

The woman gets out of her seat and walks toward me. My heart pounds faster and faster as I hear her heels click toward me. I can feel sweat building in the palms of my hands, and my face flush with warmth and fear. I scoot backwards, breathing harder and panicking, clutching onto the carpet underneath me. Swallowing air, I take a deep breath and debate the very thought of escaping. However, my paralyzed body will not allow any movement. As the woman leaves the shadows and steps into the sunlight, she reveals her face.

I gasp.

PART ONE

DANCING BETWEEN THE RAINDROPS

CHAPTER ONE
The Rose That Grew from Concrete

Sometimes it feels like I take three steps forward and seven steps backwards.
Ducking and weaving, trying to find a spot I can be dry in.
A spot where I am not drenched in this rain.
They say liquid nourishes the grains.
And yet I remain gasping for air, trying to keep my head in the game.
Back and forth I go, and then it stops…
Stops...
Stops...

My great-grandmother always tells me to dance between the raindrops.

THE MOST POWERFUL thing anyone can do is dream. Since about age seven, I have had a recurring dream where I am the star at a red-carpet event. It used to be filled with glitz and glam - lights, camera, action, sparkles - but has transformed into that of a nightmare. This night, the terror overshadows my bedside as I toss and turn on my deflated air mattress.

A white Cadillac Escalade Limo pulls up to the red carpet. The limo driver - a tall, tan male wearing a tuxedo and a top hat - gets out of the vehicle and opens the back passenger side door. I step out, oozing with confidence and basking in the bliss of a dream come true. Here I stand: an 18-year-old glamorous, beautiful, African American A-list actress. My five-feet-five-inches hourglass frame is sugar-coated with honey-caramel brown skin. I am that girl: feisty, intelligent, funny, talented, and somewhat crazy (in a "good" way).

The crowd goes wild!

I position my diamond studded shoes at the top of the red carpet, smiling at onlookers; camera ready and dressed to a tee: hair slicked back, a fur dangling around my neck, gorgeous pearls draping from my earlobes, and a long, silver, diamond-studded dress that accentuates my curves. I stand in the moment and walk down the red carpet, as gracious as a gazelle. A reporter along the sidelines catches my attention, so I walk toward him.

"Miss Fé, you are so gorgeous in your Lady Mayeline dress. Congratulations on all your success! How does it feel to star in such a revolutionary role?" says the reporter.

I smile. "It's always a blessing to -" I respond.

Interrupted by a helicopter light shining from above, I panic and look for safety. I place my hand in front of my eyes and run toward the nearest exit. Paparazzi continue taking pictures, causing more camera flashes from various directions. Overwhelmed, I run in the opposite direction of each flashing light.

Gunshots blaze. Unsure of where the bullets are coming from, I continue searching for an escape, getting lost in the sea of bright lights and squirming people. I run faster, bumping into people along the way. It seems the only one afraid is me. The gunshots become louder as the crowd grows steeper. Pushing people out of my way, I see someone chasing me. However, they vanish as I look back. I grab the bottom of my dress, sprinting across the carpet. I cannot see what is chasing me anymore.

In search for corners to cut, the exit grows farther away. I end up in the same place no matter what I do. The crowd grows steeper as the lights grow brighter, and gunshots louder and closer.

I trip and fall, ripping my evening gown and dragging my fur. Desperate and gasping for air, I attempt to get up and catch my breath. I collapse from my weakening legs, attempting to rise again. To escape, I struggle to push my body up with my wobbling arms, finding the strength to crawl; only going two steps before becoming feeble and falling to my frailty.

My vision becomes blurry as my surroundings spin around me. The people disappear. The once close and bothersome white light seems too far away to reach. I go in and out of consciousness. A dark silhouette stands over me.

"Fé!" I hear a voice yell.

I awake, looking around at my now empty surroundings. In a daze, I grow unconscious as a bright light reenters my vision.

Here we are in Washington, D.C.. The nation's capital, where most of my family and I were born and raised. To me, there is nothing like it: the rich culture, mambo sauce, Go-go music, and staple school trips to the free museums at the Smithsonian and National Mall. The place where one can see varieties of homes on the same street: some well-nurtured, the others abandoned. If I am being honest, I have not quite felt at home in my city as of late. Everything feels like it is changing - pushing us out instead of pulling us in.

"Fé!" my mother says, tugging my arm and shaking my body.

The sunlight peaks through the ripped curtains, shining into my eyes. I awake in my disheveled room: unkept walls, organized clutter, posters of Janet Jackson and Tupac Shakur (à la Poetic Justice) and an Oscar on the wall. As my mother awakens me, I can sense the worry in the air. There is something different about this morning - something just does not feel… right. Another sound drowns the usual noise outside of our home in Northeast D.C. out: the chaos happening within.

My mother, Beatrice Holley - a beautiful, curvy African American woman in her late 30s - shakes me, urging me to sit up. She has caramel brown skin, shoulder-length hair, and a graceful disposition.

She shoves me once more. "Fé! Wake up!" she says.

I sit up, breathing hard and sweating. Stuck between the world of a nightmare and what may be a living one, I realize the red carpet was just a dream; one I may prefer over what is to come. Still confused and a little disoriented, I rub my eyes and stretch my body.

"Huh?" I ask.

"Hurry and pack your things!" she says.

A US Marshall enters the room. He has bulging muscles with a presence of authority - and to top it off, a terrible attitude.

"Grab your most important items: social security card, birth certificate, purse, jewelry, etcetera, and get out!" he says.

I look at my mother, confused and still a little dazed. She swallows air, placing her head down as her face becomes flushed with red.

"I'm so sorry," she says before leaving the room.

The US Marshal has no sympathy. He gets closer to me, yelling and pointing for me to get up and pack my belongings.

"Hurry! Get your things and get outta here!" he says as he walks around the bedroom.

Still disoriented, I sit up, looking around the room for my bookbag. Five African American males from the neighborhood rush into the bedroom with a handful of black, 42-gallon contractor trash bags. They step over me, throwing every item in sight into a bag before leaving the room - making a beeline to the curb outside. While packing my important items, I grow angry and watch the guys. My identification documents, Holy Bible, and a few keepsake pieces fit into a small backpack. I then notice one guy putting my diamond necklace into his pocket. I stare at him, scrunching my nose.

"Put my things back!" I say, feeling the fire blaze from my eyes across the room.

He stares back, puffing his chest and clinching his jaw. Breathing harder, he gives in, throwing my necklace on the floor; the very necklace my Grammy gave me! *How dare he?*

Warmth overtakes my body as my mind fills with rage. I look at the necklace, then back at him.

Did he just throw my grandmother's necklace onto the floor?

I stand up, placing my shoulders back and my head up. I do not break eye contact as I walk toward him. He smirks, planting his feet on the floor, crushing my necklace. I slap him in the face.

"Have some manners!" I say.

The guy pushes me against the wall, throwing a jab. I dodge it, punching him in the face. He launches toward me while I grab everything in sight to defend myself. A second US Marshall - a Caucasian male in his 40s with a smaller, athletic build - rushes into the room and pushes him.

"I will arrest both of your ignorant behinds!" says the Marshall.

It is too late. I am already in war mode.

I hear nothing of what the Marshall is saying. All I can see is red - betrayal, hurt, pain, confusion.

How could this be happening to us?

"Keep your pet on its leash!" I scream.

My mom hears the chaos and rushes into the room, grabbing my right arm - yanking me toward the door.

"Let's go!" she says.

Yanking my arm back, I respond, "I'll stay. I've gotta keep an eye on these thieves."

My mom turns to me. "Grab your things… college girl," she says calmly.

That is just it! I graduated high school last week, and I am scheduled to attend a 4-year university in the fall; both are dreams I have pressed to accomplish. Yet here we are again: taking three steps forward and seven backwards.

Why this? Why now? Why… us?

My mom grabs my balled up fists and glides her fingers between them, bringing our coupled hands close to her heart. She looks into my eyes.

"You're the first to go to college. Don't let me stop you," she says, on the verge of tears while exuding strength and fear all at once.

Still angry from the fight, I stare at my mom with hard eyes, breathing harder and harder. I can feel anger exploding through my body and taking control of all my senses. I close my eyes, heart pounding, yet somehow grounded by my mother's soft, nurturing hands. Counting to ten, I open my eyes, noticing the tears falling down her cheeks. I take quick breaths, growing softer to my mother's care. My eyes soften.

My mother is right. We cannot let this stop us.

As my disposition eases, my shoulders fall limp. Though still angry, I back down, dragging my bookbag and following my mom out of the room.

We must be living a nightmare.

The movers place every item outside, emptying our home. Me and my family sit on the porch as they drop our belongings - clothes, food, the china cabinet, photo albums, furniture, electronics, and other keepsakes - on the curb - thrown into trash bags. My grandfather, Reno Hayworth (I call him Stoney), pulls up with a 26-foot U-Haul truck, parallel parking it along the front of our home. Stoney is brown skinned with a slim figure. He has the coolest salt and pepper beard with an even stripe of silver in the middle of black, and an even smoother swag and personality. Jumping out of the truck, he stares into our faces, losing himself in our worried eyes. Shaking it off, he hugs my mom and begins moving our items into the truck. Meanwhile, neighbors stand around and stare. Some laugh. Some do not.

It must get better than this.

Me and my siblings - Marcus Holley (age 13), Sabrina Holley (age 10), Jasmine Holley (age 9), Kayla Holley (age 6), and the twins Zoriana Holley and Quinn Holley (age 1) - sit on the porch with our heads down as my mom, grandfather, and my stepdad, Joe Brown, triple check everything is out of our home. We are all humiliated and ashamed. Our home, that was once filled with laughter, joy, and family bonding over meals and parties, is now empty of everything both tangible and sentimental.

How can a time of pleasure turn into one of pain?

Holding the twins on my lap and my bookbag in my hand, I glance around at the crowd of onlookers - growing angrier.

"What the f—k are y'all staring at?" I scream.

I become silent, clutching onto the twins, and gathering the top corners of my trash bag. My facial expression goes blank as I become numb to the movement happening around us. I daze into space, refusing to let any tears fall.

We must dance between the raindrops... just as my great-grandmother says.

CHAPTER TWO
Hope in Homelessness

IT IS MOVE-IN day at Bradford Kingsley University (abbreviated as BKU), one of the top universities in the nation. Emotions fill the atmosphere: ecstatic first-year students, family members afraid to let go, excitement, cheer, positive vibes; it is a joyous day. The campus has a city layout with apartment-style dorms surrounded by beautiful greenery. Filled with flowers, academic reminders, and anxious college students, the school's environment oozes with dreams come true.

We arrive at the campus in a gold 2009 Caravan, parking in front of my new dorm: Sturges Hall. I take a deep breath, looking through the window at a dream come true. Sliding the back door open, I step out, taking a long breath in. Then I remember sitting in my high school library for hours, looking at pictures and videos of BKU. I clutch onto my grandmother's necklace around my neck, smiling from ear-to-ear. A dream once plastered on my vision board has become a reality.

This is happening.

I shake it off, grabbing my bookbag and a trash bag filled with my items from the back seat. I release the seat lever on the second row, gaining access to the other bags piled up in the third row of the van. My mother comes around from the driver's side filled with joy and gratitude. She smiles as she proudly reads the sign.

"Bradford Kingsley University," she says, exhaling.

My father, Noah Jones Jr. (who I call DaddyO), comes from around the passenger side, joining me and my mom at the back of the van. DaddyO is a handsome African American male in his late 30s. His dimples, smile, and social skills deem him a charming man who can move around in any crowd. He hugs me, smiling.

"Daddy is so proud of you, Mu Baby," he says, alluding to my childhood nickname, Mumu.

"Yes! My baby has a full ride to the Bradford Kingsley University. I could only dream," my mom says.

Tears stroll down her now warmer cheeks. She pulls me in, wrapping her arms around me. Her smile is as wide as the ocean. She kisses me on my cheek. My father joins in, also wrapping his arms around me. A moment that was joyous has become one of mixed emotions. I clutch onto my trash bag when the flashbacks begin:

My family being evicted from our home.
Our items stacked inside of a storage room.
Needing to buy new things for college.

I think of all the things that could go wrong. Will this be another moment of three steps forward and seven backwards? I cannot stop worrying about how long this pleasant moment will last. Overwhelmed, I force a smile and bury my head into my parents' embrace.

I am truly grateful.

We arrive at my dorm room on the second level of the five-story building. I stand there in shock with the key in my right hand. Noticing my stagnation, my mom grabs the key from me, unlocking and opening the door. We see a traditional dorm room with a small refrigerator, microwave, and two twin-sized beds - just as I have always imagined.

I look around the room, observing every nook and cranny. It has traditional wooden bed frames and matching dressers, outdated floor tile, and a simple bathroom in the left corner of the room. Someone has decorated the right side - a bedding set draped over the bed, as well as items placed on the dresser, nightstand, and study desk. My parents check out the closet space while I drop my bag beside the empty bed, wiping my hands across it, then plopping down.

In walks my cheerful new roommate - a Caucasian girl with brown curls and plenty of energy, about eighteen-years-old. She seems to have a good head on her shoulders.

"Wow! You have trash already?" she asks.

I look down at my construction-sized black trash bag filled with my clothing, then look away in shame. My mom rubs my back, then turns to acknowledge her with a big smile.

"Hi," says my mom, reaching her hand out. They shake hands.

She continues, "I'm Ms. Holley, Imani's mom. You must be Amanda?"

Amanda smiles from ear to ear.

"Yes! Amanda Kingsley. It's nice to meet you, Ms. Holley!" she says.

DaddyO, who is unpacking and organizing my belongings, overhears Amanda's introduction.

"Kingsley? May I ask if you are connected to the university?" he asks.

He continues, "Oh, my apologies! I am Imani's father, Noah Jones." He extends his hand.

Amanda shakes hands while chuckling, "Good catch! Yes, the co-founder, Henry Kingsley, is my great-great-grandfather. He and Joseph Bradford started the university together. Mr. Bradford implemented the development, which is why his name appears first in the school's name - Bradford Kingsley University. My great-great-grandfather did not appreciate it since it was his idea - but, hey! Here we are!" she chuckles, snorting a little.

We stare at her, confused about what she has babbled.

She continues, "Sorry, I can be quite a talker sometimes, which is why I am studying law."

"So, I see," I whisper to myself. My mom, with her usual bionic hearing, elbows me to hush.

"Oh?" says DaddyO, smiling and looking at me, patting my back.

"So is my daughter!" he continues.

My dad has this tendency to push me into social situations. The irony? It is always during moments where I could not care less about speaking. I sigh, looking away, eager for this exchange to end. Amanda extends her hand.

"Oh great! That must be why we're roomies! It's nice to meet you, Imani!" she says, still holding her hand out.

I give her a blank look - pouting my face. Awkwardness fills the air. My mom laughs away the discomfort.

"Please excuse her, she's a little under the weather today. I'm sure she'll be as chipper as a chipmunk later!" says my mom.

Amanda smiles, "Oh, I'm sure of it!"

I give a slighted smile, placing my hands in my pockets, pivoting from side-to-side. Amanda waves.

"No problem! I'm going to grab a bite to eat. Let's chat later?" she asks.

We smile and nod at one another as confirmation. I wipe the forced smile from my face as Amanda leaves the room, turning to unpack my bags. My mom taps me.

"I'm so proud of you, My Gorgeous One," she says, rubbing my back.

I stare blankly, confused about why this moment is not all I have dreamt it to be. I sift through any negative emotions to find the highlight: I made it here! This is a dream come true, and no eviction, trash bag or anything else can stop me from enjoying this accomplishment. I am determined to show God my gratitude for His blessings. Yet, I am having trouble displaying my happiness.

My mom lifts my chin, staring into my eyes.

"Don't let anyone or anything steal your shine," says my mom. She grabs my hand. "Not even me."

I stare into her eyes, at a loss for words. Deciding to lighten the moment, I chuckle.

"Did you really say, 'chipper as a chipmunk'?" I joke.

We all burst into laughter. My mom laughs, then grabs both of my arms, pulling me in for a hug.

"I mean it, Fé. You are meant to be great," she says.

She releases the hug, extending her arms out to give me eye contact. "Shine, Gorg! Shine!"

I smile. She kisses my forehead and embraces me again, rubbing my back. The beauty of this moment is unparalleled. Yes! It is possible for a girl like me to attend the college of my dreams. Yes! It is possible to defy statistics.

Yes! There is hope in homelessness.

"I'm proud of you Mu Baby," my dad adds. "Daddy's baby girl is doing big things…"

"In a small world," my mom and I say, completing his usual catchphrase.

We laugh and roll our eyes. He lands a big, juicy kiss on my cheek as he and my mom embrace me.

"We love you and are so proud of you," says my mom.

Allowing myself to hang limp, I take a moment to melt in their hug; soon wrapping my arms around my parents. They kiss my cheeks as their love dissolves my fears. I disappear into their embrace with a single tear strolling from my eye.

I can do this. We can do this… together.

The first class of my freshman year is 'Introduction to US Law'. I am wearing a decent pair of black slacks with a tighter button-up shirt. I stop by the entrance to fix my now exposed undershirt; only to discover a button has somehow popped off during my walk to class. I understand I need new clothes; however, have I had this shirt that long? It has only been three years since I purchased it. I place my hand over the gap, praying that no one notices the atrocious outfit I have on. What is a girl to do? Locating a spot from a distance, I run to the only available seat in the second row. As I adjust in my chair, I look around at my new classmates. A Caucasian student sitting next to me pulls out a brand-new MacBook Pro, causing me to look around, noticing that most students also have laptops. I pull out my worn notebook and pen.

A student sitting next to me - a Caucasian woman with a slim physique and blonde hair - glances over with a smirk.

"Nice notebook," she says, turning to type on her laptop.

I look her up and down, noticing her chipped front tooth.

"Thanks, nice teeth," I say, smiling big.

The girl rolls her eyes and toots her nose upwards, typing faster and harder than before. She reminds me that no one will stop me from being proud. I made it to college with a full ride; I don't have a laptop yet. Who cares? I will just have to add it to my goal list. Proud of myself, I open my 5-Subject spiraled notebook with wide ruled paper, flipping to a blank page. Smiling from ear to ear, I breathe deeply. Clicking my pen open, I write at the top page, 'Imani Holley… Introduction to US Law'. I sit up straighter in my seat, aligning my shoulders and lifting my head. I will take up as much space as possible.

No one can stop me now.

The classroom comprises with majority Caucasian students

and a trickle of diversity. Despite being one of the few minorities, I am certain I belong. I earned my place just like anyone else sitting around me. Smiling, I inhale - holding it for three seconds - then I exhale; taking in the moment's gratitude, releasing all tension. My dream has finally come true.

I am a first-generation college student!

A fine guy stares at me from across the room as class starts. I lose focus while admiring his chiseled face structure and toasted lighter-skin tone. He has a crisp goatee and hair like the ocean's tides. Why is this man so… beautiful? I go into a trance, staring at each blink. He glances back and forth at me, exchanging looks - somehow, I do not care that he notices me checking him out too. He smiles at me, exposing his almost-lethal gorgeous smile. Goodness, how is this man so fine? My cheeks turn red and become warmer than the sun on a hot summer's day. I tuck my hair behind my ear, smiling, and then turn to focus my attention on preparing for class. He smirks, pulling his laptop from his bag, hiding the redness all over his cheeks.

This experience feels surreal.

Class ends and students disperse through the two double-doors at the back of the classroom. I grab my belongings, heading toward the door. As I exit, I bump into the fine-specimen-of-a-human, spilling my papers everywhere.

"Oh… wow, I am so sorry," he says with a smirk on his face, picking my papers up and handing them to me.

"Really? The cliché accidental bump?" I say, rolling my eyes.

He laughs, turning his head and blushing. "A brother has to try, right?" he clears his throat.

"I guess…" I joke back.

Laughing and shaking my head, I hope he does not notice how red my face has become. As his almond-shaped eyes rest upon my image, I feel a sensation of goosebumps all over my body. Time freezes for a few seconds and the room seems to go empty - with no one there except for us two. The classroom door slams, causing me to snap back into reality. I motion my hands to cue him to get to whatever point he wants to make. He rubs his face and laughs.

"My bad. I'm Damari," he extends his hand.

"Damari…" I respond.

"Jackson…. Damari Jackson," he says, gesturing a bow.

Damari, a freshman, is a pretty boy jock with a tough side. Though one of the smartest and charming people in the school, he has a past he tries to escape.

"Hi, Mr. Jackson," I say, extending a hand and smiling, "I'm Imani… Imani Holley."

We shake hands, blushing.

He clears his throat. "It's nice to meet you, Ms. Holley."

He grabs my right hand and bows before me. Tickled, I laugh and roll my eyes again.

"You are something else… you know that, right?" I respond.

"I guess that's a good thing?" he smiles.

"Yeah. I guess you can see it that way," I smile.

We continue talking as we walk through campus. It feels like I have known him forever - a feeling I have not experienced since, well, my ex, Mike. Even then, I have never felt a chemistry so strong, and I have never felt so safe with anyone as I do now. As we approach the clock in the middle of the courtyard, we realize over an hour has passed. How does he make me feel so comfortable, so fast?

"Where are you headed to next?" he asks, adjusting his backpack on his shoulder.

"My next class isn't for another hour, so I'm going to head to the Financial Aid office to take care of a few things," I answer.

"Oh cool. Well, my next class is in about thirty minutes. Would you like me to head over with you?" he asks.

I smile, "No, I'll be fine. Thank you for offering, though. I appreciate it."

"Is everything okay?" he asks, touching my arm.

I giggle, tucking my hair behind my ear. "Yeah, yeah, everything is fine. I just - I just gotta handle some business… you know?"

He chuckles a little, sighing, "Yeah, I know how it is."

I nod in agreement, fiddling with my shoulder bag.

"Well, Ms. Holley," he says.

"Oh my gosh, call me Imani! Please and thank you," I joke.

He laughs, "Alright, Imani… how about I take your number? Maybe we can study together sometime tonight or tomorrow?"

"Yes, to my number. I'll let you know about the studying part. I'm a busy woman, you know?" I say, saving my number in his phone.

"Yeah… I get it. I like that, though," he says, looking me up and down.

Trying to be cute, I do my signature sexy turn while walking away - only to trip on an invisible object. Seriously, why am I so clumsy? I look back at him, making sure he did not notice. He has this sexy grin on his face, so I can only assume he is doing the polite thing by keeping his laughter to himself. What a gentleman. Did I mention he is fine? Goodness.

"I'll see you later," he says.

I look over my shoulder as we smile and wave at each other. He takes a deep breath, squinting his eyes as he watches me walk away.

I arrive at the Office of Student Aid. Grabbing a scholarship verification form from the lobby, I walk over to an available table to complete it. As I scan the form, I notice the "Address" line. I tap my pen on the desk, debating on which relative's address to add: Should I put my grandmother's address, which is where we have been staying since the eviction? There are so many people in the house, it could get lost. Or should I list my dad's address, with the risk of important documents going missing? Overwhelmed, I sigh and toss the paper into my shoulder bag, heading toward my dorm room.

I see a group of girls in the quad as I walk through campus. As I admire them from a distance, I cannot help but fantasize about joining their sorority. I tap my school ID on the access reader, smiling and wandering into space. No one has exposed me to the college lifestyle, so everything feels new. I wonder what it is like to join their sisterhood.

I will just add it to my goal list.

Entering my room, I toss my bag onto the arm of my desk chair, finding joy in kicking my shoes off. I need to finish unpacking, so I do one bag at a time. Blasting music, I organize my room the way I see fit by fixing the bedding set, hanging my Poetic Justice poster on the wall, and lastly, placing my Bible under the pillow; a tradition my late paternal grandmother, Lucy, passed down. I plop down onto my bed and clutch my necklace when flashbacks begin.

The guy throwing my grandmother's necklace.
People laughing at us during the eviction.
The woman judging my worn notebook.
Struggling to purchase supplies for college.

Tears trickle down my face as I fall onto the bed in fetal position.

There must be hope in homelessness.
There must be a way.
To make it out of this storm,
To see a better day.
I must make it through this,
And help to define a better path.

Lord, help me break generational curses.
Help us be prosperous, at last.
Lord, we are trying.
We're trying to believe in Your bigger plan.
We need your help.
Just please, please… take our hand.

And so, the rollercoaster begins.

CHAPTER THREE
Don't Roll, You Might Get Dirty

THREE YEARS LATER

TO WHOM MUCH is given, much is required. College has
been challenging but rewarding. Three years ago, I hated waking
up and being exposed to challenges. Now, I am prepared to take
on the day. I am a junior who is on the leadership board of my
sorority, Gamma Alpha Gamma, and I have a campus television
show, amongst other things. I am studying pre-law, but my
genuine passion is for media. Therefore, my television show is
my way of merging the two by having legal topics on a media
platform. I am almost twenty-one, so I have blossomed much
more in life: curvier curves, stronger ambition, more sass, and
more determination. My family has not found a home yet, but we
will not stop believing.

I decorated my dorm room with pink, sorority letters and
paddles, and *Poetic Justice* posters. Above my bed is a vision board
with pictures of an Oscar award and Oprah, as well as multiple
certificates and trophies. I fix my queen-sized bed (two twin beds
pushed together), shifting the Holy Bible under my pillow.
Dancing toward the mirror, I add the finishing touches on my
wardrobe.

I sing aloud, placing the cap on my lipstick and puckering my
lips toward my reflection. Looking in the mirror, I take a deep
breath, inhaling, then exhaling.

"Imani… you got this!" I say to myself.

Today is a big day, so it is mandatory that I show off a little (okay, maybe a lot): dark denim jeans with a mauve pink blazer jacket tucked, matching pumps, and my favorite YSL pendant, which Damari gave me as a gift. I accessorize with a clutch, dangling earrings and a good nude lip. All of which coordinates with my leather laptop bag. My makeup is a light foundation with a good brow and a slight contour. My hair is curled under, falling below my shoulders.

The beauty of writing down goals is that it makes them more concrete. I have pushed until I achieved everything on my goal list so far: a laptop, a better wardrobe, more resiliency, and a more active role on campus. Saving up from campus jobs, internships, and other jobs earned me most of my money.

I am proud of myself.

I look in the mirror one last time, twirling and checking out my grown-woman curves. Feeling myself, I fluff my hair and strut out of the door.

Life is about getting back up.

We are on the set of my campus television show, *Defying the Odds*. Today's segment surrounds the Black Student Union, so there are a range of panel members. I sit center of a six-person panel whereas my two best friends sit at both sides with Damari (now 21) on my left and Claudia on my right. Claudia Johnson, also a junior, is an average-sized 20-year-old who is very outgoing and can be prissy. Her chocolate-kissed skin attracts most eyes. There are three other guests from the Black Student Union executory board sitting with us. We filled the studio with about thirty students, which is the max capacity for the small set. Damari pivots toward the audience, continuing the conversation.

"We need to raise our voice for the voiceless, stand for the weak and continue to educate ourselves. It is imperative that we expand our horizon," he says.

Claudia adds on, "Yes. We have a responsibility to make this world a greater place. We will never accomplish our goals if we continue to rely on others to take a stand for us."

The audience applauds. I look at the camera. "Well, there you have it. In the words of James Baldwin, 'Not everything that is faced can be changed, but nothing can be changed until it is faced.'"

The audience applauds.

I continue, "A special thanks to the Black Student Union for joining us today. Thank you for watching *Defying the Odds: The Black Student Union Special.* I am your host, Imani Fé, and I look forward to conquering with you."

I give my signature smile as the audience gives a standing ovation. The cameraman signals a wrap and the crew powers down equipment. We all break - shaking hands and mingling as we disperse. My other best friend, Chante Allen, approaches us. Chante is an almost-20-year-old woman with brown skin, curves, and misunderstood ways.

"Girl, your baby hairs are everything!" she says to me.

"You know I gotta stay on point!" I say. We do a dance, laughing.

"Great show, Fé!" Damari says, hugging me.

"Thanks D," I blush.

He blushes back, "No. Thank you for having me."

Chante and Claudia both roll their eyes, nudging each other and shaking their heads. Noticing this, I roll my eyes.

"How could I not have my besties on the show?" I say, "C'mon, bring it in!" I pull them in for a cheesy group hug.

"Squad goals," Damari jokes. We all laugh.

Claudia turns to Chante. "Hey Tay, don't you have a routine tonight?"

Chante gives her the side eye. Damari nudges her.

"Yeah, Lady Chocolate," he teases.

She rolls her eyes, grinning, "first of all… it's Chocolate Thunder. You know what? Screw y'all!"

I chuckle. "You know we love you, girl. Exotic dancing and all."

I squeeze Chante's shoulders. She tightens up, brushing us off with a smile.

"This tuition doesn't pay itself, chile," Chante responds.

"Yeah," I add, dazing off into space:

We sit and watch as they drop our things off on the curb.

"Fé?" says Damari, causing me to snap back into reality.

He continues, "she's asking for a picture."

In front of me stands an excited young woman named Melissa. She is a sophomore with a weird fashion sense.

Melissa cheeses big, "Hi Imani! I'm Melissa. I really love you! Your show… your efforts… may I have a picture with you?"

"Sure, gorgeous!" I answer with a huge smile on my face.

Damari takes the picture. Melissa hugs me before skipping off in excitement.

"She's so sweet," I say, smiling at Melissa as she skips off.

"You have fans already," Damari teases.

He blushes and puts his head down, giving me one of those stares that only we can understand. I blush uncontrollably. I am not too sure how we can remain friends when our chemistry is so strong. All I know is I cannot grasp the thought of losing him. I would assume he feels the same. In fact, I know he does.

Claudia interrupts, "Just get together already!" She shakes her head.

We blush even more; this time, it becomes harder to hide how we are feeling inside. Have we gotten to where everyone else notices, too? I mean, sure, people have speculated since our freshman year, but I feel we have done a great job at hiding our… well… love for one another.

Shaking it off, we turn our heads and move on to other topics. Damari steps aside to catch up with a classmate while Chante comes closer to me, whispering.

"I haven't forgotten about you. This weekend, I am working at a party. I'll text you the info if you're interested," she says.

Forgetting what she is referring to, I look at her, confused. Then I remember, I am behind on helping my family with a bill. My phone buzzes in my pocket.

"I gotta go. Love y'all," I say.

I hug everyone and rush out of the room. Damari follows behind me.

My family is celebrating the twins' fourth birthday at my grandparents, Stoney and Grammy's, home in Northeast D.C.: music blasting, fingers snapping, feet stomping, grilling, laughter, and a genuine good time. It is a five-bedroom, two-level home filled with mirrors, nice furniture, and my grandmother's artwork painted onto the walls. Because of the added basement and spacious backyard, it is the spot for our family get-togethers.

Wherever my grandmother is, is a place of comfort and joy; she is the rock of the family. In fact, many of us live with her and Stoney, including us and my cousins: Keisha, Tracy, Tony, Mindy, Walter, and occasionally Fabo.

Grammy, named Sylvia Hayworth, is a gorgeous African American woman with a lighter complexion, beautiful brown eyes, and a calm demeanor. Though her dream is to be a truck driver, she has stuck with her love of art: sewing, hair, painting, crafting and more. She is talented in every way possible and has the classiest of diva tendencies. Humming a song in the kitchen, she relaxes while cooking candied yams and tending to her fried chicken, greens, macaroni and cheese, and potato salad. She is wearing a white button-up shirt with casual yellow slacks, her shirt peeping her eight-inch chest scar from a recent open-heart surgery. In walks my mom, who appears disheveled.

"Hi Mommy!" my mom says.

A huge smile spread across her face. She hugs and kisses Grammy on the cheek. Grammy smiles and places her hand on top of my mom's, leaning her cheek in for the kiss.

"Good afternoon, baby girl," she says.

My mom heads toward the refrigerator, grabbing a can of beer. Grammy shakes her head.

"Mm... What's cooking?" my mom asks.

She cracks open a cold fresh can of Bud Ice. Grammy stirs her yams, scooping a little onto the spoon.

"Want to taste?" she asks.

"Is that a question?" my mom says. She leans in to taste her mom's delicious, candied yams. "As delicious as usual," she says, licking her lips.

Grammy smiles, rinsing the spoon and getting back to her stove. "How's my college girl doing?" she asks.

My mom smiles from ear to ear. "She's doing great… honor roll and campus involvement, all while working and hosting a campus tv show. I don't know how she does it."

Grammy places her cooking spoon down, turning to her daughter. "You can too."

"I can what?" my mom asks.

"You can do all of that and more," she encourages while rubbing her arm.
She continues, "Just trust God."

Frustrated, my mom sits the can down on the kitchen counter.

"Come on, Ma! Why are you always coming down on me?" she says.

"I'm not. I'm just showing you a better route. Your children need you, Tricey," says Grammy.

My mom rolls her eyes and picks her beer up from the counter, goggling it down. Once finished, she leaves the empty can on the kitchen counter and exits with an attitude.

Grammy sighs, "the trash can is right here."

She throws the beer can away, shaking her head in disappointment. She rests her hand on the counter, deeply exhaling and closing her eyes.

Damari and I arrive at my grandparent's home, making it just in time for the party. My cousin Tony and his friends have lined about five cars at the front of the home. As we walk by, he grabs my hand. Tony is 24 years old with brown skin and a husky build; he wears a short haircut, and a simple wardrobe: white tee, jeans, and the newest sneakers. I stop to talk to him while Damari continues walking, heading to the backyard.

"You good, cuddy?" Tony asks.

"Yeah. I'm good, cuzzo. You good?" I respond.

"Yeah - Aye, let Unc know we ready. You know him… grilling and talking," he laughs.

"Aight, y'all be safe out here," I say, hugging him.

I give him a stern look, learning not to ask too many questions. In his normal chill fashion, he nods his head and smiles. I rub his back, hoping to pass any good energy his way; this triggers a memory:

Me and my cousins are all bunched onto one pullout sofa at my grandparent's home around Paradise. We pillow fight and jump up and down on the bed, taking turns falling onto the floor. My grandmother

*pops up from beneath the bed with a flashlight beneath her face. "Boo!"
she screams, with her eyes bulging. We all scream and scatter as she falls
out in laughter on the floor.*

I walk to the backyard where my relatives are all gathered. Family
members, both big and small, fill the space, dancing and enjoying
good conversation.

"Fé!" Grammy yells.

"Hi Grammy!" I say, hugging her.

We do our usual smooches, touching cheeks on both sides. I sit
next to her, catching up about school, family, and any other
updates. The advantage of going to college in my hometown is I
can visit when needed by taking Metro transportation. This,
however, can be a hinderance since I visit often. My grandmother
always reminds me to live my life and make the best of my college
experience. After much conversation, she grows tired. She must
be careful to not exert too much energy after her open-heart
surgery.

"Fé, do me a favor and take the food out of the oven. Sit it over
on the food table," she asks.

I help her to her room before taking the food outside. Placing
the aluminum trays down, I decide to spy on my family getting
down on the dance floor from afar. My cousin Keisha is gyrating
and hyping others to dance with her. Keisha is an attractive 23-
year-old with brown-skin and a taller build.

"Yesss Unc!" says Keisha.

She taps my dad on the shoulder as he busts his famous moves,
moving his shoulder side to side while spinning his wheelchair.
He used to do his notorious two-step, moving from side-to-side
while bouncing his shoulders up and down and side to side.
However, doctors amputated his right leg a couple of years ago
because of a staph infection. What I love most is he continues
living and thriving the best way he knows how. He is one of the
strongest people I know.

"Y'all youngin's don't know nothing about this!" he says,

grooving to the middle of the dance floor.

He sees my mom walk by and grabs her hand.

"Stop it, Noah!" she says, giggling.

They hand dance, laughing and switching up to the music. Keisha dances next to them.

"Aw, look at Auntie and Unc! Trying to get that old thing back. I'm telling!" she jokes.

My mom waves her off. "Keisha, we're both married. Don't nobody want Noah!"

My dad shakes his head and laughs.

"Is that so?" Keisha teases.

They brush her off and continue dancing. I head to the dance floor and show them how it is done. My parents separated when I was four years old but have remained good friends since. My stepmother, Paula, and my stepfather, Joe, join in for the fun. Paula is brown skinned with a curvier figure and a cute pixie haircut. She and my dad have been married for a decade. She is usually the loudest voice in the room, her personality beaming through her beautiful smile. Joe is about five-feet-eleven-inches with a chocolate skin tone; most say he favors K-Ci from Jodeci. He is a silly, chill person and one of the first to hit the dance floor. He and my mom have been married for about nine years.

Sliding away from the dance floor, I approach Damari and my uncle who are grilling food toward the back of the yard. Uncle Jimmy is my dad's younger brother. The two are especially close given their history of learning to survive and mature together. He is in his late 30s, with a caramel skin tone and thicker build. He wears a white tee, jeans, glasses, and a bald head to hide his ever-receding hairline.

"Oh goodness! Y'all betta not be talking bad about me!" I joke.

"Who? Me?" Damari says with a huge smile on his face.

"Both of you!" I respond, hugging my Uncle Jimmy.

We all laugh.

"Nah, Young Championette. I'm giving this pretty boy a lesson on this battle called life," Uncle Jimmy says in his usual comedic yet serious tone.

I smile, finding the perfect opportunity to throw Damari under the bus. Giving him a look, I turn to my uncle.

"So... Unc... did you whip out your Bible yet?" I tease, looking at Damari to gage his reaction.

"Good idea, young one," Uncle Jimmy says.

He places his grilling tongs on the table and wipes his hands on his jeans. Meanwhile, Damari gives me the "Why'd you have to say something?" face. I burst into laughter, trying to hide it once my uncle looks my way.

"Gotta stay sharp!" I tease.

"That's right, Championette. Stay sharp... put that fancy degree to use!" says Uncle Jimmy.

I attempt to hold in my laughter, but it is much too complicated. Damari uses the opportunity to try one of his jokes.

"I stay pointed," he says.

Silence and a lack-of-laughter fill the atmosphere. Damari chuckles while looking around for brownie points. Instead, Uncle Jimmy stares at him, shaking his head in utter displeasure. I palm my face, placing my other hand on Damari's shoulder.

"Pointed? You couldn't just say sharp?" I ask with my hand placed under my chin.

"I'm different," Damari says, straightening his jacket in his typical fashion.

All I can do is shake my head and laugh. How is he so

endearing, yet so cheesy? Either way, he is my best friend, and I would change nothing about him - not even his failed comedic attempts.

My uncle grabs Damari's shoulder, "that's right, Young Champion! You are different. Do you know the three keys to life?"

Damari counts on each finger, "Girls, Girls… and Girls."

"Boy! That's all you think about!" I say, joking, yet irritated.

"You know you're my rib, girl!" says Damari, blushing hard.

I burst into laughter. "Boy, you're always hungry!"

Uncle Jimmy chimes in, "Speaking of ribs, do you know God took one of -"

"Adam's ribs and made Eve," I say, completing his routine random fact.

Damari erupts in laughter. "Yes! We know, Unc!"

Uncle Jimmy smiles: he is so proud that we remembered. I look over the grill, noticing the pan of ribs on the table.

"About those ribs though… They betta not be too burnt," I add, salivating over the food.

"Young Championette! Burnt is the way to go. Matter of fact, this barbecue sauce is sweet - just like sweet melanin on an African Queen," he notates in his frequent dramatic form.

"Come on brotha! What about us light-skin folk?" Damari jokes.

I roll my eyes and shake my head, trying not to laugh.

"Y'all got melanin, too - just not as much as my sweet Nubian Queens. They ooze with melanin goodness and sweetness - just like the sweetness of barbecue sauce," says Uncle Jimmy.

He picks up a barbecue rib, eating it in our faces and licking the sauce from his fingertips. Damari and I laugh. I shake my head and pooch my lips - he is something else.

Uncle Jimmy pauses, shaking his head.

"They tried to mess up my meal, but I'm going to have some ribs before I go," he says, staring at us.

He takes off his glasses, wiping them on his shirt. He places them back on, then looks at me.

"It may be my last one," he says.

We stare at him, realizing what he was referring to. He rushes to the front of the house after grabbing a plate of ribs. All five cars screech off. I sigh.

"Not again," I say.

I look at Damari, who stares back at me, rubbing my shoulder.

It is now nighttime. Damari and the rest of the crowd have left for the night, including most of everyone that lives here. My grandfather and grandmother rest in the backroom as we continue celebrating outside. My mom, Joe, and I are sitting on the wooden benches in the backyard listening to music and enjoying the warm temperature. The two of them do their usual thing where they argue for minutes, then get back to regular conversation. Amused, I laugh and shake my head because I know it is nothing too serious. My little sister, Kayla, now nine years old, comes running from the house.

"Mommy! Hurry and come inside!" she urges.

We all rush inside. It feels like the worst night after a family celebration and good times go wrong. We get into a family dispute, whereas authorities are called - causing us to leave the home. Thankfully, Joe's sister, Aunt May, can pick us up so we will have a place to sleep tonight. My grandparents stayed steadfast asleep as my mother and us leave the home, packing what we could into the sedan car.

Seven of us are lapped on top of each other in the backseat of Aunt May's car. We stare out the window as we leave our grandparent's home. Drying tears and holding back anger and pain, we wipe our blurred vision to witness the transparency of family interacting as we peek through the car's foggy windows. Perplexed and hurt at the night's events, we sit quiet and stunned at a loss for words.

"How could they do this to us?" Jasmine says.

My mother looks over to Jasmine, now 12, rubbing her leg. She stares out of the window in anger, hurt, and pain. Her face balls as she shakes her head, wiping each tear that strolls down her face. Speechless, she grabs Jasmine's hand, squeezing it. The pain of tonight goes far beyond anything we have experienced yet. Filled with anger and rage, I cannot stop the tears from flowing down my eyes. Then I remember:

My mom enters the house with a box filled with her office items. She looks down as she places the box on the dining room table and walks toward her bedroom. I snoop in the box and notice a pink slip tucked inside.

I look over at my mom, whose spirit looks broken - she slouches over, leaned against the window. Anger and humiliation overwhelm me as thoughts scurry through my mind:

Where will we sleep?
What will we eat?
Will we all stay together?
How much longer will this struggle last?

My heart weeps more for my mother than for myself because I see how she tries to be good to everyone. Our home was once a haven for everyone - family, friends, and more. Why is she the one to suffer? She deserves much better than this. We all do.

We must push on.

Though disappointing, tonight has relit a fire like never before. I am more empowered than ever to break barriers and give my parents and siblings a better life. Perhaps they will follow a similar path in the future. Regardless, I am determined to blaze a fresh path so we will no longer be at the mercy of everyone but ourselves.

CHAPTER FOUR
Don't Let Anyone Put Their Junk in Your Trunk

SOMETIMES THE PAIN in defeat is not the loss, but the disappointment of a win unrealized; the disappointment that hope did not prevail. There is no happy ending to our journey thus far. The tides have swept us with its power, no matter our faith in its outcome.

My family and I drag black plastic trash bags into the motel parking lot. The kids look confused as they rub their eyes, figuring out where we are. It is a standard motel - a janky exterior with a sign that blinks, dulling a few of the letters. Aunt May and Joe drive off as we continue toward the main office.

"C'mon babies," my mom says, touching the twins' backs.

"They are not babies anymore," Marcus says.

"Yes, we are!" both Zoriana and Quinn respond.

Marcus, now 16, chases after them as they giggle and run around the parking lot. Kayla joins in for the fun while Jasmine and Sabrina, now 13, roll their eyes. It is amazing how kids can make the dullest of moments more interesting.

"Ugh! These kids are so annoying!" exclaims Jasmine.

"Stop all that noise," says my mom, hushing everyone.

We arrive at the lobby, where we drop our bags in the corner.

My mother and I stand in line at the front desk while my siblings plop on top of our clothing bags. I can see the stress flood her face as she negotiates payment. It costs about sixty-nine-dollars per night for a double occupancy room. She wipes her face as she stares blankly at all of us. I offer to help, but I am honestly not in a better financial situation myself. If only we could rise above this… above poverty; above homelessness; above the struggle.

My mom made a few phone calls to ask for help. Thankfully, Bishop S from my grandmother's church, and my grandfather Levi, offered to cover the motel expenses for a few days. They told us we could have two double-occupancy rooms for now, but afterwards we may need to share one room to save money.

The twins pounce on the beds as we enter the rooms. My stepfather stayed at his sister's place since it seemed easier that way - as the church only covers women and children. It is a basic motel - old-fashioned furniture, dusty appliances, and a bed that one may hesitate on jumping into. We do not have food or money, and there is no microwave or refrigerator. So, we have called on my great-grandmother, Mama, for help. We just need the basics; thankfully, Aunt May had given my mom a cooler, so it comes in handy for keeping the food cold. In addition, Mama has offered to go to the grocery store and bring food for us to eat.

This moment is bitter-sweet: God has blessed us with shelter and food to eat. Yet, how could we be staying in a motel when we have opened our home to so many? As we unpack our rooms and wait for Mama to arrive with groceries, I examine my mother - she has glossy eyes, yet still smiles and says endearing words to us. She does not cry. She does not complain. She just simply… exists. She exists as a mother, trying her best to take care of her children.

Then I remember when I was five years old. A little before the rest of my siblings came along, she would walk me to the library to read books. I was the only kid who knew how to count to one hundred, say my alphabets forwards and backwards, and spell my entire name - all by kindergarten. Not to mention her enrolling me into tutoring, extracurricular activities, and even getting me my amazing mentor, Pru. Oh, and the best times? Going to her office after school when she was an accountant at a nonprofit organization. My mother is simply… amazing. She has only hit a bad time in life that would impact anyone. I could not deny the beauty and warrior that is my mom - I am just trying to figure out where and how her light dimmed.

The phone rings. It is Mama! She arrives at the motel with Uncle Nick, pulling up in a late-model gold Nissan Maxima. My siblings and I jump for joy as we see their smiles peeking through the open windows. There is something about seeing them that makes my soul happy. My great-grandmother has been instrumental in my life and teaches me how to be a humble diva with a quick yet gracious tongue.

They stop in front of us, opening their doors for the usual hugs - my uncle on the driver's side, and my great-grandmother on the passenger.

"Hey, Missy Gorgeous!" says Mama, with the biggest and most beautiful smile.

I do not know how young she is, and I dare not ask! I tried asking a few times when I was younger, but all she ever said was, "A lady never tells her age". Either way, grace transcends her years. She stands about five-feet-one-inch with a nice shoulder-length style, a long black skirt with a matching shirt and shawl, a classy hat, red lipstick with the nails to match, and some cute heels. Did I mention she is a diva? Yes, she is that and more. Where else would we get it from?

She hands over bags of groceries while we chat. We have the essentials - a bag of ice, four loaves of bread, ham, cheese, milk, and water. We thank Mama and Uncle Nick for bringing us food; honestly, the ice seems to stand out the most. It is crazy how much we take simple things for granted - like a refrigerator to keep our food from perishing. After chatting for some time, we hug and say our usual "see you later's".

"Remember, Missy Gorgeous," Mama chuckles as she covers her mouth.

I crack up and shake my head, "don't say it!" I joke.

"Never let anyone put their..." she says, waiting for me to complete her statement.

"Junk in your trunk," I say, chuckling and beaming with embarrassment.

"That's right, Missy! Never let anyone put their junk in your trunk… and never forget it!" she laughs, tugging at my arm.

We both laugh as we hug and say our "I love you's". As much as her statement cracks me up, she is correct - I should let no one put their junk in my trunk. Meaning, I should allow no one to fill me with their negativity. I need to stay focused and remember why I am aiming to reach my goals. Little does she know, her words are right on time, per usual.

My siblings and I make it back to the motel room where my mother and the twins are waiting. The events that took place at my grandparent's house live rent-free in my head. I run to the bathroom, locking the door, and turning the light off. I put on my headphones, blasting "I'll Be There" by Tiffany Evans in my ears. Each lyric reminds me of the struggles my family and I are experiencing. I slide down to the floor, crying my eyes out. I do not understand why my family goes through so much pain, especially since we have remained steadfast in our faith.

"Never Let Anyone Put Their Junk in Your Trunk."

Mama's voice echoes through my head. I chuckle a little through the tears, sifting through the beauty of Tiffany's lyrics. We remain forever grateful for all who support us through our toughest times. My greatest goal is to succeed and give back everything they have so beautifully given to us.

I sit on the bathroom floor crying, somehow picturing a new reality. Then my siblings bang on the door in panic.

"Mani! Mani! Mommy needs help!" they yell.

I rush from the bathroom, heart pounding harder and harder with each step. I find my mother curled up on the floor as the kids attempt to assist her. Bending down, I try to comfort her as I look to see what is happening.

"Marcus, call the ambulance!" I yell, trying to keep tears back.

We all rush and panic as we come to our mother's rescue. One thing after another; will this rain ever stop?

Why now? Why ever? Why my mom? Why… us?

I stand there, attempting to escape reality:

I recall when I was 10 years old. I was lying on my mom's lap while she stroked my hair. Marcus, Sabrina, and Jasmine ran around the Christmas tree in laughter and joy. We filled the living room with cookies, milk, candy-stuffed stockings, holiday decorations, and an eight-foot-tall tree. The Christmas spirit rings throughout our home as our gratefulness for togetherness strengthens.

"Imani?" says my mentor Pru.

I snap out of my daydream, clasping onto my necklace while staring at my mom who is asleep on the hospital bed. My mentor, Prudence Jackson, better known as Pru, hugs me. Pru has been my mentor since I was six years old. She is a beautiful Caucasian woman with blonde hair and brown eyes. Never failing to have the sweetest demeanor, she is always inquisitive and helpful, and one of my favorite humans. I do not know where my life would be without her, as she is a true blessing to me. I want for nothing more than to make her proud.

"Please gather… let us pray," Uncle Jimmy says, motioning for everyone to grab hands.

Because of the severity, an ambulance took my mom to the District Hospital Center, in which they immediately assigned her a room and completed evaluations. Family gathers in a semicircle around my mom's hospital bed. My siblings join the prayer, worried about our mother's well-being. Grammy, DaddyO, Joe, my Aunt Eva, Damari, and a few of my cousins also connect hands. Aunt Eva is my mom's sister; she is a beautiful light-skinned woman with a curvier build. She is the mother of Keisha, Tracy, Tony, and some of my other cousins. I would spend nights at her home, hanging with my cousins when we were younger. It is a good feeling to have our family here.

Uncle Jimmy holds his Bible over top of my mom's chest and prays. Everyone bows their head to pray along. The nurse walks in behind us.

"Lord! You make the birds in the air go 'tweet, tweet', you put skin on my feet, feet," Uncle Jimmy prays.

Meanwhile, everyone chuckles, peeping at one another from one eye during the prayer.

"He's popping caps and scriptures, huh?" Damari whispers to me.

I chuckle, nudging him. "Shut up!" I whisper, closing my eyes and refocusing on the prayer.

Uncle Jimmy is still praying, "You raise me high, Lord! And protect me when I'm a lowdown dirty shame! Heal! Heal! Heal this Melanin Queen, Lord! Awaken her from her holy dream! Amen!"

"Amen," everyone says while chuckling at Uncle Jimmy.

The nurse steps up, changing the mood in the room.

"Hi. I'm Nurse Gathers. I'm assisting Ms. Holley," she says.

Checking my mom's vital signs, she records them on her clipboard. She is a woman with an average build and grey hair, looks to be in her mid-fifties.

"She fell asleep about twenty minutes ago. I am sure she has had a rough day, so let's allow her to get some rest," says Nurse Gathers.

"What's going on with her? What happened?" I ask, panicking.

"Allow me to grab Doctor Nayam so he can explain everything to you," she says.

I nod in agreement, "thank you."

The nurse nods and leaves the room. My family and I continue to comfort my mom as she sleeps, glancing at one another to ease the worry. Soon, Nurse Gathers returns with Dr. Nayam. He is about six-feet-two-inches and of Indian descent, with a slim, fit build and dark hair that is cut short. He has a great bedside manner and takes his expertise with pride.

"Hi, I'm Dr. Nayam," he says, shaking one hand at a time. "I am here to answer questions you all may have regarding Ms. Holley."

"Thank you, Doctor Nayam. I'm her oldest daughter, Imani, and I'm wondering what happened to my mother. One moment she was sitting there talking, the next she was almost paralyzed. We just want to know what is happening. Will she be okay?" I ask, holding back tears.

"First, it is a pleasure to meet you, Imani and family, although under extreme circumstance," he looks around to acknowledge everyone.

He continues, "Unfortunately, Ms. Holley suffered a stroke."

Everyone gasps. The room fills with concern.

"But how?" I ask, near tears.

"She has four aneurysms: two in her brain, two in her neck. One aneurysm in her brain leaked, causing her to have a stroke," explains Dr. Nayam.

"What's an aneurysm?" Jasmine asks.

Dr. Nayam turns to Jasmine, "Great question. An aneurysm occurs when there is a weakness in the artery, causing it to balloon and fill with blood. It is most caused by high blood pressure or also what is called atherosclerosis, amongst other culprits. In Ms. Holley's case, we believe the cause is high blood pressure."

Jasmine stares at him, confused. He smiles, then grabs a cord to show.

"So… imagine this cord is an artery, which is a type of blood vessel that transports oxygen-rich blood to your entire body," Jasmine nods. "Now, imagine it swells like this and fills with blood," he says, making a loop in the cord.

"But how does a stroke happen?" Marcus asks.

"Another brilliant question," he says, "one aneurysm in her brain leaked, causing her to have a stroke. Thankfully, it did not burst or else it would have been fatal."

"Oh my gosh," exclaims Marcus, placing his face in his hands.

"Is she going to be okay?" Sabrina asks, near tears.

"We hope so," Dr. Nayam says.

Sabrina cries. I comfort her. Marcus, Kayla, and Jasmine also cry. The adults comfort them. Grammy wipes her tears while holding Kayla in a tight embrace.

"What are the next steps?" asks Grammy.

"We will need to perform a procedure called a craniotomy, which is an open skull surgery to clamp the aneurysms in her brain. Since we can only operate on one side of the brain per procedure, we will perform a second surgery if we cannot clamp both aneurysms from one side. The hope is that we will go in from the right side, clamping the aneurysm closer to the left as well," Dr. Nayam explains.

"How about the two in her neck? Will you all clamp those as well?" Grammy inquires.

"The good news is we won't need to perform surgery on those because they pose no risks. However, she will need to be careful regarding her habits after the procedure," he responds.

"When is the surgery?" asks Joe.

"We are hoping to have her scheduled for the morning. We will have an update in just a few moments," he says.

"Thank you, Dr. Nayam," says Grammy.

The entire family thanks him as well.

"My pleasure. Let me know if you have questions. Nurse Gathers and I will be back to check on Ms. Holley. We will update you on the surgery time once confirmed," says Dr. Nayam.

We all nod. Joe and DaddyO shake the doctor's hand as he exits the room. Nurse Gathers studies my mom, then follows behind him.

"I just don't understand," I add, crying.

"I know, Fé. We don't have to," says Grammy, kissing my forehead.

Damari grabs and holds me. Nurse Gathers knocks on the door, getting everyone's attention.

"Hey family, letting you know visiting hours are almost up. It ends at 9 p.m., so you have about fifteen minutes remaining," says Nurse Gathers.

We acknowledge her, nodding. She smiles and walks away.

"I'm going to stay with her," I add, wiping tears.

"Okay, that's fine, Fé. We're going to head home so these kids can go to bed. Call us with updates," Grammy responds.

"Okay," I say.

Grammy smiles, wiping my face. "Smooches," she says.

We touch cheeks on each side before she walks off. Damari hugs me.

"Want me to stay with you?" he asks, hoping for a yes.

I smile, "That's okay, D. Get some sleep. We'll be okay."

He hesitates.

"Thank you though, I appreciate you," I continue.

"Okay… so… I'll see you tomorrow?" he asks.

I nod my head "yes", looking into his eyes to give reassurance. Still reluctant to leave, he grabs my hand.

"I love you… friend," he says.

"I love you more… friend," I say.

Uncle Jimmy approaches us with his normal sense of humor.

"Come on, Young Buck. She can fend for herself!" he says.

This lightens the mood. Everyone chuckles - hugging me and kissing my mother before exiting. Sabrina stops to check on me before turning away. Pru walks up to me, rubbing my back.

"Hey Sweetie," says Pru, smiling. She places one hand on my shoulder.

"Your mom is going to be okay. I want you to know your mentor is proud of you and is always here for you. You've worked so hard to get to where you are," she continues.

"Yet I remain chained to this place," I whisper, looking away and wiping tears.

"Oh, sweetie!" she says, hugging me.

She keeps a hand on each shoulder as she releases. She does her signature grin, letting me know an embarrassing story is coming. I smile back, presuming which story it will be.

"I remember when you were eight years old," Pru says, laughing. "You and T were the cutest little things with your little 'sprouts'!" She motions two ponytails with her fingers above both sides of her head.

We both laugh.

She continues, "you always spoke about graduating from college. Now look at you… you're one of the top leaders on campus at BKU!"

She is right. I am accomplishing my dreams, step-by-step: I

have stepped outside of my comfort zone on campus, aim to get good grades in school, and I also try to become more in life. Yet, it does not feel like enough. My family is struggling. Despite my best efforts, I am not able to help them. My smile fades.

"That's not enough," I say.

"Why not?" asks Pru.

"Because I have so much more to do," I say, fighting tears.

I continue, "Every night I lay my head on my pillow at a luxurious university; sharing the same opportunities as someone that makes three times more than all my family members combined… And while all of that is great, I live with the guilt of knowing my siblings are sleeping on the floor with no confidence of where they will be tomorrow. I proudly rock my BKU gear but do not have a solid address to put on applications. It's like a dream that disappears when the bell rings."

Pru's face fills with concern. She grabs my shoulders, smiling.

"Well, sweetie, live like the dream never ends," she says.

My mentor embraces me, causing a single tear to stroll down my face. I look over to my mom, who lays there resting. Emotions fill the atmosphere as Pru's warming love and support melts my numbing demeanor. My great-grandmother said to not allow anyone to put their junk in my trunk. However, what if I am the one filling myself with negativity? Will life get easier once I change my perspective? Either way, this rain seems to pour again, no matter how much we have danced between the raindrops. No matter how much we have guarded ourselves, hard times always seem to seep in. Perhaps my mentor is right, maybe I should live like the dream never ends; perhaps then I would not feel the impact of what is happening around us.

CHAPTER FIVE
When Your Hero Falls

WHEN ONE FALLS to their knees, one is in the best position to pray. My mother has been in the hospital for a few days now. My family and I are dealing with her healing the best way we know how: by sticking together. Yet, no matter how positive I try to be, I cannot help but show my angst to everyone around me. I try to contain myself, but sometimes it just seeps out.

Prepared for the day, I strut down the street with a pencil skirt, bouncing hair, and six-inch heels. Guys catcall and women roll their eyes in jealousy as I glide like only a queen can. Sass. Confidence. Class. I walk to my beat and could not care less who feels intimidated by my light.

As I am walking on the crosswalk, a taxicab stops past the lines, almost hitting me. Music screeches - he just killed my vibe. The driver is dismissive and unapologetic about his actions.

"Did you not see me walking on the crosswalk?" I say, staring him down.

"You shouldn't be in my way, lady!" he says, shaking his arm out of the window.

I can feel the blood boiling in my veins.

"I have the walk sign… see?" I yell.

I point to the pedestrian signal that clearly reads "Walk". He disregards it, and me.

"Get your vision checked!" I continue.

I walk away, dismissing the situation. I have things to do. The taxi driver honks his horn twice and yells out of the window, "Yeah? Stay out of my way!"

I stop in my tracks, trying to keep my composure. Until… he gives me the finger. The audacity of this guy! Does he not know I have a lot built up within me? I want to let it all out!

"And f—k you!" he screams.

He leans majority of his body out of the window, almost falling from it. I hear Kendrick Lamar's "Don't Kill My Vibe" blasting in my head. Escaping the emotions that quickly bubble inside of me, I close my eyes. Despite controlling my composure, my body twitches at the feeling of rage exploding outward. Then, it happens. He has gotten what he is looking for. I shake my wrists, turning around enough to look at him, giving him the side eye.

"What did you just say to me?" I say.

The taxi driver leans out of his window again. He yells at the top of his lungs, "I said, f—k you!"

That. Is. It! I am in my crazy mode.

My eye twitches as I yell at him and jump in front of his cab. My head touches my knees as I bend from side to side.

"Oh! You're not talking to me, honey!" I say.

I can feel my demeanor shift, and a complete loss of control. I am officially in my f-it mode.

"Who do you think I be? I'm the queen of these streets… 'reppin them 123s and ABCs!" I continue while moving from side to side.

The taxi driver is officially afraid out if his mind! What did he get himself into? More rambunctious, I climb on top of the cab.

He drives to toss me from the car. People gather around, recording the incident with their phones. I run up the hood of his car, dangling from the roof of the cab, obscuring his view, making weird faces, and yelling while hanging upside down.

"I probably shouldn't have done this," I think to myself.

He halts the cab, causing me to fly off and hit the ground. Damari is walking down the street to the Metro station when he notices the commotion. He runs up to me, laughing a little. I jokingly shake my head and cover my face. He sits on the ground next to me and we both laugh.

I must get it together.

Damari and I are studying in the study area at the campus library - an area with multiple desks, surrounded by countless bookshelves. We stacked our textbooks around us. He is rocking his school football gear while I wear a baggy top tied in the front with jeans and a pair of pumps. I have one leg propped on him while taking notes in my textbook. He has his face buried in a book, then peeks his head above it.

"Fé," he says with his usual cheesy grin.

"What?" I say, popping up as well.

He hits the table twice. "Time to go, baby! Let's get them. It's game time baby!" he says.

I am genuinely confused. What is this guy talking about now?

"Oh, right… class!" I say, jumping up to pack my belongings.

We laugh and play fight while packing our items.

"Be careful now! We don't need you jumping on top of any cabs today!" he jokes.

I punch him in the shoulder, laughing and leaving the library.

We feel eyes on us as we walk through campus together. Some consider us to be the school's "it" duo. Rumor has it we are a couple. However, we are only friends with drip, grace, and class. Everyone waves "hi" as we pass by - Damari dapping guys along the way, while I wave and hug.

"I hope you have your case under control. I heard you killed them in debate last week," he says.

"You know I'm a pro at this ish!" I respond, boastfully dancing.

"My beautiful, intellectual queen," he says.

"Stop," I say, punching him in the arm.

"Why?" he says.

"Because sir! We are not a couple!" I exclaim, laughing aloud.

"But we will be," he says, kissing me on the cheek. "Soon."

I jump backwards, "Whoa! Crossing the friendship zone there, buddy!"

He laughs, grinning from ear to ear. He stops, placing his foot back. Then, launches the other forward as if he is in race mode.

"If I beat you to the pole, you'll be mine by the end of the semester," he says, launching forward.

I burst into laughter, "But I have on heels… ugh… fine!"

I take off my heels and run after him barefoot, holding my shoes in my hands. Meanwhile, I hold my lady parts while attempting not to drop anything. Damari reaches the light pole, tapping it and doing a victory dance.

"I won!" he yells, teasing me with his silly dance moves.

I catch up to him, trying to catch my breath while checking the bottom of my bare feet. He stares at me in awe.

"I guess you're my world after all," he says in a serious tone.

His energy sifts through me. Silence overcomes us as we stare into each other's eyes. Pushing down what I feel inside, I decide to shake it off, punching him in the arm.

"You cheated! I wasn't ready!" I exclaim.

"I'll go great lengths for your love, baby," he looks down at my feet, "And judging from your bare feet, the feeling is mutual." He laughs.

"Ew! You're so corny!" I say, rolling my eyes.

I punch his arm again, this time, harder. He grabs his arm and rubs the spot. We laugh as I place my heels back on. He checks his watch.

"Whelp! Time for class!" he says.

He picks me up, placing me over his shoulder. I crack up laughing and snorting a little, as my feet dangle in the air. People watch us, noticing the chemistry we continue to deny.

Chemistry, I am afraid to accept.

I am in debate class, a standard lecture hall with lined tables and uniform seating. I present my case today, so changed into a skirt suit. Adjusting to the role, I am wearing well-manicured hands, a button-up blouse, and my hair curled under (à la Michelle Obama's hairstyle). Two students are presenting their debate at the front of the classroom. In the meantime, I sit with my notebook open for notes, focused on the current debate at hand. Then, I remember:

"Oh, my gosh! Did I cover my tracks this morning? I hope they're not showing," I think to myself.

The thought of my weave being exposed made my eyes bulge from my head. I scan the classroom, seeing if anyone is looking. Running my hands over my head, I check for exposed tracks. Then, I see a chick staring at me.

"Dang! She all up in my hair!" I think to myself. I am annoyed at the nosiness of it all.

I refocus on class, studying my notes and preparing for my case. The two students finish their debate. The class applauds as they walk back to their seats. Professor Smith, a curvy woman with eyeglasses and a quirky personality, walks to the front of the classroom to introduce the next debate.

"It is time for our last debate. May Miss Imani Holley and Miss Donna Carroll please come to the front of class," says Professor Smith.

I remember my first day of class as I get up.

Donna Carroll, a Caucasian woman with a slim physique and blonde hair, glances over with a smirk. "Nice notebook," she says, turning to type on her laptop.

I snap out of it, becoming even more empowered for my debate. We walk toward the front of the classroom, going on our respective sides. This time, I take my time strutting to my space, swaying my hips with each step, placing one heel in front of the other. My hair bounces and my curves flow as I walk like the lawyer I aim to be.

Professor Smith continues, "The debate is about welfare. I normally pre-assign a side to argue; however, you all had the leisure of selecting your own perspective. Now, let's have a clean and informed debate. Remember to start with your opening statement."

She goes back to her seat and allows us to prepare for our debates. We place our briefcases on the table, setting papers and other items out as needed. I sit my paper down on the desk, heading to the front of the class for my opening statement. Memories emerge:

My mother smiling while me and my siblings ate at the motel.
Me crying on the bathroom floor.
My mother laying in the hospital.

Coming back to reality, I begin my opening statement:

> "I stand before you today with my heart in my
> hand. Debating about a system rich men refuse to

understand. I come with a mission, slamming the competition to prove I resist and refuse to be a statistic. How can you complain about a lifestyle you know nothing about? Walking around with your nose up. Saying we're lazy pigs for being on government assistance. What would you do if you had to start from the ground up? Shoveling for scraps of metal. Wondering what you'll feed your kids for dinner. Have you ever curled up on the bathroom floor, crying in the dark? Have you ever stood in line for shelter, just to be told your case is not important enough? No. So how can you reject a system that feeds the children? Giving them a little hope for something bigger. The moment you debate between Ramen noodles and hotdogs for dinner or water your milk and stretch it for a month... we can talk. Otherwise, be quiet and listen Welfare is to help create solid ground while we build the foundation. Rising like roses growing from the concrete. Surprise! You did not expect a child raised on welfare to be your classmate. Did you? Let me tell you something you never knew. It does not make me any less qualified than you."

The class stands, giving a standing ovation. Donna sits in her seat with her mouth open, not uttering a word. Meanwhile, I return to my seat, organize my papers, and stand in pride with my arms folded. Smirking and beaming with confidence, I await Donna's response. Donna sits in her seat and ponders what to say next. Professor Smith steps in to fill the silence.

"Wow, Imani! Quite the opening statement. I'm quite speechless myself," she says, clearing her throat.

She straightens her glasses and looks back at me; then to Donna, who is still sitting in her seat, stuck.

She continues, "From the looks of it, so is Donna."

She looks to Donna. "Miss Carroll, would you like to present your opening statement?"

Donna shakes her head "no." Professor Smith gives her a few

extra seconds to change her answer, then turns to the class.

"Well, class," Professor Smith says, clearing her throat again, "It looks like Imani wins the case in favor of the benefit of public assistance." She turns to me. "Interesting argument, Miss Holley."

She smiles, giving me her nod of approval. It is clear I am a favorite in her class. The class dismisses early because of the brevity of the debate. Filled with happiness, I leave the classroom as people congratulate me on my win along the way. I approach Donna, extending a hand, but she rejects it, mean mugging me instead. Meanwhile, Donna's friend, Ashley, a twenty-year-old petite Asian girl, smiles at me.

"Great job today!" she says.

"Thanks, Ashley! I appreciate it," I respond, smiling back at her.

Donna rolls her eyes and turns away. I disregard her actions while holding my head high, strutting out of the classroom. I head toward the bathroom, emanating elegance and grace.

I walk into the restroom, heading straight to the sink, tossing my bag onto the counter. Then, a woman appears from a stall and stands next to me to wash her hands. I fumble through my purse and grab my powder foundation, pretending to fix my makeup. We exchange smiles and polite gestures. Soon enough, the woman washes and dries her hands and exits the restroom, smiling as she leaves. Free to let go, I throw my briefcase onto the sink, kick my heels off and grip on to the counter. My head throbs as I fight inaudible whispers. I hold my temples, fighting memories from resurfacing.

My mother going into an ambulance.
A crowd of people staring at my family as they evicted us from our home.
My family leaving my grandparent's home.
Us arriving at the motel.
Us struggling to find food to eat.
My siblings' smiles.

What should I do?

I grab the bottle of prescription pills from my bag, pouring about ten into my palm. My hands tremble as I stare at the engraving on each white pill: "50mg", it reads. I stare at myself in the mirror as a single tear falls from my eye. Swallowing air, I become numb. Whispers overcome as I consider the pathways I could take. Then I remember my family. So, I place the pills back into the bottle, listening to the sound as each hits the bottom. Throwing the bottle back into my purse, I scream while pulling my hair back, falling to the floor beside the sink.

I cannot let myself crumble. Not now. Not ever.

I arrive at the District Hospital Center to visit my mom. While entering the building, I hold the door open for a woman approaching behind me. The woman struts through with her nose up, failing to say thank you. This! This is one of my biggest pet peeves: a lack of manners. Attempting to remain calm, I take a few deep breaths. It does not work, so I grab the woman by her hand, pull her outside, and then shut the door in her face.

"Next time, say thank you!" I exclaim to the woman.

I strut away while flipping my hair. The woman is in shock, clutching her pearls while staring through the glass door.

I arrive at my mother's hospital room, spying on her through the window. I knock on the door, opening it to her sitting up on the hospital bed. She is eating a cup of fruit while reading a book. Smiling from ear to ear, she places her book on the bed.

"The Gorgeous One!" she says with the hugest smile, reaching out for a hug.

I smile as we embrace. "Hi, Beautiful. How's My Anointed One doing?"

"Blessed," she responds.

I sit on the bed next to her.

"How are you feeling?" I ask while examining her vitals on the monitor.

She takes a deep breath. "Good, actually."

I examine her head. A bandage covers the right side of her skull. That same portion has her hair cut off, revealing a noticeable dent in her head.

"Doctors tell me you've recovered quicker than most," I say, filled with gratitude.

"So, I've heard," she beams, "it surprised them to see me up and talking after only a few days following my procedure."

I smile, holding her hand, stopping tears from escaping as I smile through the emotions of the moment.

"How are my babies?" she asks, eyes gleaming with joy.

"They're fine. School is going well," I answer. "We met with Child and Family Services to find out who would have temporary custody of them."

"And…" she responds.

"No decision yet. Without Grammy and Stoney able to help, there really is not anyone who can, except -" I say.

I grow quiet, taking a deep breath and looking at my mom.

"Except?" she asks, sitting up a little straighter, though she still struggles to move.

"There are a few teachers from their school willing to take them in - Ms. J and Ms. V," I answer.

My mom wipes a tear away, smiling, at a loss for words.

"My God," she says, overwhelmed with joy.

"We're going to have another meeting to discuss how to handle everything. I don't mind helping to buy a few items they may need while they're with them. Are you okay with that?" I ask.

Still wavering in opinion, myself, I grow more and more uncertain about splitting them up. My mom thinks a little, nodding her head.

"Yes, baby. I think the kids are safe there. I appreciate them stepping up and offering their help. They do not have to do that," she says, getting emotional.

I fight back my tears. I want to tell her how much me and my siblings are missing her. How I barely sleep at night because I am worried about her health. However, that would be selfish of me. She is sitting in front of me smiling with stitches in her head from an open skull surgery - it does not matter how we feel. She made it out alive, and that is all that matters.

So, I hold my tears and conjure up a smile, "Yeah, but overall, the kids are okay… worried about you, but okay."

She smiles, "Everything's going to be alright!"

How does she know? Anything could have happened in the operating room. Well, who am I kidding? She is still alive, right?

"Yeah," I say, forcing a slighted smile.

She grabs my hand. "How's school? Did you shut it down at your debate earlier?"

"Oh, she already knows I did! She knows I am one of the best!" I think to myself.

"Yep!" I respond with the hugest smile on my face.

"Of course, you did! You were passionate about it," my mom says.

I cannot help but chuckle and blush. I cannot lie, I did that!

"Yeah, everyone was speechless when I presented my opening statement - an automatic win, baby!" I say, brushing my shoulder off with a substantial amount of pride in myself.

She gets more excited.

"That's what I'm talking about!" she says, squeezing my hand.

I can do nothing but smile. My mommy is proud of me, and I'm just as proud of her. For once, I see her smiling. No alcohol. No depression. There were no wandering thoughts. Just pure happiness and gratitude for life.

The feeling of joy subsides from me. Why does this always happen? I look around the room. I notice each flawed spot on the floor that they could have mopped better; how the monitors beep at a rhythmic pace; the smell of hospital fluids in the air: a distinct smell I could never describe. I hate that smell.

Then I look back at my mother. Her head is still half shaven, and a huge smile spread across her face. This is a miracle! She survived the unthinkable, and I am grateful. However, what about my siblings? I have seen how brutal the system can be, so I do not want them in foster care. Thoughts swirl in my mind.

My exams are coming up.
I must clean my room.
I missed a shift for work and was late to class this morning.

How do I balance it all?

In my mom's usual perfect timing, she notices my change of demeanor. She lifts my head up with one finger. I somehow did not notice my head was down. I guess it is getting harder to keep the truth hidden.

"You know, ma… it's like I take three steps forward and seven steps backward. Like I could never get ahead," I confess, holding back tears.

In her usual fashion, she smiles a smile only heaven could make.

"That's a thing called resistance, baby. Most resistance happens when you're breaking through. Like when a caterpillar transitions into a butterfly, you're earning your wings. It may get difficult, baby, but you must keep going. You hear me?" she says.

A tear falls from my eye. I nod yes.

She continues, "Stick it through and you'll soar like an eagle."

She wipes my tear and pulls me in for a hug. I cuddle up next to her, being careful not to sit on any tubes or wires. Her head is healing, and here she is comforting me. I guess a mother never stops being a mom. In the same, through thick and thin, I must continue to be a dutiful daughter and big sister.

Me and my girls are at one of the hottest parties of the school year, BKU's Greek Night. Some of the finest fraternity guys are strolling and doing their thing. There are several sororities here, but me and my sorors (sorority sisters) stand out the most: the ladies of Gamma Alpha Gamma. We are strolling through the party, doing our signature moves, letting everyone know we are still number one. As the line disassembles, I strut away and give props along the way.

I head to grab a drink, gliding through the party with my drink in hand, nodding and smiling at familiar faces throughout the crowd. Then, here comes crazy Chante; she always knows how to bring out the D.C. in me.

"Bae Fé!" says Chante, trying to pop my eardrums with her high-pitched voice.

I jump back, holding my chest. I always transform into the 'Ratchet Queen' with Chante.

"Dang Chante, don't be scaring me like that!" I say.

She laughs in her usual "Chante" fashion, slapping her leg and making a scene. I roll my eyes and giggle at her melodramatic behavior. We continue catching up and cracking jokes when a guy bumps into me, spilling my drink all over my dress. I look way too good tonight for some guy to be interrupting my flow.

"I don't have time for these vibe killers," I express loud enough for him to hear me as he walks by.

He looks me up and down. I know he does not think I am interested after that lame introduction.

"Sheesh, I bumped into a beautiful angel," he says, smiling and trying to kiss my hand.

Chante and I sniff around. There is this sudden unbearable odor that is just outright disrespectful.

"What is that smell?" Chante yells, holding her nose and stomach.

The smell is horrid! I kick my right foot up, landing in a karate pose with a forearm block. I somehow thought this would stop the smell from attacking my nostrils, but it only made it worse. Blowing air out of my nose, I attempt to un-smell this tragedy of an odor. Then he has the audacity to whisper in my face. Oh my gosh, the smell makes me want to cry and run for cover.

Then I realize…

"Is that your breath, man?" I yell at him.

He puts his hands to his mouth, checking his breath. Instead of taking ownership of his foul play, he shrugs his unhygienic shoulders and walks away! The audacity of it all.

"Colgate is great!" I yell toward him as he strolls away.

Chante bursts into laughter, "girl, you are so rude!"

"He's the rude one! Burning my nostril hairs! I ought to sue his behind…. Ugh, I need a drink," I say.

We both laugh as we head toward the bar. I grab more napkins and wipe down my dress. Then comes Claudia's silly self.

"These combs ain't loyal!" Claudia jokes.

"Neither is your edge control," I say, sooner than I thought to filter, but whatever.

"Oop! Disrespectful!" says Chante.

We all laugh. I rub my edges, dazing off into space. The alcohol is clearly kicking in.

"I was so lost without my edges. They're so loyal when you treat them right," I say, taking another sip of my drink.

"Mm... so are your split ends, boo," Chante says, touching the ends of my extensions. "Did that chick in India trim?" She perches her shady little lips.

I smack her hands away from me. "First of all, Brazil. Second, mind your Perm Yaki!" I respond, rolling my eyes.

"Well, boo, it doesn't matter cause your edges are still from Northeast DC!" Chante says.

"Ew... Snitch! Why are you always exposing my weave? Leave the bundle exploration up to me!" I joke.

Claudia laughs, "Girl, let me explore your bundle collection, 'cause you have all the options."

I pat my hair, swinging it, "Well, I am a Weaveologist, so..."

The DJ blasts my song. I lose my cool. Damari is dancing nearby, so I grab him and begin mouthing the lyrics while dancing for him - and yes, he loves every second. My sorors pull me into the line. We do a prepared dance to the song: shaking, dropping it like it is hot, and strutting like we are on the runway. On campus, we are the life of the party. The crowd's attention is great, but I focus my attention on Damari while dancing with the girls, giving him flirtatious glances and smiles along the way.

The DJ changes the song. We all disperse, laughing and giving each other props. Damari approaches me, smiling and pulling me closer to him. He grabs my hand, gliding it up his chest and placing my arms around his neck. He then wraps his hands around my waist. We lock eyes and slow dance. I lay my head on his shoulder and caress him, smiling. He kisses the top of my head and then glides his fingers along my jawline, leaning in for a kiss until...

My messy sorority sister, Rachel, interrupts, causing us to snap out of the moment.

"Hey Damari," says Rachel, grinning in my man, I mean...

Damari's face.

She rubs her hand across his chest. He shoves it away and looks at me. I step back, waiting to see how he handles the situation. I cannot believe he has been messing with her the entire time. Then again, I do not put it past him. In fact, I put nothing past anyone.

"Rachel," Damari says.

She yanks him by his collar and kisses him.

"You miss me, baby?" she says, grinning and looking me up and down.

Appalled, I smack Rachel and launch toward her, getting the best of her. However, Damari's civil self pulls me back, holding me. She scurries away while I push him off me. Catching my breath, I glance at him for a moment, then shake my head and leave the party.

I walk down the street at about midnight. It is dark and there are not too many people on the streets. I sway from side to side while dragging my bare feet down a street known for prostitution. It looks sketchy: trash all over the sidewalk, boxes, and homeless people scattered with no one in sight. People honk their horns while driving by; some stopping to see if I am interested. I ignore them, avoiding any eye contact.

A man wearing a jacket, face mask, and khakis jumps out and attacks me as I walk by an alley He pushes me against the brick building, choking, and fondling me, licking my cheek. I try to stare into his face but cannot see, since he has everything covered. He feels very familiar, almost a little too familiar.

"Who are you?" I ask. I am unsure but certain at the same time.

I scream for him to get off me, but he chokes me harder instead. It becomes harder and harder to breathe, and I lose consciousness. My vision becomes blurry and my surroundings spin. Damari appears, knocking the man to the ground with a punch. I fall to my hands and knees, trying to breathe. Damari pulls the guy up by his shirt and points a gun to his neck.

"If you ever touch her again, your life is over!" Damari says while pressing the weapon against him.

The guy flees. I throw up. Then I faint, laying my head in my puke. I see a vision:

There are spinning surroundings, and a white light seems too far away to reach. A black figure stands over me as I reach for it.

It is Damari bending down to check on me.

"Fé!" he yells, picking my limp body off the ground.

It is about one in the morning as Damari bathes me in his tub. His apartment has a Batchelor-style layout of basic furniture: a king-sized bed with a simplistic headboard, a bedroom set with two nightstands and a dresser, and a 70-inch flatscreen television mounted to the wall. He has a few pictures of family members hanging on the walls, and layers of cologne on top of his bathroom counter. He takes pride in having a clean home; perhaps it is because of having strict parents. I assume those tedious chores throughout his youth came in handy as an adult, as he was always required to keep his room tidy as a child.

While bathing me, he shampoos the puke from my hair with a sponge, scrubbing my body ever so gently to make sure every piece of dirt is gone. The amazing thing is he does not seem to get aroused. He cares for my well-being, and that makes me love him more… as a friend. I must admit, though, I am falling for my best friend. His genuine care for me, and the worry in his eyes for my safety, only grows my almost-inevitable adoration of him.

I daze in and out of consciousness as he rinses the night's pain from my physical skin. Although the damage feels internal, the external cleansing somehow helps soothe my inner heartache. With each squeeze of the sponge onto my skin, I have somehow forgiven him for hurting me earlier in the night. Yet, each time he pulls away, only to grab more water, I feel the dagger in my heart evermore.

He has somehow reversed the vibrations of disappointment; somehow, he has flipped the script. With each wash, I feel his eyes dagger into my soul, screaming with disappointment, yet a forgiving sense of empathy.

"You're more than this," he says to me, squeezing the last bit of water from the sponge onto my back.

He repeats, "You're worth more than this."

He is right; I am worth much more. However, this is not the time to make me the bad guy. This is his time to prove he loves me, despite my flaws. My grudge was fading in and out. I guess honey works better than vinegar, after all.

"You are the most beautiful woman I know," he says, grabbing the towel and jotting specks of water from my face.

He continues, "Be the queen you are destined to be."

He kisses my forehead and hugs me. That is it. His embrace has somehow unlocked the floodgates of my emotions, releasing the deepest love I have tried to hide for all these years. Our friendship is too special for me to ruin with my drama - my ex, my indecisiveness, my secret I have yet to admit to him. As I melt into his arms and my heart melts into his power of vulnerability, he holds me close, helping me to dry off. I feel like a new woman again, finding a remedy by being protected in his arms throughout the night.

I could get used to this.

Damari and I cuddle together in his bed, sound asleep. He has his sculpted, warm arms wrapped tight around me as we lay in a spooned position. The essence of my favorite candles lingers in the air as the meditation sounds play in the background. I feel so… safe.

It is about 3 o'clock in the morning when my nightmares begin:

I am walking on the red carpet as gunshots blaze. Lights flash, almost like those of paparazzi cameras, combined with helicopter spotlights. I run in the opposite direction of each light that flashes, searching for an escape. Looking for corners to cut, I go in the same circles - always ending back where I began. I stop in my tracks and hold my stomach, falling to my knees.

I sit up, awakening from my nightmare. Panting, I attempt to catch my breath, checking my chest for gunshot wounds. Damari awakens.

"What's wrong?" he exclaims, holding me.

I cannot speak. All I can do is stare at him, shaken by my demise. Near tears, I find the strength to utter the words "the dream." He hugs me, soothing my now cold skin with his affection. I bury my head into his shoulders as we embrace.

It is about 5 o'clock in the morning as Damari and I approach my dorm room door. He attempts to come inside to get me settled in, but I reject his offer.

"I'll see you tomorrow?" he says, leaning in to kiss my cheek.

"Talk to Rachel about that," I respond, turning my cheek away from his lips.

He shakes his head and looks down, shaking off the energy. He places his hands in his pocket, takes a deep breath, and straightens up, looking me in my eyes.

"How's ma?" he asks, staring into my eyes with the hopes of a positive conversation.

"Good. I'm going to visit her tomorrow morning," I answer, staring at him with a blank expression.

"What time? I'll take you," he says.

"I'll find a way," I say, staring at him, then looking away.

"I asked what time? Stop being so stubborn," he says, placing more bass into his voice.

I roll my eyes and sigh, "9."

"A.M.?" he asks.

"I said morning, didn't I?" I say, rolling my eyes and looking away with my arms folded.

"Cool! I'll be here at 8 so we can get there early. Are the kids coming?" he asks in another attempt to change the tempo.

"Yeah," I say, attempting to block the images of him and Rachel from my mind.

"How are they?" he asks.

I daze off into space, striking him to ask again.

"They good. You know, school and everything," I respond.

I am annoyed with him and his questions, so I fumble for my keys while avoiding all eye contact. Regardless of how I try to hide, I am afraid he will find out my secret without me uttering it to a soul.

"We should take them to the movies or something," he suggests.

He leans in closer, placing his hand on the wall above me. I stop fidgeting with my bag and look up into his eyes. There it goes… he is trying to find the truth again. I look down. Finally… my keys!

"Yeah, Kayla's birthday is coming up. Christmas is around the corner. I just don't know what I am going to do," I say to him, positioning my key in my hand.

"I'll help. I have money saved up. We can pick the kids up from wherever they are, take them to see your mom, and give them the holiday they deserve… and you too," he says.

He grabs my chin, directing my eyes to meet his. I get lost in his brown pupils, somehow swallowed in the abyss of his care for me and my family. How could I not tell him? Why am I hiding this from him, the very person who knows my secrets the most? It is not the time. I can feel bags form under my eyes and wrinkles on my forehead as stressful thoughts of finances swarm in my mind.

"Don't worry," he says, looking into my eyes, "I got you."

He grabs my hands, massaging my pressure point with his strong, warm, manly grip. I just noticed he smells so good today and is wearing my favorite sweater: the grey one with the crew neckline. His hairline is especially crisp today, with the goatee lined beautifully to his chiseled facial features. His lips seem moist with a tint of natural pinkness, revealing his beautiful, authentic smile.

Then I realize, those are the same lips that kissed Rachel last night… right in front of me.

"About last night…" he says.

"I don't want to hear about her," I interrupt.

I turn away from him, unlocking my door and turning the knob to go in. He goes to follow behind me. I stop him.

"Look, there's nothing there, I swear," he explains.

It feels a little too late for me to accept any excuses.

"We're not together anyway, right?" I say, stepping into the door.

He sighs, tucking his hands into his pockets. "I'll see you tomorrow at 8 - actually 7:30 - so we can get the kids on the way."

I swallow air, tucking my hair behind my ear. "7:30 a.m. tomorrow. Cool."

I lean in to give him a friendly hug, but he pulls me in for a deeper caress. I cannot help but accept his sincere act of affection. It feels good to be loved. To be seen.

He catches my attention as I turn to go into my room.

"Hey," he says.

I look at him, searching in his eyes.

He continues, "I believe in you."

I smile, attempting to stop tears from forming in my eyes. "Goodnight, D."

He smiles back, "Goodnight, Fé."

I close the door behind me.

He leans in on the other side of the door, whispering, "I love you… so much."

The void shifts through my bones as I lean against the inside of the door. I can still smell his cologne, see his smile, feel his touch. I can still feel his arms wrapped around me. Somehow, I can hear him say "I love you".

I love you too, Damari.

I stumble into my room, knocking over every item along the way. It is dark, so I glide my hand along the wall to find the light switch. Soon enough, I find it, squinting my eyes from the brightness of the light. My head is throbbing, so I head to the bathroom to get relief.

I stumble toward the restroom, bumping into the walls and the sink. As clumsy as I am, I trip from thin air, so grab onto the counter to balance myself. It is then that I get a glimpse of my new reflection in the mirror: disorderly hair, somehow smeared mascara. What happened to the woman I have worked so hard at keeping together?

I open the medicine cabinet, taking a pill from one of my prescribed medicine bottles. Closing the mirror, I toss one pill into my mouth, watching as it travels down my throat. Catching another glimpse of my horrid reflection, I close my eyes to escape my reality. Then, I see:

I see a hand opening a door. A white light shines through, overtaking whatever is beyond that point. As the light fades, a pill bottle appears.

It seems my dreams and visions are no longer safe, either. I open my eyes, staring at the distorted image of myself yet again. My face, filled with dry patches that I have worked hard to exfoliate away; my skin cracked from a lack of proper moisture;

and my eyes forming a slight dark circle underneath. The worst part of it all, I do not know when the pieces started falling apart.

I turn on the water faucet, twisting both knobs to get an even flow of warm-temperature water. Cupping my hands together below the faucet, I gather enough water to splash some on my face; then toward the mirror, on the stranger that appears in my reflection.

How could I allow myself to retreat to who I was three years ago?

I throw myself onto the floor, crying. Snot bubbles fill my nostrils, making it harder for me to breathe. My head spins as I fight to stay sober and prevent my migraine from growing worse. Somehow, this moment of despair feels more real than anything I have done this past year. Yes, my purpose feels on track with my campus television show and pre-law classes, but what else am I doing toward my purpose?

How will my family survive this storm?

My baby brother, Quinn, walks into the bathroom, making a beeline toward me. He leans down, rubbing my back and drying my tears. I raise my head from my tear-saturated arms.

"Mani?" he says, sitting down in front of me with his legs crossed Indian style. He moves my hand from my face.

"What's wrong? Are you okay?" he asks.

Now I feel even more embarrassed. He is too young to worry about how I feel. So, I suck up my tears and retract every ounce of snot that now dangled from my nose. He grabs a piece of toilet paper, blotting my eyes dry. This makes my heart smile.

"Quinny Bear, what are you doing awake?" I ask, blowing my nose with the few squares of toilet paper he grabbed from the roll.

"I heard you crying. Do you miss mommy?" he asks, leaning closer to my face.

That is it! I cannot hold my tears back any longer. I weep, losing a slight grip of life with each sniffle.

"I miss mommy too," he says.

I need to be stronger than this. He is only four years old; yet he is trying to console me. I must be better than this. We all cannot take care of someone older than us, from a young age. For it is not his responsibility to worry about me; he needs to focus on being a kid. So, I attempt to get it together, even throwing in a smile.

"You know, Quinny Bear… our mommy is okay!" I say, pepping up, "let's get you back to sleep!"

I stand up, losing my balance a little along the way. My head is still pounding, but I try to focus on my baby brother instead. Picking him up from the floor, I throw him onto my hip.

"How was school?" he asks, dangling his little arms around my neck as I carry him back to bed.

"It was great, cutie pie. How about you?" I respond.

"It was fantastic! I learned so much!" he says, throwing his arms into the air.

How does he have so much energy at five in the morning? Where did he learn to say "fantastic"? I am impressed.

"Oh yeah? What color is… this?" I say, pointing to a random flowerpot in my room.

"Blue!" he exclaims.

"How about… this?" I joke, pointing toward his shirt.

He giggles, "Green!"

"Good job! How about… this?" I laugh, pointing toward his nose.

"Brown!" he celebrates, giggling loudly with joy.

"You're so smart," I say, hugging him tight before releasing him onto the bed.

I make room between my four siblings already scattered across the queen-sized bed. Thankfully, my housing advisor, Ms. Trinity, helped me with my rooming situation. So, I do not have to worry about a roommate this year, leaving more space for my siblings. I sit on the bed, placing Quinn on my lap, pulling a cover over top of him and rocking him in my arms. He relaxes, melting with each rock.

"Mani?" he asks, looking up at me.

"Yes, Quinny Bear?" I respond, smiling at him.

"I love you," he says, kissing me on the cheek.

A tear falls from my eye. "I love you too, Quinny Bear."

I kiss him on the forehead and continue rocking him to sleep. The rain is not stopping, so I must learn to dance between the raindrops. Even when one's hero falls, we must learn to get back up again.

PART TWO

A VANISHED HOPE

CHAPTER SIX
Picking Up the Pieces

I never want to be a vanished hope.
Roughly thrown aside.
Never expected,
Or even tried.
I am a bird,
Soaring through the sky.
Blessing everything I pass by.
I am a blooming flower.
Never a coward.
I am me…
IMANI
An actual miracle in reality.

THE SNOW FALLS in D.C., and trees have lost all their leaves. While looking forward to winter break, students prepare for the most difficult exams of the semester. Everyone gossips about the expensive gifts their parents may or may not get them, when their flight leaves, and which family members they look forward to seeing at dinner, or not. Me? My mindset is a little different. It feels great to hear the jingle bells ringing; however, there is a piece of me nervous about what the day may bring.

My siblings and I exit the Metro bus and walk a block to my dorm room. I examine each child - Sabrina, Kayla, Jasmine, Zoriana, and Quinn - checking that they are warm. The twins fight with their shoulder straps as their bookbags droop from their shoulder blades sagging onto their arms. I do my normal routine of checking our surroundings. It is easier to go unrecognized this year since my dorm is on the far edge of campus. God knew what He was doing.

As we approach my dorm building, Country Hall, I tap my student ID on the badge reader. We enter the lobby, which resembles a hotel - gold rails, brown diamond tiles, and sturdy old-fashioned furniture. Thank goodness there is no student security at the front to detail each visitor that enters. Yet, despite the freedom of adulting that I am provided with my dorm, my heart palpitates each time.

My palms become sweaty as we press the elevator up button. I shake my leg and pat it as I wonder why the elevator is taking so long. It dings, opening the doors to a group of students chatting as they exit. They ooh and ahh at the adorableness of my younger siblings. I smile and thank them for the compliments, the usual small talk. As scary as it is, I am grateful to have them in my care.

As we enter my dorm room, the kids plop on the bed and couch. I drop my items, kick my shoes off and run to the restroom, finding relief in releasing the day's stressors. I inhale gratitude while exhaling any tensions. My phone rings from the living room area. Jasmine knocks on the bathroom door.

"Mani, somebody is calling you," she says with her mouth pressed between the crack of the door.

"Who is it?" I yell from the toilet.

"It's a 202 number," she responds.

Confused, I hurry and finish my business in the restroom, and open the bathroom door to retrieve my cell phone. I call the number back, hearing the voice of a social worker from the Child and Family Services Agency on the other end. I called them to discuss how I can find aid to help me take care of my siblings while my mother is in the hospital. It has been a few days since I left a voicemail, so I am glad they called back.

We agreed to meet later in the week to discuss any services they could offer. They instructed me to compile a list of relatives that could attend the meeting as well. I am almost certain no one is fond of the foster care system; in fact, I have heard no positive feedback about it, ever. Therefore, I want to prevent my siblings from being spread across a system that was purposed to protect but seems to cause suffering. Despite our homelessness over the past three years, my mother has always kept "her babies" together. I do not want us to be torn apart on the account of me.

So, that is what my mom and I did - we reached out to several relatives to see if they could take part in the agency meeting and consider taking temporary custody of my siblings while my mom heals, and I finish college. We put together a list of relatives to attend the meeting by phone or in person.

There must be a way.

The day arrives. It is time to meet to discuss my siblings' shelter arrangements. We scheduled it for the evening to make sure the teachers were present. I dropped my siblings off at a relative's house before arriving at the agency building. They assigned us to a small conference room with about ten chairs positioned in a circle. The social worker has a phone and chair in the middle.

As I arrive, a few of my loved ones are already here - Mama, Pru, my mother's best friend Tameka, my cousin, and two teachers from my siblings' school, Ms. V and Ms. J. On the phone is my father, my great-grandmother Nana, and my Uncle Rob and Aunt Chelle. We allowed my mom to rest and agreed to update her after the meeting. So, I asked her what her thoughts were beforehand. Having my loved ones' support makes everything feel a bit more manageable. I feel we can get through this, and maybe the storm will end soon.

I hug and greet everyone and thank them for their support. My mentor approaches me, pulling me aside. I smile. Although we spoke when I first arrived, there is something about her that brightens my day every single time we speak.

"Sweetie, how are you feeling about all of this?" asks Pru.

I take a deep breath in, exhaling. "I'm… okay. My mom is okay, so I feel like I can't complain, you know?" I respond.

"Sweetie, you know I am always here for you. How are the kiddos? Where are they right now?" she asks, rubbing my back.

"They're doing good. I dropped them off at Keisha's house. After the meeting, Mama and Uncle Nick will take me to pick them up," I say.

"Sure, Sweetie. How's your mom? Is she healing okay since her surgery?" she asks, leaning in closer to examine my facial expressions.

"She's doing okay, progressing well. In fact, Dr. Nayam says she's progressing quicker than most patients who have had an open-skull surgery. She's talking, moving around, and is independent," I reply.

Pru holds her chest with a sigh of relief. "I am so glad to hear. I know your mom will be okay sweetie," she rubs my back, "She is a strong woman with amazing kiddos. She has a lot to fight for. I'll go to see her tomorrow after I drop my kids off at school."

I nod my head in agreement, smiling and hugging her. The social worker, Ms. Robertson, announces it is time for the meeting to begin. We all sit down in a circle, everyone directing their attention to me. I could feel it in the air, the love and concern of adults watching me fight for my siblings when I should just be focusing on school. That does not alter me, though. I love my siblings so much that I feel like a second mom to them. Their health and safety are important to me. However, so is my education; so is defying statistics and breaking generational curses. In sum, I attribute my determination to break chains to them.

"So, Imani. Why don't you start us off by letting us know why you called for this meeting, and what you hope for the resolve to be," says Ms. Robertson.

I look at each person's face. Some give an encouraging smile, and others show gestures of concern. The common themes: love and support. I inhale and exhale before beginning.

"First, I want to thank everyone for coming out to show support for my mom, siblings, and me. Your love and support mean a lot to us during this time. My mother is doing okay. She had her brain surgery where they clipped both aneurysms in her brain from one side. Her recovery will be restrictive and progressive because two more remain in her neck. So, that will be a process. Regarding shelter, we haven't had a place to call home in a while. We were staying with my grandmother for a bit, but that ended. So, we've been going between relatives' houses and motels since then. Sabrina, Jasmine, Kayla, Zoriana, and Quinn are doing well. They've been staying with me at my dorm. Although I love knowing they are safe, I am afraid someone will find out and I will lose my student housing. With all our things in storage, it's the only stable shelter we have right now. Plus, I do not want to risk being put out of school in my Junior Year. I could use help with someone keeping them while I complete the semester. I'm hoping we could work something out where we keep them together as much as possible," I state, stopping tears from falling.

Ms. Robertson gives each person the floor to say how they can help. My father agrees his house is open if no resolve. My mentor offers to bring us to her home during winter break; however, she would be out of town for Christmas. Everyone else said they would help purchase any needed items for the kids and myself. Their teachers, Ms. V and Ms. J, spoke up and offered their homes. Ms. J would house Sabrina and Jasmine while Ms. V houses Kayla and the twins. The benefit is that the kids would be at school every day. Thankfully, my little brother Marcus is staying with his grandmother, so he does not need any accommodations.

The kids would join them after the new year; this way, they can be with family during the holidays. I am satisfied with this arrangement because both Ms. V and Ms. J are women my mother and siblings trust. We agreed to go shopping for the kids and I bring everything to their home when the time comes.

The beauty of having a great support system is priceless. I feel a relief like none other. It feels great to know we are not alone.

The days draw closer to Christmas.

I am still worried about how I will supply my siblings with gifts for the holidays. With my mother in the hospital, and my grandmother still healing, I do not feel I have anywhere to turn. Somehow, I know that is not true. Each day brings a new level of anxiety and gratefulness. The storm seems to get stronger and may honestly get the best of me. I do not know how I can make it past the rain.

Thankfully, the kids are now on winter break, so I do not need to worry about getting them to school. Therefore, I just go to class and come straight back to my dorm room. Since it is time for finals, there are not too many campus activities, so I can save face a little better.

As I study, I realize that I have not heard from my job regarding my hours next semester. My palms sweat thinking of all the days I missed because of having to handle family business. It was worth it - my siblings are safe - yet the thought of losing my job at a time like this simply scares me. So, I pick up the phone to call my supervisor.

I got fired.

The rain is pouring harder and harder, and although I attempt to pick up the pieces, they continue to fall from my hands; only shattering into smaller pieces. I run to the bathroom, dodging toys, clothes, and bookbags that cover the floor.

"Are you okay?" asks Sabrina.

"Yes," I say.

I run to the restroom and lock the door, holding my mouth and crying as I slide toward the floor. The weeping causes my head to throb as my body temperature increases. I do not feel good. I turn off the light and lay in a ball on the floor, rocking and contemplating whether I have the strength to go on. Then, after minutes of crying, I hear the playful sounds of my siblings outside of the door. The tears stop and my worries end. I need to figure out how to get back on my feet. So, I turn to prayer, crying and screaming at God like He owes me money; like He had stolen my best friend.

"God! I've given you my all, but it seems I only get scraps! I try to follow my purpose and do what you have given me to do but look how I am rewarded! When will the rain stop? Lord, I am drowning! I don't know how I will afford to buy the kids anything for Christmas, let alone how we will afford to eat. God,

I'm grateful for the help you have given us, and that my mom is still here today, but please help! I cannot bear this pain anymore!" I pray.

Balled up into a ball for a little longer, I take deep breaths while counting to ten. Then, it is amazing, I feel a renewed strength. I realize He has heard my cries. I leap from the floor and look in the mirror. Boy, do I look a mess! My makeup is looking crazy - eyes like a raccoon, hair looking like the twins brushed it, and a nose as puffy and red as Rudolph's. I must get it together. Everything will be okay.

I leave the bathroom and head toward the kitchen to fix dinner. My siblings surround me, tagging each other and running circles around my legs. Why do kids do this? Of all the space in the place, they come to bother me! I would tell them to take the playing elsewhere, but this time I take part. So, I tickle them and chase them around the room while we laugh and enjoy togetherness.

Now that the kids have eaten, I sit on the couch and check my bank account, turning away to make sure no one oversees. "-$36.14" it reads. I scroll down, noticing an automatic payment that overdraft my account by only $1.14, and a $35.00 bank overdraft fee. Highway robbery. It is late in the day, so I choose to put it aside until the call center opens. I swipe out of the banking app and massage my temples for relaxation. Then, Pru calls.

"Hey Sweetie! How are you and the kiddos?" she asks with a tone of love and care.

"We're doing okay. The kids are on winter break, and I am almost finished with finals. How are you and the family?" I ask, excited yet somehow discouraged.

"Everyone is doing well! Hey, listen sweetie. What are your thoughts about you and the kids staying with us during the holiday break? We'll be out of town for Christmas, but I'd love to spend some quality time with y'all and see your adorable faces," she says.

I jump for joy, "yes, please! We'd love that!"

"Okay, great! Let me know when you finish with exams, and I'll come and swoop y'all. Love you, sweetie!" she says.

"Okay, we're looking forward to it! Love you too!" I say.

I hang up the phone and announce to the kids, "We'll be going to Mama P's house!"

They jump for joy and chant "Mama P". We are all excited to spend some time with my mentor and family. We are all beyond grateful for Pru's unwavering love and support.

I sit back, fulfilled, watching my siblings play. Thoughts swim as my mind remembers the uncertainty of the days to come. I cannot help but worry about money and where we will go for Christmas. Instead of basking in apprehension, I choose to set it aside and enjoy the beauty of the moment - my siblings are here, safe, and we all look forward to seeing our loved ones.

We received a Christmas miracle.

We ended up spending about a week with my mentor. Then for Christmas, my Uncle Rob and Aunt Chelle surprised us. Uncle Rob drove from North Carolina to D.C. on Christmas Eve, to be sure we had family to open gifts with on Christmas. They went shopping while we were asleep and stayed up till the wee hours of the morning wrapping our gifts. I will never forget their love in a time of chaos and pain. They and my cousins (their children) Chrissy, Kiara, and Bobby, all made us feel like we were at home. For that, I will always be indebted.

Between my mentor's house and my aunt and uncle's home, I learned a new way of looking at family and raising kids. Both were healthy two-parent households that were wholesome and well-taken care of. I admire that. A part of me indulged in the feeling of having parental figures taking care of me and my siblings. I could feel like a young adult again. Like a big sister. I did not have to worry about food, or money, or shelter. I simply just made sure everyone was okay, and that felt good. The smiles on my siblings' faces felt even better, filling my heart with joy and my soul with ambition. I could smile again.

From the bottom of my heart, I will always cherish their love and generosity. Tears cried a good cry, and yet it remains one of the most beautiful Christmas holidays of all, thanks to my mentor, aunt, and uncle.

For even when the pieces fall, it takes a village to build a home.

Thank you, Pru, Aunt Chelle, and Uncle Rob… forever more. We love you.

CHAPTER SEVEN
XO, Ex… Ohhhh

IT IS THE last semester of Junior Year, and things are going well. My siblings are back at school, and my new classes have begun. They have not gone with Ms. V or Ms. J just yet but will soon. Snow covers the campus, along with patches of ice and excessive "Watch Your Step" signs. I am more than ready for the season - wearing some boots, jeans, a sweater, and a trench coat, and of course a cute hat to match. As I enter the school building, I hear someone call me.

"Imani!" they yell.

I look back, noticing my ex, Mike Brennan. He is about five-feet-nine-inches with a slim, athletic build. He is lighter skinned with curly hair that stops just past his shoulders.

"Imani! It's Mike. Hold up a minute," he yells again, running to catch up with me.

My heart races and palms become sweaty as I look who was once my lover in his eyes. As he gets closer, I notice his dimples have gotten deeper, and his teeth a little whiter. Yet, I wonder what he wants from me. Has he not hurt me enough already? Am I just a puppet he can control when convenient to him?

"Mike, I-," I say, at a loss for words.

"Listen, Mani, I know I hurt you - I just miss you and need you in my life," he says.

He gets closer to me… all in my personal bubble!

"Mike, you don't have to do this, okay? I don't need -" I say.

Interrupting me, he kisses me, pulling my body closer to him. For a fraction of a millisecond, it feels good. He still has warm arms and sensual lips. Then I realize he is not the one for me anymore. So, I slap him and turn to walk away. He grabs my arm, pulling me back closer to him.

"Look, I'm trying to show you I love you, but you're going to embarrass me like that?" he says.

His grip gets tighter around my arm as he pulls down, digging his fingers in. Then I remember why I left. I step back, holding my arm, then my face, as if the bruises are still there. I shake my head and walk away.

"Imani, I need you in my life!" he says as I walk into the academic hall.

Too bad. Too sad.

I exit the school building, looking around each corner before approaching. Seeing the sight is clear, I breathe a breath of fresh air. Then he reappears.

"Imani -" he says.

"No, Mike!" I attempt to walk around him, but he blocks me in.

"Just give me one minute. Just hear me out," he says, cradling my hand.

I look down at our cupped hands, then back up into his eyes, somehow searching for something good to see in him again; only to be disappointed in the reopened wounds I once thought were healed.

He looks into my eyes and says, "Mani, I miss you. I miss your smile. I miss having you around me. I miss you correcting me. I just miss you a lot, Imani."

Unphased. I ask, "Mike, have you ever heard the saying 'you never miss a good thing until it's gone?'"

"Yeah," he replies.

"Exactly. So, what does you missing me have to do with me?" I say, pulling my hand away.

He grows frustrated. "Look!" he catches himself, exhaling. "Look, I love you, Imani, and I apologize for hurting you. I never wanted to cause you any pain. I've been working on myself - I've been seeking treatment and now I'm confident I can love you right," he says, taking my hand again.

"Mike, I am going through too much to deal with your narcissistic behavior. I love you, but I cannot allow you to bring me down, especially at a time like this," I say.

A tear drops from my eyes. Looking away, I wipe it, gather myself, and look back at him.

I continue, "I love you, but I cannot love you anymore."

I squeeze his hand, giving a slighted smile before walking away. My heart is pounding, and about seventy-five percent of me wants to turn back and accept his apology. However, I cannot. The physical abuse runs further than skin-deep, and that pain is irreparable. He must watch as I walk away, but for real this time.

As I head to my dorm, I realize it is Thursday, my father's dialysis treatment day. He goes on Tuesday, Thursday, and Saturday each week, so I always feel there is something happening on those days. We talk every day, but I have not seen him in a while. So, I figure it is the perfect time to surprise him by picking him up from treatment. Marcus is watching the kids in my room, and I am now making a little more coins from my campus library job. As I arrive at The District Hospital Center, an eerie feeling overcomes me, triggering a memory:

My father and I were sitting in his room at the District Hospital Center Rehabilitation Facility. He pivoted his body to sit up, scooting toward the edge of the bed. This was a monumental achievement. Since his hip disarticulation (amputation of his entire right leg from the hip down), this was the first time he sat up on his own. I jumped up and down, celebrating his maneuver we learned during his rehab training. He smiled big and wide, basking in the joy of his accomplishment. As he should!

I smile, shaking off the feeling. Hopping off the Metro bus, I walk to the dialysis center. It is located inside of a building toward the corner of the hospital's campus. Its building is white with a gray interior. The lights illuminate outward, but if one has no business in the building, it is easy to miss. However, it is all too familiar to me because my dad has been on dialysis for over a decade. Therefore, we frequent the building a lot.

I enter the building, nodding, and greeting people as I walk by. Some dude tries to holler at me, but I keep walking; though he is fine, and I am single! Hey - anyway - back to the point. So, I walk through the maze-layout of a hospital, arriving at my father's dialysis center. I can feel my blood pressure go up as I grab the handle to the door. My heart paces with excitement, yet my nerves blur all the good feelings that come up. I am so excited to see my dad but know all too well the pain his body experiences with each tug at his heart.

I ring the doorbell and announce myself as his daughter. The nurses become excited and notify my father, pointing me in his direction.

"Mr. Jones! Your daughter is here," says a nurse.

"Are you the one that attends BKU?" she asks

I smile, "yes, I do!"

"Oh my gosh, we have heard so much about you! Your dad talks about you all the time. He is so proud!" she says, pinching my arm.

We chuckle and talk as we walk toward his station. There he is, my father, sitting in the dialysis chair with his shirt halfway off - one side drooped over the top of his shoulder, and the other still placed correctly on his body. He wears a long sleeve thermal shirt for dialysis since it gets cold. Because of the recycling process of blood from the machine, he becomes colder during the process.

To give a little back story, my dad first went on dialysis after I was born. During his diagnosis, he was only 20 years old, and my mom was seventeen when he received the news that both of his kidneys failed because of hypertension. They notified him he needed to undergo dialysis to stay alive and detox his system. He got a transplant shortly thereafter, only for it to fail about eight years later. He has not received another transplant since then. Although, his primary doctor promises he will be at the top of the list, only to list absurd conditions before considering him. These include attending all hemodialysis treatments, three times per week, four hours each visit. My dad has been undergoing this for a long time, so he becomes discouraged at the thought. Undergoing this rough process of having a machine pull the blood from his body, cleanse it, then place it back has weakened his heart.

It surprised his doctors to see him survive for this long. I assume that is due to him starting so young. In fact, he is one of the youngest in his dialysis treatment center, which is populated with mostly older patients. Therefore, he always feels prompted to advise and inspire younger patients upon the rare occasion that one comes along. My father's story pains me till this day, because despite his athletic background in boxing, football, and other sports - as well as his time in bootcamp - he also believes in eating healthy. I am still perplexed by how he experiences the most health issues of anyone else I know. His strength is truly remarkable.

"Hey, Mu Baby! Daddy didn't know you were picking me up today," he says, reaching out for a hug and kiss.

"I know! I missed your face so wanted to surprise you," I chuckle, embracing him.

My father and I have an interesting bond. I am his eldest daughter of seven - Shauna, Quill, Vell, Daisy, Neb and Zan - three of which are by marriage. Yet I have always remained a daddy's girl. In fact, all my sisters are. Now, the term "daddy's girl" does not negate my relationship with my mom, who I am also close to. However, even she will agree that I have always been attached to my daddy's hip, and he made it that way!

We both cheese as we catch up, excited to see one another. I help him into his wheelchair and push him over to the scale. The nurses weigh him, comparing his body weight from before the session to his current one. This shows how much fluid the machine removed during the dialysis treatment, as the purpose of dialysis is to remove toxins the kidney would normally filter out.

"I lost 3, that's good," he tells me, rolling himself back onto surface level.

"Good job, Mr. Jones!" says the nurse, patting him on his back.

"Let's keep up the great work, daughter. Let's keep Daddy coming in on time, okay? He's doing good," she says, snagging my arm.

"Oh, I will!" I respond, helping my dad get his items together.

Gathering his bookbag, he realizes something is missing. "Oh, Mu Baby, go get Daddy cup from off the chair," he asks.

I head to his station to grab a large-sized plastic convenience store cup. As I walk, I cannot help but notice specks of blood nearby, and his TV station set to a sports network. I grab the cup and head back to him.

"Alright, pretty girl! We'll see you next time. Make sure you keep your dad on track!" says the nurse.

I help my dad put on his big puffer coat with a fur-lined hood. I zip it up and check for any gaps in wardrobe coverage, making sure he is nice and bundled up. My dad places his left leg on the foot holder at the bottom of his wheelchair as I begin to push it. We say "see you later" to the nurses, pressing the exit button to leave the facility.

"Wait, baby. Take Daddy around the corner to get some ice," he asks, turning back to me.

I snicker and shake my head. Why am I surprised? This is his usual request.

"Okay, DaddyO. I got you," I say, making a U-turn to the

dining room.

I fill his large cup with ice and a small amount of water, per his usual request. I hand it to him, then submit an order for the rideshare.

"Thank you, baby. You have a rental car? Let's get some Popeyes," he asks, with his eyes bulging out with excitement as he crunches on ice.

"DaddyO, I do not have a rental car today, so no Popeyes. But I can walk and get you some carryout once we get to your place," I respond, cracking up.

"Oh, you ordered a ride?" he asks, sipping on the water.

"Yes, DaddyO. I got you. He'll be here soon," I say, showing him the map.

We sit and chat at the front of the hospital while waiting for the ride. He continues crunching on his ice while telling his usual "back in the day street stories". I cannot help but stare at him as he narrates each story. His strength, his story, his love. He is truly the best father I could ask for, but I still wonder if he understands it.

I zone out a little, staring at every little detail: the stubbles of hair on his face; his hands, wrinkled and scarred from hard work, yet moisturized and well-groomed; his shaped-up hairline that complements each wave in his low cut; how his dimples show each time he talks or chews his ice. Then he smiles. His smile is still beautiful - teeth perfectly aligned and strategically positioned to form a Colgate smile. I wonder if he knows how handsome he is. I mean, that is where I get it from! My mama and my daddy. Quick brag moment, I know.

The car arrives, pulling into the hospital valet, which is shaped like a semi-circle. My father and I head to the sloped part of the curb that is designed for disabled patients. It is about 8 o'clock at night, so the wind is brisk and harsh. We bundle up as I push him to the car. We do the routine we learned in rehabilitation, where we position the wheelchair parallel to the car while he pivots his body into the seat, using the car's frame to adjust himself. I hand him his bookbag and cup of ice, then break down his wheelchair, placing it in the trunk of the car.

Normally, the rideshare sends a WAV (wheelchair-accessible vehicle) where the driver pushes him up a ramp and locks his wheelchair in; however, they were unavailable. Thankfully, we are both versed in regular car accommodations. I sit in the backseat, enjoying the conversation between him and the driver as he radiates his charismatic charm.

We arrive at my father's home, where my stepmother Paula greets us. Our relationship has always been interesting - because although she has always made me feel welcomed and loved - her and my dad's marriage is, well, more dramatic than most. However, I can do nothing but respect their love and simply exist in their world when around. I smile and hug her, then wheel my father backwards up the two steps in the backyard, entering the kitchen. He notices every object out of place, dishes in the sink, and everything else that has shifted out of order since he left for dialysis at about 2:30 p.m. He wheels himself through the home, calling for my younger siblings.

"Daisy! Neb! Zan!" he yells.

My stepmother reemerges. "They out with their friends, Junior," she says.

She heads up the stairs. He then does his routine of taking off his coat and lifting his shirt to check his colostomy bag. After seeing it is clean and intact, he heads toward the kitchen, where he washes the dishes. He hands me a washed cup from the sink, asking me to fill it with ice and a swig of juice. I notice soap suds still on the cup, teasing and pointing it out to him as I rinse it. He laughs, as he is used to me pointing out his half-rinsed dishes.

"Mu Baby, Daddy just wants you to know I'm proud of you. I know I haven't always been there the way you want me to, but I love you and know God got big things in store for you. You've been such a big blessing to Daddy, and stayed by my side when I was sick," he says to me, turning the sink water off and drying his hands with a towel.

He continues, "you know, I remember you laying in the bed next to Daddy's bed when I was in rehab," he stops tears from falling from his eyes, "Daddy could never say I appreciate you enough. You are a true blessing to me, and God knew what he was doing when he sent you into my life."

He gestures for my hand. I pat tears from my eyes as I step closer to my father, adjoining hands with him.

"No matter what happens, Daddy will always be here for you, okay?" he says, staring into my eyes.

I know that look. It is the one my great-grandfather gave before he left. The same one my dad has been growing into more and more with each surgery, dialysis treatment, and vicious verbal and physical attack. I could not look into his eyes, for my heart did not want to know the truth of what he was leading to.

"DaddyO, please don't say that. God has so much planned for you! You heard your doctor. You're going to get a kidney next month… and they will find you a prosthetic leg… and your colostomy bag can be reversed. DaddyO, I just need you to stick it through, okay? God got you," I respond, fighting to convince myself everything will be alright.

He looks down, swallowing air, "look, Mu Baby…. Daddy is tired. I want you to look after your little sisters, okay? Daddy has been through a lot and my body is getting weaker and weaker."

"Don't talk like that, daddy! I hate when you say those things," I say, near tears.

How could he be content with leaving me when I have done so much to live for him?

"Mu Baby, I didn't want to tell you this… but Daddy flatlined at dialysis on Tuesday. They brought me back right away, but my heart weakens more and more with each treatment. I used to take it, but now I can feel my heart cramping when the machine is cleaning my blood," he says, clasping his hands together, "I just need you to know Daddy loves you, and I never want you to think I want to leave you or your sisters, but I need you to be prepared just in case Daddy does not make it."

He dries my tears, pulling me in for a hug. He consoles me as I cry at the unthinkable. There is something about his hugs that always calm my fears. His love renews my strength.

I pep up, smiling, "DaddyO, I love you… and everything is going to be fine!"

He stares at me, worried; then softens his eyes. He forces a smile and puckers up his big lips and places a juicy kiss on my cheek.

"Muah!" he says, smiling.

"Ew! I don't know where your lips been!" I laugh, wiping my face.

We both laugh and converse, enjoying the moment of love and family time. I am not too sure what tomorrow holds, and I am not interested in finding out. What was once an anticipation for a better future now feels more like fear that overshadows any thought thereof.

After a good night at my dad's home, I arrive back at campus. There is something lighter about the air, but I cannot help but worry about what tomorrow may bring. My family has been having so many health challenges, I feel each moment is one to savor.

There stands in front of my dorm room door, a bouquet of pink roses. A crystal vase that is lined with specks of gold holds it. I pick them up, smelling them while searching for a card. "I miss you. With love, Mike," it reads. Somewhat disappointed, I take the bouquet into my room, placing them on the dining room table.

"Mani!" my siblings yell.

There they are - feet kicked up in pajamas, watching a movie. They jump up with excitement and jolt toward me.

"Hey y'all," I say, hugging them, "why y'all not in bed? You have school in the morning."

I turn off the television. "Did y'all finish y'all homework?" I ask.

"Yes!" they answer.

"Marcus helped me with my alphabets!" Zoriana exclaims.

"Good!" I respond with a big smile, tickling her.

"Yeah, I'm still wondering why they have homework in Pre-K," says Marcus, chuckling.

I laugh, "I guess they gotta train them early."

We both laugh. Marcus is a great help when he visits from his grandmother's house. Since he is in high school, he only visits when he can. We have somewhat of a love-hate relationship, so throw slight insults at one another while participating in competitive chatter - as brothers and sisters do. Meanwhile. the kids chase each other around the room.

"Alright! Stop all that noise… Let's see those homework folders!" I say, clapping my hands together.

They each grab their bookbags, handing me their homework folders. Marcus and I triple check their answers, then we all get ready for bed - placing out uniforms, shoes, and making sure bookbags are in one spot. Thankfully, the kids have already bathed and brushed their teeth. They lay down on the bed and fall asleep. The rare quietness provokes me to deliberate between sleeping and studying. Because of my hectic class assignment schedule, I choose the latter.

It is the next morning. Today is a lovely day because it is Friday, and I only have one class today. I look forward to freedom, bringing joy to my anxious spirit. Until I remember, I have work tonight. Okay, great. As I walk through the campus quad, wearing some cute jeans and flat boots, Mike approaches me.

"Imani," he says, grabbing my hand.

"Mike… how do you know my class schedule?" I ask, annoyed at his persistence.

He gives me a look. I catch his drift. He and Chante are close, so I am sure she is the informant in this situation. If only she knew the abuse he has caused me.

"Never mind," I say, rolling my eyes and walking away.

He grabs my arm again, "Imani, just listen… please."

Still with my back turned, I stop and take a deep breath. Inhaling a peace of mind; then exhaling all fury, pain, and regret. I turn around to face him, finding him on one knee.

"Boy! I hope you're not about to propose! And I know your knee is cold on this ice!" I say, somewhat flattered by the gesture.

He laughs and gets up, brushing the ice residue from his jeans.

"Did you receive my flowers?" he asks, gazing into my eyes.

I look at him confused - why is he playing the role of Prince Charming, knowing someone sent him from the pits of hell?

I sigh. "Yes, Mike. I got your roses," I say.

"Did you like them?" he asks, beaming with curiosity.

Dodging his question, I drop my head, placing one hand on my hip. "What do you want, Mike? I don't want to be late for class," I say.

Somehow, I can feel him chipping away at my heart's protective barrier. The wind collects a remedy of his cologne, passing it by my nose. I close my eyes, inhaling what feels like the pleasant moments of our past. Then I remember, this is the first man I fell in love with. We were young and - as some would say - stupid; yet my heart remains curious about how things would be if we were more mature.

"Let me take you out. Just for one day. If it goes bad, you won't ever hear from me again," he pleads, grabbing my hand and pulling me closer.

He gets face-to-face with me, teasing the thought of our lips adjoining. I can feel his sincerity. His love. Why is he doing this to me?

"You promise?" I ask with a smirk.

"Promise what?" he replies.

"You promise I won't hear from you again?" I tease.

He fights a smile, brushing his hand across his face.

"Only if it goes wrong," he teases back.

"Okay. Let's do tomorrow at noon," I say, smirking.

"Aight, bet!" he shouts.

He steps back, noticing the purposeful, judgmental look on my face. "I mean, cool... cool," he says, straightening his jacket.

"Aight, bye," I say, smiling as I walk away.

He clears his throat. "Aight then!" he projects.

A guy walks by him as he waves goodbye; he searches for who Mike is waving to.

"Oh, I was talking to her... she's... Never mind," he says to the guy.

Laughing at himself, he places his hands in his pockets and walks off.

So, I have decided to give Mike another chance. I dropped my siblings off at my dad's place, where Mike picked me up, taking me to his place to get ready. As I shower, he sits on the couch watching game highlights on his smart tv. I get out of the shower, putting cocoa butter all over my body, dabbing doses of his favorite perfume on me. Something about this moment makes me happy. Although, a piece of me is afraid.

"I'm so nervous about leaving the kids," I yell from the bathroom.

"They'll be okay with Pops and them," he responds, turning the television down some.

"Yeah, I guess you're right… I mean, I know they are. I just feel super overprotective," I say, getting dressed.

"We sound old," he laughs.

I strut into the living area with my signature date look: a black dress with minimal accessories. I curled my hair into spiral curls and wore a red lip. From the look on his face, I can tell he approves of this dress hugging every curve on my figure.

"Is this what adulting has come to?" I joke, grabbing the earrings from my overnight bag.

He stares at me with his jaw dropped and his body peeled to the couch.

"Wow, you look… stunning," he says.

"Thanks," I say, blushing and cheesing from ear to ear.

He gets up, spins me around and hugs my waist from the back.

"We're not making that reservation," he whispers, kissing my neck.

He spins me around, stopping me once we come face-to-face. He looks into my eyes, dips me, then leans in for a long, passionate kiss. How can something feel so right, yet so wrong? Here I am, feeling those same emotions I felt when I was sixteen. The only difference being it does not feel like Lala land, or a fairytale. It feels real; scary; this one feels more like a roller coaster at a kid's theme park - the type that you underestimate, thinking it will be an easy ride, only to be as afraid as the kids you are chaperoning? Yeah, that kind.

I am especially impressed because he took the time to make reservations at my favorite restaurant in Georgetown. It is such a beautiful night - romantic strolls on the Waterfront, playful tickles, and sporadic heart pouring's of "I love you". It is a perfect date, and it does not stop there.

Over the next couple of days, we become closer again - playing his video game together, strolls in the park, study sessions, cuddling. It feels right… it feels safe. Until… We are sitting on a bench at the National Mall enjoying the sunset. My head is resting on his shoulders, our fingers intertwined. Then he sits up, nervous.

"Baby, I'm so proud of you," he says, looking into my eyes.

"Why is he so nervous?" I think to myself.

"I'm even more proud of you, babe," I reply, smiling and landing a slow and passionate kiss.

"Really… You are the most resilient, beautiful woman I know. I don't know who I'd be without you," he says.

At a loss for words, I swallow a huge gulp of air, searching his eyes for what is coming next. He grabs my hand.

"Imani, all my heart knows is you. Your love. Your kiss. Your touch. I want to spend my life with you," he says, gazing into my eyes.

"Mike, I -" I stumble my words, finding the right words to say.

He places one knee down into the gravel that lines the pond of the National Mall. Holding my hand, he uses his other to grab a small black box from his pocket.

"Imani Fé Holley, you are my rock, my Queen, my beginning, and end. God has truly blessed me when He sent you…. I never take that for granted," he confesses.

I wipe a tear from my eye. "Yes, Mike."

"Yes, what?" he asks.

"Yes, I'll marry you!" I answer.

"Oh! This is just a promise ring. My bad!" he laughs.

"You some trash," I joke, pushing him and gushing with embarrassment. "So stupid, ugh!"

I attempt to pull my hand away, but he holds on tighter.

"I'm just playing, baby. Will you marry me?" he laughs, waiting for a response.

"I guess," I say.

He tilts his head to the side.

"Yes, I will marry you Michael," I say, smiling,

He places the ring on my left ring finger. I pull him up and we come eye-to-eye, embracing one another with a kiss.

"You know, I really don't like you," I joke.

"Yeah, I bet," he laughs, continuing the passion of the moment.

We return to Mike's home, where we remain in lovers' bliss. The moment feels so good. Yet I cannot seem to quiet the voice in the back of my mind that tells me it is only a temporary feeling. As we cuddle and watch television, I fight roaming thoughts. The room feels like it is closing in on me, and I feel alone, though I am right in his arms.

Why does it feel this way? My first love proposed to me, and all I can do is think of everything that could go wrong. Is this a sign? Then, my phone dings. He jumps up, fuming with anger.

"Who the f—k is that, texting you?" he yells.

Startled, I jump back, reminded of why my guards were up in the first place. I reach for my phone, but he jumps and snatches it before I can get to it.

"Damari?" he exclaims.

He throws my phone, grabbing me up from the bed.

"Why the f—k are you still talking to that lame n—a?" he yells, spit flying in my face.

"He's not a n—a," I respond, stuck in his grip.

He cocks his hands backwards, slapping me in the face.

"Oh, so you gonna defend that n—a? Aight!" he pushes me on the floor and takes my phone.

We tussle around his apartment, breaking my phone screen. He tosses me against the wall, choking me and yelling in my face.

He leans into my ear, and whispers, "I will kill both of y'all."

"Mike, I can't… breathe," I say, struggling for air.

With tears flowing down my face, he releases me from his grip. I fall to the floor, remembering the night after the party:

A man wearing a jacket, face mask, and khakis jumps out and attacks me as I walk by an alley. He pushes me against the brick building, choking, and fondling me, licking my cheek. I try to stare into his face but cannot see…

"It was you, wasn't it?" I ask, looking up at him with a blurred vision and a sore face.

"What?" he yells loud enough for the entire apartment building to hear.

"You attacked me that night. I thought it was you, but I convinced myself you would never go that far to hurt me," I say, still catching my breath and stopping tears.

"Nah. Nah. I don't know what you're talking about!" he says.

I can tell he is lying. So, I get up and grab my things. He pushes me, snatching my bag and tossing my items onto the floor.

"Where you think you going?" he yells.

"Mike, I need to go!" I push past him.

"You ain't going nowhere!" he grabs my arm, tossing me onto the bed.

"Get off me! I knew it wasn't real!" I say, jumping from the bed.

"Nah, you ruined us! I proposed to you! But you texting that college n—a!" he says.

"Mike! Damari is my best friend!" I yell, picking my things off the floor.

"Nah, I don't believe you," he says.

I am on ten, and he is calming down.

"Why does it matter? It's not like you've been around to love me anyway!" I say, standing firm.

"What you just say?" he says, balling his fist up.

He launches his fist back, holding my body in place. I place my hands in front of my face, ducking from his blow. I breathe harder and harder, bracing myself for the pain… something much too familiar. Why did I let my guards down… again? He stops. Taking a step back, he releases his fist and takes a deep breath. He swipes his hand across my face.

"He could never love you like I do," he says, glaring into my eyes.

His lips are sealed, yet I can feel his breath steaming from his nostrils onto my face. I have seen him upset before, but this monster is one I do not quite recognize. How can he love me while showing me more hate? It cannot be love. I cannot believe that for myself.

In the nick of time, my phone rings. Only it is not the lifesaving call I thought it to be.

"Mani! Daddy is in the hospital! I have him on three-way," my sister Neb says through the phone.

I panic, gathering my belongings.

"Hey Mu Baby, Daddy wasn't feeling well, so Neb called the ambulance. They say I have some fluid in my lungs," my father says, his voice trembling.

I become angrier and angrier.

"What's wrong?" Mike says, suddenly "concerned" about my well-being.

"Just leave me alone, Mike," I respond.

I grab my things and head out of the door, slamming it behind me.

I deserve better than this.

Another night of sleeping alone and crying my eyes out. Curled into a ball in the dark, worried about what he may do and why he is not answering my calls. How can someone treat me so wrong but have the power to make it right? How can he go on a heartbreak spree, then change his mind and decide to be nice to me… and I comply?

My heart feels like it is bleeding yet exploding with an uncontrollable number of emotions and pain. Humiliation fills my face as I conceal it with emotions of anger and fury. I pick up my phone and blast love songs as each lyric pierces my heart more and more. They are right… I cannot wait to hate him. I cannot wait to act like he never existed on my heart's canvas. Like his fingers never touched my soul. I wish I could forget his smile, his charm, his unique ability to press every single string of my heart's instrument. The good thing is, he makes himself easy to forget.

His egotistical view of ignoring my calls and texts only leads me to mistrust more. I can see him now, puffing his chest up while I call him back-to-back. I must get it together. I must fix my crown. I must get back up again.

Girl, Stand Up!

So, I cry a good cry, blowing snot bubbles and wiping them on my forearm. I delete all our pictures from my phone, then block his number and all social media accounts. I debate removing his contact, then decide to delete that too. I log into my email account and delete every thread with his name attached, blocking his email, too. I must rid him of my mind. I must get his claws out of my soul.

I stand up to take a shower, stepping over my siblings' sleeping bodies on the floor. Why do these kids sleep there when there is a bed? I digress.

I stare in the mirror, gliding my hand across my face. I go through each ripple, exploring and assessing for lumps that were not there before. My eyes look darker, but I cannot recall him striking there, so maybe it is because of stress. Why is everything falling apart… even me?

I remove my clothes, allowing each piece to hit the floor. Like slow motion, I turn on the shower, gauging the temperature with my hand. I jump back at the hotness, but the pain feels good this time. With each scrub, I allow the cut of heartbreak to bleed from my soul. This feels good. This feels… new. Painful, but new.

As I dry off, layering my body with cocoa butter, I fight with tormented memories of Mike. I have a flashback to his hand striking backwards; I close my eyes and flinch, as if he is in the room. How can someone feel like a monster and a knight at once?

I stroll to the kitchen, wearing my robe, and a towel wrapped around my head. This moment feels… still. As I make a cup of hot green tea, I hear someone creaking up to my dorm room door. My heart, once filled with fear, renews with peace. There are three knocks. I can feel the energy sifting through the door. They knock again. I throw on a pair of sweats and a crop top, then look through the peephole.

How did he know I needed him?

I crack the door open, peeping my head through. There he is, six-feet-one-inch with a sun kissed tan that is overshadowed by the paleness of winter. My heart flutters as our eyes meet, almond to almond, brown to brown. Damari, my heart has missed you.

"Imani. Open the door, please," says Damari.

Why is he at my door? Doesn't he know I am on an emotional tirade about his love? Against all love! Doesn't he know the thought of him fulfills every fiber of my being? A love so abundant that it overflows like the Nile River; only contained by the perimeters of the reality surrounding us. I cannot love him the way I want because the pain of my past could be like venom in his veins.

"Imani, I love you. Please open the door," he says.

I cannot. He must leave now!

"Please go away, Damari. I cannot take any more pain right now," I say.

He twists the doorknob, "Fé, please..."

As my heart flutters through my body, I skim my face with my fingertips, triple checking for any truths that may expose of my fight with Mike. Checking my hair and breath, I open the door.

"Yes, Damari?" I say to him. Although my face looks jaded, my heart is looking for him to pull me in.

"I miss you," he says, pushing his way through my door.

"Um, who told you to come in, sir?" I say in a high-pitched voice.

Dismissing my question, he giggles, "Oh, hush that up, girl." He laughs and pulls me into his arms.

I look into his eyes as he holds me face-to-face, searching for every lie possible. I cannot find any. *What is he hiding?*

I attempt to pull away, pushing my arms from his torso. He grabs me firmer, pulling me in closer, rubbing my back. Pain strikes through my abdomen like never before. I slouch over, hitting the floor and screaming with pain.

"Imani, what's going on? Are you okay?" he asks.

I shake my head "no".

He sits on the floor next to me, wrapping his body around mine. I lay my head on his shoulder, allowing each tear to touch his cashmere sweater. As he rubs my head, shushing my quiet tears with each stroke, I battle with the thought of telling him my truth - how my siblings are asleep in the other room and have been living in my dorm room with me; how I ran back into the arms of the man he saved me from; how my dad is in the hospital with pneumonia; and how I fear losing it all, including my sanity.

Instead, I just sink into the moment, rocking in his arms and sulking in his embrace.

They say it is better to love and lose, than to have never tried to love at all. Although that very saying sinks into my soul and inspires me to become hopeful of love like never, it also scares me. The thought of never finding love makes me feel like the room is closing in on me. The thought of loneliness and gloomy nights scare me into submission. I am convinced. I should open my heart up to love again.

Just as quickly as it comes, hope goes. The painful remembrance of... pain... takes away every bit of false courage I thought I got. What is it about my happiness that triggers my pain? Am I bruised beyond lovability? *Is that a… thing?*

Damari's touch comforts me like none other. Just being in his presence causes me to forget every worry I have. Yet, while my thoughts go blank, my emotions run ramped once he walks into a room. I feel like a puppy that whimpers without knowing why. He is the Superman to my Superwoman. Yet, the thought of turning my cape in to him is frightening. What if he fell in love with my strength so much that my weakness pushes him away?

Am I capable of love? Or any good thing at all? Everything is going wrong, and I am not too sure when it will be right again. Only God and time will tell.

CHAPTER EIGHT
Allow Your Heart Time to Grow Strong

MY ALARM BUZZES. The time reads 5:00 a.m. I smack the snooze button and roll back over. Then I realize, the kids have school! I get up, rolling to my feet. I stretch my arms and yarn, making a noise loud enough to wake the entire floor. My morning breath is getting out of control. I stroll to the bathroom, enjoying the ambiance of sleeping children. Showering, brushing my teeth, and journaling in peace, I am now ready to hit the go button on today.

So, I wake the kids, one-by-one, and head to the kitchen to grab cereal bowls. They get dressed, wash their faces, and brush their teeth, yawning and stretching along the way. I line them up, checking for eye crust and brushing edges. The day is ready to start. We grab their bookbags and I grab my workout gear. We say a quick prayer before leaving my dorm, then continue along our way.

My father has been in the hospital about a week. His condition has worsened, and therefore so has my faith. As he has now slipped into a full coma. I cannot help but think of the words he last spoke to me, and how he somehow wants me to be okay with his likely transition. Keeping a grip on life has felt difficult. I can feel myself falling into this pit of emotions, where I somehow always end up back in the same place: miserable. My campus life has decreased. I have missed classes and could not care less about socializing. I try to look normal, but everyone who knows me best knows I am lying.

Both my parents battling health challenges is a hard pill to swallow. So, to cope, I exercise. After ensuring the kids arrive at school, I head to my campus gym to get some cardio in before class. I present a project in class today, then will go to visit my father afterwards. My mother has been doing better, so I feel he needs the most attention right now. I must admit, I am nervous. Doctors have limited visitation for the past few days, so I had to request special permission to see him. This is much different because I am always by his side - watching every health provider that enters his room, every drop of medicine in his IV, and every beep and graph on his monitors. But this time I cannot, and that hurts.

Until my scheduled time to visit, I drown myself in work, school and, honestly, self-sabotage. I cannot help but cling to worries. Feeling positive bothers me now… how do I get out of this?

I enter the gym, grabbing a clean white face towel from the student towel station. As I am logging the linen out, Chante and Claudia approach me.

"Fé, is that you, girl?" exclaims Chante.

We all smile and hug. I am happy to see them but cannot help but crack a crooked smile.

"Hey! How y'all been?" I ask, hugging them.

"Girl, we've been worried about you! Where have you been? D says you're going through some things," says Claudia

"Mm, yeah, but everything will be okay," I say, fidgeting with my towel and combo lock.

"How's your mom? Your dad? How's your family?" Chante asks.

I can see she is sincere. I know my girls care about me, but I cannot help but feel the guilt that I have been a terrible friend.

"Everything is… well… it's okay, I guess," I fight the urge to cry, faking it off by wiping my face with the towel.

I continue, "The good news is my mom is getting out of the hospital soon, and my siblings have been good," I say, smiling and nodding my head. As I think of what to say next, my emotions go through the roof.

"My dad... he... umm..." I swallow air, still fighting the urge to run away.

"His condition has worsened. The doctors are pressing me to unplug him from life support, but I'm not ready to do that. They tried to convince me he was dying the first time, and they lied to me! That was two years ago, and he is still here! They stopped me from seeing my father for some days, and now, suddenly, he won't survive! Why do they target him so much? I just can't!" I burst into tears.

Chante and Claudia console me, rubbing my back and taking me to the women's locker room. We sit and talk, catching up on everything that has transpired.

"How are your brothers and sisters? Who are they staying with now?" Chante asks.

"Oh, they've been staying with some relatives," I respond, clearing my throat, "look, loves, I gotta get going. I present in a couple of hours, then heading to the hospital to visit my dad," I say, standing up and drying my face.

They stand up too. "Okay, Fé, let's do something this week, alright?" says Claudia.

"Yeah, girl! We miss you!" Chante adds, giving me an annoying big bear hug.

We laugh, just like old times. This feels... good.

"I miss y'all too. And okay, just let me know and I'm there," I say.

We all hug, and I go my separate way. The beauty of friendship is remarkable. Especially when friends understand you may fail just as much as they can. My girls having my back, though I do not feel I have had theirs, is a feeling worth staying strong for.

As they leave the restroom, I head to the sink, throwing water in my face.

I am beautiful.
I am smart.
I am resilient.
I am powerful.
I am a child of God.

I repeat to myself, staring at every flaw in the mirror. With each repeat, I somehow feel those things. I am beautiful, smart, resilient, powerful, and I am a child of God! No matter what I see, I must remember that.

I place my items into the locker, blast my favorite music playlist in my headphones, and then head toward the treadmill. I lean onto the machine, stretching and breathing through every thought. Inhaling faith and healing, and exhaling worry and fear. I jump on the treadmill, taking out every piece of frustration I have on the machine. Running faster and breathing harder with sweat dripping into my face, falling between my lips. I feel a little more rejuvenated.

I arrive at Unison Medical Center. The feeling is eerie. I do not trust this hospital to save my own life. The building looks like an abandoned high school that kids never cared to attend. The security guard is dismissive and nonchalant, yet somehow resourceful. He talks, texts, and stream shows on his phone while guests are in front of him, with no shame. Some nurses are professional, some are sketchy. The doctors all seem like a political party to get rid of my dad, like they have a check riding on it. Everything just feels… wrong.

I know great healthcare when I see it. I know amazing doctors, nurses, and caregivers that treat patients with genuine care. In fact, medical professionals saved my dad. However, they hired the wrong batch of medical staff at this specific medical center, with a few exceptions. Therefore, I am terrified.

As I walk down the hallway, I can feel eyes on me. The nurse meets me near the Nurse's station and chaperones me to my father's room. I am immediately on defense and simply do not trust anyone, no matter how big their smile is. For I have seen wolves smile, too.

I enter my father's hospital room. There is the smell again. The hospital smell: the smell of fluids, tubes, and life flashing before my eyes; but forget about me. My dad is in this situation again! There he is… with a breathing tube inserted into his throat, and IV tubes coming from every direction. Is this infusion pump machine even on? Why do they treat my dad like a guinea pig? Does he not matter to them? Do they now know, or understand, the beautiful and powerful man that he is? That he would give the shirt off his back if they needed it!

Do they even care?

My head is throbbing. I massage my temples to stop the splitting pain that ping-pongs around my head. Feeling faint, I grab a seat and pull it next to my father's bed. Scooting closer, I grab his swollen hands and look for a signal of awareness inside his eyes. They are not open. They are closed. He cannot speak. He cannot see… me.

What are they doing to him?

I jump up to my feet, boiling with thoughts of anger and vengeance. Do they know who they are messing with? They cannot get away with this neglect! Then I realize, he confessed to me he was ready to go. Fighting my thoughts, I go to the window, taking a quick glance at the half-empty parking lot. The sun is setting, and I am seeing my reflection in the big, dark, and empty window. However, my reflection does not matter right now… only my father's.

I return to his bed, examining every inch of his body: the blisters on his arms, the fluid throughout his body, and the peeling dead skin. It does not seem like they have taken care of him in days.

Why would they treat him this way?

He does not deserve it. He has fought with surgeries, dialysis treatments, tugs at his heart, harsh words, and worse for years! I just want a happy life for him. Yet perhaps I need to live with his truth instead of mine: maybe his peace on earth looks different than what I imagined.

DaddyO, please don't tell my heart the truth.

I cannot lose him. I cannot understand why he would want to leave his baby girl. Yes, my sisters, brothers, and family, too… but what about me? I have had his back through every storm. I have lost jobs behind him and almost lost my mind when he nearly left us the first time. Why would he do this to us again? Why would he do this to me again?

"Imani, it is not about you," I tell myself.

But why not? Why is this not about me? Yes, he is hurting and wants to be free, but so am I! I am hurting too! What about me?

What about me, DaddyO?

Stopping tears, I gather myself. I take videos and photos of every bruise, bump, blister, tube, monitor, and more. So many machines. So many tubes.

Daddy, I am sorry.

I am sorry I could not be there the way you needed me to be. I am sorry I did not sleep with one eye open, watching every hand that touched you. I am sorry I did not dispute every medical decision, but I tried my best, daddy. I really did.

Can you see how this is hurting me, daddy?

I can feel myself going crazy. I need to breathe. One. Two. Three. Four. Five… I count, trying to breathe slower. Yet nothing is awakening me from this nightmare. That is what it is, right? A nightmare? Please pinch me so I can wake up.

I want my father back. I want to see his slanted eyes, his dimples as deep as the blue sea, his Colgate smile, and his charismatic demeanor — but I cannot. So, I must live in the moment. I must trust God.

But I am not giving up the fight for my father.

I whip out my Holy Bible, turn to his favorite gospel song, and then untwist my bottle of Holy Oil. Blessing the atmosphere, I pray over my father - his healing, his well-being, and his protection. *Is it time to tell my heart the truth?* Did he mean the words he confessed to me saying he was tired, and I that may have to live the rest of my life without him? Why make such a cold decision with a heart so warm and beautiful?

The sun has set, and the moon is the only light shining. Still, there is no light shining within me; and if there is one within my dad, I cannot witness it. All I know is if he wants to fight, I will fight. If he wants to go, I will… well… I would not know what to do. Maybe, just maybe, I need to tell my heart the truth.

I grab my father's hand, speaking to him and sharing my good aura until nurses ask me to leave. We are in this together… always and forever.

DaddyO, I love you.

I have been fighting with the decision regarding my dad's healthcare for a couple of days now. My father listed me as his power of attorney; therefore, it is my duty to make important decisions regarding his healthcare when his condition prohibits him from doing so. This includes surgeries, healthcare methods, and any other important decisions regarding his life. The irony is, when he listed me as his power of attorney a couple of years ago, he ended up needing one a few days later. Here is a little backstory:

Two years ago, my dad suffered a staph infection. He recalled getting a random cut on his leg and thought of it as just a scratch. Unsure of where it came from, he assumed it resulted from the rusted gate on his back porch. One day he was chasing after his dog, and the dog collided with the gate door, causing it to fall. A wire on the door ripped through his jeans, scratching his leg. He disregarded it as the usual scratch, not knowing the impact it would have on his life. He lived in public housing, so a lot of things went unfixed, no matter how many times he called. The gate was one of them.

He continued along with what he was doing. A day or so later, he was heading to dialysis treatment at The District Hospital Center when his right leg fell limp. He described it as losing all feeling in his leg — becoming numb and nearly collapsing onto the ground. Thankfully, he was on the hospital campus so called for help. He later grew a fever and fell unconscious. Doctors called me, informing me of my father's condition. I will never forget it because it was about a week before Christmas. What is it with my family, the holiday season, and health?

They discovered it was a rapidly growing staph infection, so immediately placed him in a medically seduced coma. Therefore, as his power of attorney, it was up to me to make crucial decisions since he could not speak for himself. The infection was quickly spreading throughout his right leg. Therefore, doctors worried it would travel into his central region, effecting his heart and other organs. To prevent this, they suggested I consent to multiple procedures to remove the infection. I did. Unfortunately, the surgeries helped slow the infection but did not cure it. Before we know it, his condition worsened.

I was out of town when I got the news, so took the first flight to D.C.. I will never forget the look on my relatives' faces upon my arrival; everyone looked as if all hope was gone. Shaking it off, I made a beeline to my mother, bracing myself for bad news.

"Is he still alive?" I asked as she embraced me.

She swallowed air and looked down. I could tell she, too, was fighting with her faith. I do not see my mother discouraged too often, so her sadness caused me to panic. Though she kept her composure together for me, her eyes revealed it all. My heart dropped to my stomach as I awaited the looming news.

"Yes, baby. He's still alive, but they say we may lose him in the next 24 to 48 hours. They're advising us to take him from life support," she said, rubbing my back with tears streaming down her face.

The words "he's still alive" is all I needed to hear. Relieved, I shook off the news and tried to stay encouraged.

"Which room is he in?" I asked.

I must admit, I was petrified. My mom escorted me to my father's room where he laid unconscious. Family surrounded him as they mourned the impending news. Everyone looked at me, waiting to see what I would say. I took one look at my father and said, "Oh, he'll be okay." Then I rubbed his arms, kissed him, and left the room.

Little did I know, a war would follow. I slept in the hospital with him for weeks. Since they did not allow visitors to sleep in the Intensive Care Unit (ICU) rooms overnight, I bunked up in the family lounge, jumping up and running to the secured unit every few minutes.

Nurses often swapped my blankets, giving me fresh linen to sleep with. I remember lining my favorite reclining chair with a sheet, then covering myself with a thicker blanket. Fear often awoke me from my sleep, so I constantly rushed to his room - checking his vitals, taking care of his skin, and saying a quick prayer - speaking encouraging words in case he could hear me.

God had bigger plans; so, we kept our faith. Our prayers became stronger and louder. Gospel music rang in his ears often as we covered his body with Holy Oil daily. He once told me to keep the Holy Bible under my pillow as I slept, as his mom, my grandma Lucy, once told him. So, I kept my Bible under his pillow as he healed. Whenever our family visited, I felt comfortable leaving him for long enough to head to the hospital's chapel to pray. In prayer, I promised to have faith over fear.

"Faith over fear. Faith over fear," I repeated.

My God is greater than any fear. I believed that since He made our bodies, He could heal them, too. So, that is what I reminded God of in each prayer. Each praise. Each worship. That I believe in His power to heal.

I did not do it alone, though. Family came and prayed, bishops, deacons, and more. Everyone showed my father love; often coming to spend the night with me, bringing food and changes of clothes. I remember growing closer to my Aunt T during this time. She oozed with love for her little brother like none other: singing New Edition songs to him, making sure I ate, and watching his back while I slept. We took turns making sure he was safe.

My mom's strength also kept me. She worried and often asked our bishop and prayer line to cover him in prayer. She brought me changes of clothes, and always made sure I ate. My cousins and family, too. Everyone, including my little sisters, used the Holy Spirit and prayed over his healing. Because of this, God moved:

We prayed for a stronger heart so he could get approved for surgery. God did that.

We prayed for him to awaken from his sedation. God did that.

We prayed for his breathing and lungs to grow stronger so they could remove the breathing tube. God did that.

We prayed for safe surgeries, and the infection removed. God did that.

For what could God not do? Nothing. All things are possible with Him!

Eventually, the same doctor that tried to persuade us to unplug him from life support was the same one amazed at God's glory. A moment I will never forget.

"Is that Mr. Jones?" he yelled in amazement. "Wow! He looks great. Let's get him to a regular floor this week," he said.

My father's surgeon remarked, "Have you all been praying? I can tell!" He smiled, informing us that my dad's heart was now strong enough for surgery.

What could God not do? Nothing!

We have experienced the glory of God: my father lived when doctors thought he would not survive; my mother survived two brain aneurysms; my Grammy survived an open-heart surgery; and he continues to provide us shelter during our homelessness. We have no right to complain! God is good all the time.

On another note, though I have witnessed his miracle-working power, I know when His plans may be a little different from mine. My spirit tells me this may be one of those times. Yes, God brought my dad through a staph infection a couple of years ago; he lived years later when doctors said he would only have hours! In the same, God could heal my father from this pneumonia. He could heal his lungs and give him more life to live. Yet, as much as my heart wants to believe it, my spirit knows different.

So, I fight.

I fight with my spirit, my heart, my mind. This cannot be true. Why does he not want to fight? He has been through a lot, I know, but does he not want to see his future grandchildren? Does he not want to see how God can bring him through, again?

I do not want to give up on my father.

For the past day or so, I have done nothing but think of my father: his smile, his hugs, his juicy cheek kisses; the way he boosts my mood with his proudness in me. I just miss him. To be honest, I could use my mother's touch right now. Thankfully, she gets out of the hospital today. She amazes doctors with her progress. They say she has healed quicker than most craniotomy patients. I am grateful for her, no matter what trials we are going through.

So, I head downstairs to the lobby of my dorm. I see the gold Nissan Maxima pull up at the entrance. There she is: my beautiful mommy. I jump for joy and run to the car, hugging her, my Uncle Nick, and my gorgeous great-grandmother. Mama and I do our usual chitter-chatter before I escort my mother to my dorm room. She is walking a little slower, but everything seems normal. I cannot help but wonder if she is staying strong for me; for us. I want to know the truth: is her head hurting? Does it hurt when she walks? What is she battling? I do not want her to battle it alone. For I feel her burden is mine to carry, too.

The kids are staying with their teachers for a little, which gives me time to gather myself. It also gives my mom a period to get back into the flow of things before they return to us. It has only been a few days since they left, so we will get them in about another week.

We arrive at my room, smiling and appreciating the time. God is so good, and we know that to be true. She opens my fridge and grabs a bottle of water and a banana. Meanwhile, I unpack her backpack and update her on everything that is happening. We discuss my father's health as I show her pictures I took during my visit.

"Manz, can you open this water bottle for your momma, please?" she asks, handing the bottle to me.

"Sure!" I respond, opening the bottle and peeling the banana.

"Thanks, My Gorgeous One," she smiles.

"You're welcome, beautiful!" I smile back.

There's a brief silence as she sips on water, taken aback by its coldness. I swallow air, looking down, not quite knowing what to say next. Not that I am awkward with my mother, I just do not talk much lately. I am losing myself and I am not too sure what to do about it. In her usual fashion, she notices my disposition.

"You alright, Gorg?" she asks, staring into my eyes.

The stare only she could have. The one that tells me she already knows the answer to her question. She just wants me to say it out of my mouth. You know, rhetorical. I take a deep breath and begin fidgeting with my pants.

"Umm… I don't know how much stronger I can be, ma," I say.

I attempt to stop the tear from falling down my eyes, but one escapes anyway. She places down the water bottle, scooting closer and comforting me.

I continue, "I know I'm supposed to be strong… and that I have it in me... but I don't know how much I can take. Everything is all my fault, and I don't know how to fix it."

"No, no, no, Gorg. Nothing is your fault. You are a wonderful daughter to me and your dad, and a great big sister to your brothers and sisters." She lifts my chin. "We are so lucky and blessed to have such a loving daughter. Never forget how much we love you, okay?" she says.

"It's just that… had I not given permission to amputate his leg, he would not have been mistreated the way he was... and he would not be in the situation he is in… again," I confess, still trying not to cry.

It should be all about her healing on her first day home. Yet I cannot help but release all walls with her love embracing me. She hugs me, rubbing my back.

"Manz, you did nothing wrong, okay? You are strong and I have your back. Your daddy knows that which is why he gave you permission to make those decisions," she says. "Okay?"

I nod my head yes, crying in her arms. I cannot help but feel guilty for not holding back my tears. My mom just came home, and I am putting more worries on her? She has enough to worry about. I am not sure what tomorrow brings. Every inch of me wants to save my father, like we did - well, like God did - before. I am just not sure he wants to be saved.

The doctor called to inform me my father flatlined three times back-to-back last night. So, although it pains me, I plan to visit him to pray and hear what he and God want. As I arrive at Unison Medical Center, I can feel my bones shatter within me. My heart drops as I see his room from the parking lot. I walk what feels like the last mile - passing each nurses' station, smelling the "hospital smell" in the hallways. I don myself up in PPE (personal protective equipment) - a gown, mask, hairnet, gloves, and shoe covers - and enter my father's room.

There he is, in a worse condition. However, there is a silver lining: he may open his eyes today, according to the nurse. Before my arrival, I called and asked the nurse if they can allow him to open his eyes. Although this feeling feels good - to look forward to seeing his beautiful brown eyes - it unraveled my nerves. How are they able to control that? I was told he was in a coma. Because of this, his eyes have been closed each time I visited the hospital, no matter how much I tried to wake him. Yet (this time) his eyes will open upon my request? I am on guard; I have ridden this rodeo before.

I examine his body - bumps, bruises - everything is worse. He has gangrene in his hands from what looks like an IV burn. This occurs when someone places the IV needle in the wrong location. His skin is blistering more, and his body is more swollen. As I record every detail, including details of his nails, I cannot help but breakdown and cry.

I want to fight for him.

I want to fight for my father's life. This is something I have seen before. The last time he was in the hospital, they convinced us his body had given out on him, but it was not true. I know doctors do their best, but some do not show genuine care.

I become infuriated. My father does not deserve this. He is such a good man. Why is he in the hospital, again? Why does he have to fight for his life, again? Regardless, I know his life is much more beautiful than these moments. He is still a warrior in my eyes, and in life, period. I stare at my DaddyO, triggering a memory from my childhood:

I was in fourth grade. My dad took me to school on Monday after I spent the weekend with him. However, I was so excited to see my dad that I begged to skip school that day. Hoping to get backup, he took me to the principal's office to encourage me to attend class. Instead, the principal, Mr. Woods, smiled and looked at us. "That's okay. Imani is one of our star students. If she wants to spend the day with her dad, she should spend the day with her dad," said Mr. Woods. We smiled, leaving the school to go household shopping on H Street Northeast. Our daddy-daughter time meant the world to me. A memory I will cherish forever. One he talked about till this day.

As I bend down along his bed, crying, my father's eyes open. However, they do not open all the way. He has so much fluid in his eyes that his lids have become swollen, so they open halfway. Although disheartened, I am overjoyed to see his eyes.

"DaddyO!" I scream with a huge smile on my face.

"You're awake!" I say, grabbing his hand and wiping a tear with my other hand.

He blinks to acknowledge what I said and attempts to smile around the breathing tube. I continue talking and asking questions as he blinks to respond to each one. From the look in his eyes, I can tell he is tired. His words repeat in my head, and now I see them coming to fruition. Attempting to keep my smile, I stop talking… staring into his eyes.

"DaddyO," I say, cradling his hand as he looks into my eyes, "I don't want to lose you. I know you feel you haven't been the best father, but you are the best father I could ever ask for." Bursting into tears, I continue. "I don't know why. It's just, I see you living and thriving. I see you getting a prosthetic leg and walking again, your colostomy bag being reversed, and you getting a kidney transplant, so you won't be on dialysis. You are going to meet your grandbabies for the first time and walk me down the aisle. I see you being old, Mr. GQ, dancing at the cookout with your cane. I see it all! Don't you see it, too, DaddyO? I want you to stay. I'm so sorry!" I cry.

I cry harder and harder. He looks at me. Although he cannot talk, I can hear him loud and clear. He wants me to be okay with his decision, but I am not ready for it. I do not want to tell my heart that truth.

"DaddyO, I know you are ready to go. I know you are tired. But can't you fight? I know you could win if you wanted to… please?" I say, begging him.

He stares at me, closes his eyes, looks down, then looks back at me. I can tell he has already decided.

I must learn to accept it.

"No matter what happens, DaddyO, please know that I love you. I wish I could talk to you right now. I wish I could hear your voice. I love seeing your beautiful eyes, and I am glad you are awake." I cry more. "I am so sorry you're going through this… it is all my fault," I cry for minutes.

He looks at me with sad eyes, then shakes his head "no". He wants to tell me it is not my fault, but I know it is not true.

"It is my fault, DaddyO. I was the one who agreed to amputate your leg, and I'm the one who consented with those surgeries your body went through. I wanted to save you because you wanted to be with us. But all that did was cause more pain… I am so sorry! You didn't deserve to be treated that way." His eyes lower as he looks into mine.

I continue, "I want you to know you are the strongest man I know. No matter what negative things people have said, none of them could bear all that you have. No matter how many times you wanted to give up, you hung on for us. I will never forget that."

His eyes widen, almost as if he is looking for the magic words. However, I cannot bring myself to say them. My heart cannot handle it.

"DaddyO, I support you either way. I know you are tired and

have been through a lot… I… just…" I say, struggling to say the words. His eyes widen more.

"I'm sorry, daddy. I just can't let you go." I hold his hand a little tighter, careful not to hurt him.

He closes his eyes again, shaking his head. I can tell he is sad about my denial of the inevitable.

"I am going to fight for you, okay? If they did something wrong, I will fight for you. I will always be your voice and will never give up on you," I say, kissing his hand.

I continue to talk to him and update him on everything, experiencing a rollercoaster of laughter and crying. I reminisce on memories and try to find every word imaginable to convince him to stay. However, it is different this time. We are on two different pages.

So, I grab my Bible that I tucked under his pillow and read scripture. I play gospel music and cleanse the atmosphere. I do this for only a few minutes; for my spirit tells me this may be the last time I talk to him. Therefore, I sit back down and continue talking. I look at every detail of his eyes, his face, his expressions. I am truly going to miss him.

I check the clock, noticing it is past the visitation hours. My heart palpitates as I realize my time is running out. I continue loving on my dad, as we FaceTime family so they can see his eyes too. I do not want this to end.

The nurse knocks on the door. "Hey sweetie. I'm sorry, but visitor hours are over," she says with an empathetic face.

I nod at her, shedding a tear. I turn back to my father, who is looking at me with the same eyes I do him - that of a fearful goodbye.

"Alright, DaddyO," I say, fighting tears with a crackling voice, "I'll see you later, okay? I love you and I know we can get through this. God got you no matter what, and so do we," I say.

No matter what I say, nothing feels like quite enough. No words

can describe what he means to me, and all I could express to him.
Why my father?

He could have so much more life. He is so loving, strong, charismatic. He is a remarkable human being. I guess God takes his good ones early. I look into his eyes as he stares back at me. We are not talking, but it feels like it says more than words could. I kiss his forehead and cheek, then hug him.

"I love you, DaddyO, and I will always be here for you," I cry, leaving to exit the room.

As I walk away, we stare at each other. I continuously stop along the way, wishing I could save him. Wishing I could take away all his pain. Wishing I could give him the life he once dreamt of, the one I still dream of for him.

"I'll be back tomorrow, okay DaddyO?" I say to him.

He closes his eyes, then looks back at me. I can tell this may be our last goodbye.

"I love you, DaddyO," I say, leaving the room.

His eyes never blink as I leave. The distance between us feels so far, yet he feels near all at once. I can feel the energy of goodbye, yet my heart is still prepared to fight.

I still want to fight for my father.

My dad slipped back into his coma shortly after I left; this information caused me to spiral closer to the edge. So, my girls Chante and Claudia took me out to comfort me. Damari joins us on a night out on U Street Northwest; his presence always makes me feel a little better. I put in the extra effort to look decent: heeled boots, jeans, and a nice shawl. I have been having a lot of bad hair days lately, so opted to wear a stylish hat with a good red lip. We enjoy a few drinks and some good music in the lounge. It feels great to smile, but I cannot help but drift off, thinking about my father. I keep visualizing his eyes as I exited the room the last time we saw each other.

My phone lights up: it is Mike, again. His text reads: "I miss you. Call me when you can." Since our fight, he has called me constantly, but I am not ready to talk to him yet. The last thing I need is him making me feel worse off. He does not realize that his anger may last for a moment, but his strikes and words have a lasting impact.

Fighting off the memories of Mike, and numbing the pain of my dad, I down another shot. Damari, Chante, and Claudia all surround me with good vibes, smiles, and plenty of jokes. It feels good to have a moment of bliss. For a second, I convince myself that everything is the same as before.

It is about two in the morning when I arrive at my dorm room, so I assume my mother would be asleep. I fumble with the keys, dropping them twice before fitting them correctly into the key slot. As I open the door, I block my eyes from the light. Why is she still awake?

I see my grandfather, Stoney, chatting with my mom on the couch. Since Grammy's health scare, Stoney has grown more open and vulnerable toward loved ones. He has always been a loving dad and granddad; however, those moments made him more sentimental about showing love. They ask me how my night was. I slur my words, telling them it was fine. I join them in the living room after sobering down in the shower.

"How are you doing, Pebbles? … Really?" Stoney asks me.

He calls me Pebbles in response to my nickname I gave him. All my cousins and siblings call him granddad, but I call him Stoney because of his coldhearted demeanor. We know it is not the case. In fact, he is the coolest in town.

"I'm doing okay, Stoney. Just making sense of everything," I respond, faking a smile. However, I am only fooling myself.

"I know you're not okay, Imani," he fixes his glasses on his face, and takes a deep breath, "I don't know how to say this right here… but you may have to be okay with letting Noah go. I love your dad too, but he may be ready," he says.

I become quiet, fighting my thoughts and any other emotions that arise.

"Yes, baby. Your daddy is strong, but we can't keep letting him go through that, baby," my mom adds.

They both converse with me. I hear every word, but I do not grasp what they are saying. I cannot seem to accept the fact that this is the conversation. *Is my hope not enough?* Can faith not carry us through, again?

"Listen, Pebbles. You don't need to decide now, it's really God's decision," says Stoney.

"Yeah, baby. Remember that God has the final say, no matter what decision we make," my mom adds, alluding to my grandmother surviving through something similar.

"But I'm not ready to let him go. I just can't," I say, stopping tears.

They console me, "I know baby," my mother says, hugging me.

My grandfather rubs my back, "Pebbles, don't rush into it. Give your heart time to grow strong, then you'll know what to do."

After talking with my mom and grandfather, I realize I am not alone in this fight. The love and care they have for my dad assures me I have partners in this fight - that feels good. Yet I cannot help but feel like my father's life lies in my hands. That very thought keeps me awake at night, taking over everything I know. I have slept little since he has been in a coma. Every time my phone rings, I become terrified, thinking it is a call saying he is no longer here with us. I do not want him to go alone. It would pain me, but I want to be there with him.

Stoney's words run constantly in my mind, "Give your heart time to grow strong". Yes, he is correct. This is not a rushed matter. After all that my father has battled for our family, he deserves a strong heart and a peaceful spirit on my behalf. I must be at peace with his peace.

I must allow my heart time to grow strong.

CHAPTER NINE
Until We Meet Again

TODAY IS THE day, sigh. We must say goodbye to my first love. My father. My DaddyO. Words cannot explain the numbness I feel, but I guess that is fitting. How can one describe numbness except with that simple, yet complex, word? It is pain, nervousness, uncertainty, love, and fear all wrapped into one enormous ball of an attempt to remain strong. Well, to at least appear that way. On the outside, I appear much stronger than I feel inside. Everyone seems to watch me, wondering why I have not burst into tears yet. Why not? Why have I not? What is wrong with me? Nothing! Nothing is wrong with me at all! Please bear with me as I am trying to maintain what little sanity I have left. I am slowly losing my soul…

I am slowly losing my grip.

My mother gives me that look. You know, the one where she gazes into my eyes and tells me with her eyes that she knows I am in pain, is here for me, and I am free to let it all out? Yes, that one. So, I avoid her eyes. I avoid them because it will unleash the barriers that withhold my tears. It will release the waterworks that I have built up through every surgery with DaddyO; somehow, adding his tears to mine. Doubled, it feels like all those tears are waiting to fall from my very numb eyes.

Little by little, my family arrives at the Unison Medical Center. It is a miniature family reunion. It elates us to see each other–hugging and sharing jokes in the parking lot and smiling every time another relative arrives. "Ay, that's Pookie!" (Just kidding, I do not have a cousin by that name… or do I?). Reality sinks in as we release the grips of our embrace and look to the enormous elephant in our peripheral view: the hospital. It reminds us why we united: to say goodbye to DaddyO. In the back of my mind, I know my father would smile seeing all the love and support from family.

After about twenty family members arrive, I call the doctor to let him know we are ready to make our rounds to see my dad. He informs us the elevator is out of order and we can either come back tomorrow morning or wait for it to be fixed, though there is no guarantee it will operate soon. I pray to God, asking for His perfect timing, asking He allows my father to go when He is ready, no sooner and no later.

I pull my little sisters - Neb, Zan, and Daisy - aside, asking them what their preference is. From the look in their eyes, I can tell this is not a conversation or decision they are ready for. I understand, as they are all under 18. So, I place on my "big sister hat", and call for my family's undivided attention. That is when security comes down, informing us that elevators are still not operating, and we may need to return another day. This does not settle well with our spirits. Therefore, we ask him to give us a little time to decide what we will do.

"So, who wants to leave tonight and gather again tomorrow?" I ask.

Everyone looks around at each other, and no one raises a hand. I smile inside. It feels good to see extra love and support.

"Okay, who wants to wait it out tonight?" I ask.

Everyone's hands shoot up.

"I'm going to see my Unc! He needs to know I love him," my cousin Carl shouts.

"Yeah, my Unc is the best man I know. I'll sit here all night if I have to," Tony adds.

I agree, I ain't going nowhere! So, we wait. We pull out lawn chairs from the trunks of our cars (did I mention we are always prepared for a cookout?). My cousin Rozzi looks out by having an ice cooler filled with fresh ice in the trunk of her car. How did she? … never mind. I chuckle at her preparedness. All that matters is that we have each other, and some fresh ice, to go with our non-alcoholic (not really) beverages.

The security guard returns, and we inform him of our decision to stay. We wait a few hours, exploring the emotions of the night, leaning into each other's strength. Security returns around midnight. He is a darker-skinned male with a heavy-set frame and average height, a low haircut and long facial hair. By now, he has come back so many times with updates that we are more comfortable with him, as he is with us.

"Hey, he is a blessed man to have this type of support," he says to us as we gather around for an update.

He continues, "it looks like they cannot fix elevators until tomorrow. We have looked at different angles, but not one elevator in the building works right now. However, I spoke with the doctor, and they have approved me to take you through the stairway. Me and my colleagues would escort you up to your loved one's room. The only restriction is, there can only be three visitors at a time, so we will need to make multiple rounds until everyone can go upstairs."

We all agree without hesitation, jumping for joy that we get to see him. My father's room is on the fifth floor of the hospital, which means we must all walk five flights of stairs to get to him. We talk amongst each other, agreeing on who goes in which rounds.

I am going up last since I am the one who must decide to remove him from life support. As time passes, my heart sinks to the pit of my stomach. I can no longer fight what is to happen next. Yet, I somehow wish I could turn back the hands of time to save him from going through this again.

It is my time to go up and make that decision. A decision that will change the course of all our lives. One that has haunted me for over two years. I look around at my relatives, almost praying someone would save me—save me from reality. Save me from the inevitable. Yes, that is the word of this chapter: inevitable.

However, they could not. They all look at me with sad eyes and offer their love and support as we all get through this difficult time.

I ask one last time, "Has everyone gone up?" everyone replies "yes".

That leaves me, my mother, and my oldest cousin, Keisha.

I ask Keisha, "Are you sure you want to go up for this?"

She has already experienced so much with her firstborn, my baby cousin, Nylah Love, who has battled cancer since a toddler. Throughout it all, she remains one of the sassiest, smartest, tell-it-like-it-is little girls I know. She is a true princess warrior; how could she not be? She stems from a long line of strong men and women, including her mommy. How can Keisha handle this again? She insists, and I can do nothing but respect and appreciate her for doing so. I am grateful.

So, here we are. All three of us walk up each flight of stairs together, often taking a break for my mother to rest. I admire her willpower to get up the stairs despite the physical pain she feels. I wish there was a way I could help soothe her pain - the physical torment she feels with each step, her fight for her own health, and the emotions she experiences as we get closer to setting her first love free.

We make it to the fifth floor. I can smell the neglect in the air. I cannot help but grow angry at the memories of my dad's physical state. The floor has an aroma of sickness, yet no actual presence of professionals who care to cure their pain. Eyes are on us as security guides us through the empty floor. People are stunned that so many visitors are allowed in during such a restricted time. Only patients who are considered as being on their "death bed" can have loved one's visit. Therefore, this only meant one thing: DaddyO would soon depart us.

My father's nurse greets us at the door to his ICU room. I will never forget his kindness. He keeps a Catholic faith and continues to offer prayer and comfort for support. We tell him we may accept his offer. I peek in the room at my DaddyO. He is the same: unconscious and on a ventilator. My heart shatters one more piece. I take a deep breath, trying to control the many thoughts fleeing my mind.

"Maybe he'll be okay."
"Is this the right decision?"
"What if he wakes up?"
"Are the doctors telling the truth?"
"Is his body deteriorating, or are they lying to us?"
"Am I a murderer?"
"Am I killing my father?"

In her usual impeccable timing, my mother rubs my back. "It's going to be okay, baby," she says.

I nod my head, getting donned up. After we put on the necessary PPE, the nurse permits us to enter my father's room.

"Why?!"
"Why do I have to enter his room?!"

My heart beats a million miles a minute. I cannot give up on him. I cannot be the person who pulls the plug. My mom and cousin are in front of me. They both gesture for me to enter the room first.

I can't.
How?
Why?
Let's just go home.
Let's just give him more time to come around.

The truth of the matter is, he is already gone. We just have to let him go within the physical realm. So, I muster up the energy to enter the room. Tears fall as my body falls limp. Then, I feel a strength like none other. We must be strong for him, just as he has been for us.

There he is—so handsome with skin like brown sugar and a head shaped like an egg. The strongest man I have ever known. The first man to hold me, to tell me I am beautiful, to speak life into me, to hold me to heaven and give me to God as an infant. There he is: my DaddyO. Muted by a breathing tube and poked and prodded with every critical care tube known to man.

How could he endure this?
What is he thinking?
Is he in pain?
Or is his spirit already enjoying the milk and honey of the promise land?

I will never know the answer to my questions, for only he and God know that. However, what I know is I cannot stand to see him this way.

We surround his bed. Silence and grief fill the room like a thief in the night. How dare they do this to him? I blame the medical care team! How can they have tubes coming from every side of his body and IV tubing that has nothing traveling through it? They turned his feeding machine off... why are they starving him? Is this their fault? Have they singled-handedly decided my father's fate as if they are his creator? I am fuming with anger. Questions. Pain.

In walks Doctor Nubian with a smirk on his face and an even more relaxed posture. I cannot help but see him as a suspect. Is my father just a check to him? Again, I know there are some skilled doctors, but has he even been working today? Did he just come from sleeping in his office? Maybe not. All I know is I did not want to see his face.

"You must be his daughter, Imani?" says the doctor. I reply yes.

"Are you ready to remove the ventilator?" he asks.

"No, not yet," I firmly respond.

My mother, cousin, and I continue examining my father's body, checking for all bruises, tubing, blood, dirt, and any other signs of neglect. As we are examining him, the doctor motions for the nurse to grab other medical professionals. How rude! My family and I look at him, wondering what is going on. A man enters the room, no greeting or anything - just mute. He makes a beeline to my father's bed and begins taking the tube out of his mouth.

"What are you doing?" I exclaim.

"Oh, you're not ready to remove the ventilator?" asks the doctor, still with a slight smirk on his face.

"No!" we all reply.

"Sorry, we thought you were ready," he states.

"No, we need to pray over him first," my mom says.

The doctor and medical tech apologize and leave the room.

This makes us so angry! Why is he in such a rush to kill my father? My mother's first love and my cousin's uncle? Feeling the negative energy in the room, we decide to bless the atmosphere. We play his favorite Gospel songs, read scripture, bless him with Holy Oil, and touch his body, letting him know we are here. We profess our love for him, laughing at distant memories and allowing our tears to touch his nearly cold skin.

The nurse returns. We let him know we receive his offer to say a last rites prayer over my dad before we let him go. He obliges, grabbing our hands as we form a circle around his bed. We place the Bible on his bed as we send our positive thoughts and good vibrations to him. The nurse says the prayer, as we all stand in agreement. The nurse leaves the room, giving us more time with my dad before he returns with the medical team. My stomach falls, and I imagine my mom and cousin's too. I still cannot believe this is happening.

Someone, please awake me from this nightmare.

It is time. We look at one another, nodding our heads in agreement. Rather than call him in, we decide to wait until the nurse returns to the room. This gives us more time with DaddyO. In the meantime, we cry, laugh, and speak a blessed spiritual life over him, caressing him every chance we get. The nurse returns with the medical team.

We take a deep breath.

We step back toward the wall, making space for them to approach his bed. I breathe hard, gasping for air. My mom links her arm around my left arm; my cousin links hers to my right. We watch as the doctors remove the tubes, awaking my father.

He goes through his transition, attempting to breathe, yet struggling with the fluid that has overtaken his lungs.

"Put it back! I change my mind! Put the tubes back in! He's not ready!" I scream, falling to my knees.

My vision becomes blurry as tears fill my eyes. I beg them to turn the machine back on, to reverse my decision. My family upholds me, telling me he is ready. They pull me up, consoling me as we all witness this decision.

"Hold him. He needs to know you are here," Keisha says.

I run to him, hugging him, and kissing his forehead. I place my hand over his heart as I whisper loving words into his ear. My mom holds me up as I battle with my strength. My cousin stands on his right side, cradling his hand and looking into his eyes. I cannot see them. He continues to breathe, fighting with the fluid. His breathing slows down.

"No, Daddy! Please don't leave me!" I cry aloud.

He breathes harder and harder. Each time I cry, he tries to keep going. I fight with the thought of letting him go. Why would he want to leave me? Leave us? However, there is this glorious voice in my spirit telling me to be at peace. It tells me to say the words that I cannot bear to say. So, I cry, and my father tries harder to survive.

I go back and forth between telling him to stay and uttering the words that it is okay to be at peace. Only for him to go along with whatever I ask him to do each time. Each time I beg, he breathes harder; each time I seem at peace, his breathing slows. Weeping, I rub my father's chest above his heart and kiss his forehead. I tell him I love him and that I will never stop fighting for him. I am filled with anger, sadness, loneliness, and uncertainty.

Then, a peace overfills me. I can feel God and my father telling me it is okay to say those words. So… I hold him… allowing my tears to fall onto his beautiful brown skin. I feel his heart beating into the palms of my hands as I kiss his forehead over and over and over again.

"DaddyO, I love you so much. And I will never stop loving you," I whisper into his ear.

I can feel a shift in the atmosphere. That inner small voice continues to nudge my spirit and has now illuminated into my mind. I take a deep breath, kissing and loving on him. Reminding him of what he means to me… and to all of us. Then I remember his pain, and his smile.

I see a happier DaddyO, smiling and dancing to Go-go music at the family cookout. He is happy, whole. He is himself.

It is well with my soul. I lean in closer to him, kissing his cheek and holding his heart.

"It's okay, DaddyO. No more pain. Be at peace. Be free. I love you," I say, whispering into his ear.

My tears fall onto his cheek. I can feel his heart stop as his body sinks in. Peace and harmony fill the room, and I see a white light float into the air. My spirit is lighter, and my heart is smiling a little. I look up, still checking for a heartbeat, but nothing is there.

"I think he transitioned," I say, looking at my cousin Keisha as tears stroll down my face.

"He did. He looked up to you, mouthed 'I love you', smiled, then he left," she says, with a feeling of peace over her.

My mom hugs me with tears streaming down her face; then she caresses my father. Tears fall, but it is different this time. This time, it feels peaceful. No agony. No pain. Just… peace.

"It's almost like I can feel the angels in the room. Like all our relatives welcomed him in," I say, smiling.

"Yeah, from how he smiled, it looks like he was happy to see someone," my cousin replies.

"I'm sure your grandma Lucy welcomed him," my mom says, alluding to my father's mom, who passed when I was five.

"Yeah, I guess so," I smile. "I love you, DaddyO!"

"Yeah, we love you so, so much, Noah," my mom adds.

"Love you, and miss you already, Uncle Noah," Keisha adds.

We wipe our tears away as we continue to love on him. The atmosphere is peaceful as we talk about cherished memories of my father. Preparing to head back downstairs to inform our family of the news, we say our last goodbyes. We gather his items, kissing his face, and gliding our fingers along his now colder skin. Tears stream as we take deep breaths, peeling ourselves from his energy field. Leaving the view of the shell that what was once my father, my cousin's uncle, and my mother's first love. Once we are downstairs, Keisha stops me, grabbing my shoulders.

"I'll tell you something that has helped me… always remember to cry with your head up. It reminds you that although everything is not okay, you will somehow be okay. You will get through it," she says, pulling me in for a hug.

A tear falls as we embrace. That explains how she always seems so strong through everything she has endured. Come to think of it, I have never seen her with her head hanging low. She always looks up at the sky. Her strength, resilience, and ever-enduring love for her daughters Nylah and Chunky Cheeks will always be remarkable to me. I will always say she is one of the strongest women I know.

How can something so painful be so beautiful all at once? I can do nothing but remember my daddy. My first love.

His smile.
His charisma.
His everlasting love.
How he shook his foot while playing the video game.
How he could talk for ages about his "street days".

My first love. My DaddyO. I am not sure how I will live on without him, but I know I must make it through. I must remember to cry with my head up.

DaddyO, I love you forevermore. We will never stop missing you.

Until we meet again.

CHAPTER TEN
Cry With Your Head Up

IT IS A rainy night in D.C.: heavy rainfall, gloomy skies, and slippery streets. The worst part of it all: I forgot my umbrella. Even worse: I put a genuine effort into my hair today. The rain has drenched my shirt, and I am covered in sweat, yet I am still trying to regain tenacity for my studying. So, I continue to head east on campus toward the library. I run around a tall grey bricked academic building where I discover a canopy shielding chairs from the storm. I shift my jacket that lies on the top of my head, covering my hair. Next, I dash from the corner of the building towards the canopy. Slouching into the chair, I place my jacket back onto my body and release a sigh of relief, pointing the heels of my (now broken) 4-inch heels toward one another. At last, there is a little coverage from the rain.

I am still trying to hang on as life has gotten tougher. My cousin's words, "Cry with your head up," ring in my ears throughout the day. I must navigate through this pain and numbness I feel every second of every day. I can tell my heart is still not ready to learn the truth. Although it has grown strong, as my grandfather suggested, it seems to hide behind reality's gates. It is a separate reality where everything I am experiencing is a delusion, believing I will wake up at any moment to enjoy life again.

Since my father's transition, I cannot help but think of his smile and battle with the possibility he could have survived. Then I remember the look in his eyes, telling me he was ready, and the peace in the atmosphere when he transitioned. I cannot help but think of his dimples, his scent, his style, his charisma, his amazing hugs, his annoying juicy kisses that never failed to make me smile, and his… love. He had a love for me that only a father could express; no one could replace that feeling. Never.

My mom and I have been working hard to plan my dad's funeral. My cousins, sister, and other loved ones are helping however they can, and it feels good to have the support. If only he could witness all the love others have for him. I want to give him the celebration he deserves. One fit for a true warrior. However, I must admit, I have struggled through the process. I bounce between classes, work, family needs, and arranging his home going celebration. Honestly, I do not know how I would survive the storm if it were not for my mom's love, support, and efforts. Each time I run back into my shell of normality, she reminds me we can do this and that he deserves the best home going celebration that we can give.

My siblings have moved back into my dorm after staying with their teachers for a couple of weeks while my mother healed. Before he went into the hospital, my father took in Sabrina and Jasmine for a few days. We all believe my mom is at a good place to take on duties again. She has been recovering from her surgery, and we are all glad to have her home. The kids are flourishing at school and are happy to be back on campus with us. Sometimes I wonder how everything is impacting them. Do they feel the weight of our homelessness, too? Or are they happy to be all together? Either way, I am grateful for God's steadfast goodness. We do not yet have a home to call our own; but He always makes sure we have a roof over our heads. It is beautiful how God can show His mercy, love, and grace through miracles, and still somehow show His hand through disappointments. To have witnessed my mom conquer such a journey is nothing short of remarkable.

To step away from the rain a little, I went to Damari's house. It is a little relief from the storm, but I cannot help but have nightmares. Nowadays, I must take sleeping pills just to get my mind to relax. I believe my body is becoming numb to them, because my mind seems to run more rampant with each dose. It is about 3 o'clock in the morning when I awake from my nightmare, kicking and screaming. It feels like my mind is unraveling, bit by bit, and all I can do is sit and watch it float away.

"No, no, no. Please, God! No!" I cry, sitting up and breathing hard.

Damari jumps up from his sleep, comforting me and quieting my thoughts.

"Baby, baby, baby, shh… Fé…" says Damari, pulling me into his arms.

He kisses my forehead and pulls me in closer. I can feel the warmth of his body easing my speeding heartbeat. For just a second, my fears melt into hope, and the hate and anger I feel within becomes less and less dominating. He rubs my back, moving his hand up and down, soothing every bit of tension I feel, inside and out. Why is his love so special? Is this only meant for friendship? Dare we dare to be more… than friends?

My breathing becomes slower and my mind races just a little less. I remember the day at the hospital.

I see my dad being removed from the breathing machine as he begins his journey of transitioning. I cry louder and louder, begging for him to stay.

The tears pour down my cheek, soaking Damari's shoulder, running down his arm.

"Please God. Please God," I whisper to myself, fighting the thoughts.

"What's wrong? Are you thinking about your dad?" he asks.

I nod my head "yes", then escape from his loving embrace.

I feel cold as I leave the warmth of his arms. Wearing his T-shirt, I make a beeline to his bathroom. I stand in the mirror, staring and analyzing every flaw; fighting the thoughts of what the future may hold. Inaudible whispers overwhelm me. So, I grab a prescribed pill bottle from my bag on the counter, take a pill out, and swallow it; watching it go down my throat.

The whispers slow down, then become rapid again. I try to fight them, but I am drowned in a sea of thoughts. Then, Damari walks in. The thoughts stop.

He hugs me from behind, wrapping his arms around my waist as we stand in front of the mirror. I wipe the tears from my cheeks until he grabs my hand and holds it. Then, blots my tears with a face tissue. We look in the mirror. No words, just… searching.

"It's going to be alright, I promise," says Damari.

I look at him in the mirror, "D, I'm trying… I really am."

"Yeah, I know," he says, shaking his head.

He kisses my cheek, overlapping my arm with his. Silence fills the room. A silence that can sew souls together. One that could light the darkest night.

"I miss you," I say, rubbing his arm and melting into his embrace.

"I miss you, too," he responds.

He turns me around to face him as he pulls me in for an even closer hug. We release, still linking arms and connecting bodies. Staring into each other's eyes, we explore all feelings we thought we lost; but are still there stronger than ever before. Then, he smiles and grabs my hands, placing them behind his neck. As I embrace him, he places his hands around my lower back, hugging me tight, digging his nose into the back of my neck.

We close our eyes and pull one another closer as we explore the ever-enduring emotions in the air. I loosen my arms, releasing from the hug; he glides his fingers across my jawline then kisses me.

"I love you," he says, breathing deep while staring into my eyes.

"I love you more," I say, basking in the love in his arms.

"I don't think that's possible," he responds, kissing my

forehead.

The love and comfort of Damari is like none other. If only I were not afraid of being hurt again. Then maybe, just maybe, he could love me the way I always believed someone would.

And yet a beautiful pain remains…

I have felt a beautiful pain since my father's departure. It is like the world closed its doors on me; yet expanded its horizons all at once. The sky is a little bluer. The atmosphere feels clean and less jaded; almost as if everything is anew. It feels like there are angels constantly surrounding me, attempting to fill my heart with joy.

In contrast, there is the pain. My heart, soul, and mind all seem to drift away from me. It feels like every piece of stained glass I have conjured up is shattering right within me, with the daggers of broken glass landing into my heart.

I must cry with my head up.

My father fought a good fight for me and my family; so, we must do the same for him. No matter what pain I feel inside, I must keep going. Seeking to balance between work, school, and planning his service, I have had little energy to accept the truth of his transition. It has been almost a month since he passed; and it has taken some time to gather money for the funeral. The need to raise money to cover the costs delayed us in having his service; thankfully, we have gotten everything straightened out right in time. As in D.C., they dispose of the body after a month and donate it; at least that is what I was told. Regardless, all things are possible with God. We are thankful to celebrate him the correct way.

And so, the day comes…

My mother, siblings, and I are getting ready in my dorm room. I stare in the mirror, finding beauty in my reflection. Analyzing the stretchy white dress that I purchased for another event but matches the blue and white theme for my dad's service; one I thought would come later in life. I fix my hair, tucking in flyaway hair strands, and slicking my edges until I cannot slick them any further. Then I stare at myself, *seeing my father in my features:* his hairline, face shape, slanted eyes, full lips. Then, I remember his smile - shattering my heart and gluing the pieces back together all at once. How am I to survive this? *How do I pretend everything is okay when it is… not?*

This time, I cannot shake it. I can no longer pretend to be strong. I must cry with my head held up; but all I want to do is run and hide, and pretend reality is as I make it. Maybe it is - maybe he is okay. Maybe he is on a long vacation where he is happy, fulfilled, and whole. One where he is at peace. For I know not what today holds. All I know is I must cry with my head up.

As I gather my thoughts, I remember:

My mother, cousins, and I arrive at the Capital Funeral Home. They guide us to the room where he lays, motioning me to go up first. My heart shatters into pieces as nerves fill my body. I take deep breaths… in.. out… in… out. Then I count to ten as I approach my dad's casket. A beautiful silver casket with white lining. There he is, still as handsome as ever, wearing a white quality tuxedo with blue flowers engraved within. They covered his hands with white gloves. His hairline is on point, as I know he would require, and his face looks at peace. He looks like he is sleeping and dreaming the most peaceful dream one could ever imagine. I feel a comfort. Forgetting what reality is, I kiss my father as if he will awake and smile again. Is my mind playing tricks on me?

My siblings knock on the bathroom door. "Mani! Mommy said, are you ready to go?" they ask, snapping me back into the present moment.

I rush from the bathroom, grabbing my purse and other items for the service: three picture poster boards of my dad, fans with his face on it, and the obituaries. I continue picking up things that fall from the pile in my arms. My siblings surround me with condolences in their eyes.

"Okay, y'all ready?" I ask, huffing and puffing for air.

"We've been ready!" exclaims Kayla.

Everyone laughs.

"I don't know why you always ask that when we've been waiting for you all along," my mother jokes.

We all laugh; then there is a deep silence.

"You okay, Gorg?" my mother asks, rubbing my back and staring into my eyes.

There she goes again, asking questions she already knows the answer to. Ones that would break down all walls I have worked to keep up. Though rhetorical, I know she wants me to talk to her; to release my emotions so I do not explode. However, I choose not to. I must cry with my head up. How can I do that if I burst into tears?

"Yes," I reply, looking down and swallowing air.

She nods, "Okay, we're all here, okay?"

I nod my head "yes". We grab our items and rush out of the door.

He wants us to be strong.

My relatives and I gather at the City of Faith church for my dad's home going service. The church is close to Paradise, which is the neighborhood my family grew up in, where my parents met, and where I was born. We stick close together as we walk into the building, displaying the photo boards, and distributing wristbands, fans, and programs. The love he has is out of this world. It feels good to see all my family in one place, though under unfortunate circumstance.

As we approach his casket, my heart shatters one more piece. Topped with white and blue flowers, it matches the theme of our wardrobe to celebrate his favorite team, the Dallas Cowboys. Blue is also his favorite color. I still cannot believe this is the last goodbye to my father, my first love, my warrior. I do not have any words to describe how I feel right now. It is beautiful. It is painful. It is… reality.

Well, is it?

Am I stuck in a bad dream that will end at any moment? Will I awake and find him happy and whole, living in his flesh here on earth? I am not sure, but what I know is that this feeling is too much for my heart to bear. As the program begins, I walk around and make sure everyone has the items for the service. There is worship dance, a word from the pastor, and more.

"Um, are you okay, Fé?" Chante asks, stopping me mid track.

I exhale. "Yes, I'm okay," I respond, afraid of the truth of what is going on.

I comfort my little sisters at our dad's casket, still in disbelief about how handsome and peaceful he looks. I must distract my mind. So, I look for places I can help, walking around the church sanctuary and lobby. Then everyone settles. No more wristbands to distribute. No more obituaries to hand out. Just, stillness.

I sit down in my seat, rocking back and forth.

"Cry with your head up. Cry with your head up."

I repeat to myself as I tilt my head to the sky, just as I have witnessed my cousin Keisha do so many times before. A tear streams down my face. I can feel warmth taking over my body. My heart palpitates as I shake my leg at a rapid pace.

"Oh no, I'm losing control. Wait… just… wait…"

I suck my tears back in, using my father's fan to dry my eyes, ignoring his smiling face staring back at me. Then, my cousin Ray strolls in, honoring my father.

That is it. I cannot hold it anymore.

I cry aloud, shaking and trembling. "I want my daddy back! I want my daddy back!" I scream.

My family and friends surround me, rubbing my back and consoling me.

"There you go, let it out baby," says Chante.

I cry until I cannot no more. My family surrounds me, holding me up as my turn approaches to say my last goodbye.

"Next up, Imani is going to say a poem for Uncle Noah," says Tony.

Silence fills the room as I walk to the podium. The walls close in on me, and my legs shake as I find my way to say goodbye to my first love. My mom joins me, rubbing my back and holding me up as I struggle to stand. I clear my throat, fiddling with the piece of paper in my hand. I am at a loss for words.

"You got this baby, do it for your daddy," my mom affirms me.

I shake my head "yes" holding back tears. A range of emotions come over me: sadness, grief, anger, contentment, confusion.

Why did he leave?
Why did they win?
Why would that matter? He is the true winner, after all. Right?

My mom rubs my back again, urging me to speak as family and friends quietly await the poem. I have a flashback to the moment I wrote the poem.

It was about midnight when I sat in the back of Keisha's car. I prayed and played "I'll be missing you" as I allowed tears and words to flow. It was the first time I had allowed myself to grieve about my dad. The hurt cut like a knife; but it felt good to honor him by writing the poem, just as he would have for me.

My mom rubs my back again, triggering me to awake from my thoughts. I take a deep breath and begin presenting my poem.

<u>*Well Done, DaddyO*</u>
DaddyO, I refuse to tell my heart you are gone.
It's wrapped in your love
I'm not sure how it could beat on.
My heart has beaten with yours, as you've defeated many wars. My
First Love.
A bond like no other since the day I was born.
My mind has gotten a clue that this earth has lost you.
Yet my spirit rejoices, whispering, "He's still here with you!"

How can I tell my heart it can't feel your touch?
Hear your voice, embrace your love?
How can I show my children your love?
Or see your Colgate smile as you walk me down the aisle?
DaddyO, I am lost without you.
Each time you hurt, your heart's pain poured into mine.
Powerfully intertwined through each IV-line, dialysis treatment,
surgery, and insult, too.
DaddyO, I need you to understand that I really, really LOVE you.
I'm not ready to come to grips. You are gone too soon.
Who knew that day would be the last I'd hear you say, "I love you. "
DaddyO, your fight was not in vain.
Your sleepless nights. Your strength to love through the pain.
I hated watching you go through hell.
I tried to save you, but God's plans prevailed.
Now I've been in a trance, dancing between false hope and reality.
You left a legacy; you conquered the storm.
I thought you'd live forever; I guess I was wrong.
I'll never be ready, although you prepped us for this.
So I lift you toward Heaven, just as you did me when I was a kid.
I praise Heavenly Father for welcoming you into His Home.
Although my heart has a void for you, I celebrate you at His throne.
Enjoying milk and honey, pain-free.
I am happy you have gained your wings.
But please, DaddyO, don't tell my heart your truth;
For I am not sure it could carry on without you.

As the service concludes, we all gather to honor my dad. It is a beautiful moment - we take pictures, find joy in each other, and say our tearful goodbyes as we rub his casket in the hearse. The love of my family, and the support he received in his transition, is something I will never forget. I pray he was there watching as we celebrated the warrior he was. I pray his soul is at peace and pain-free, just as he wished. He is free; and that must matter to me.

Life must go on…

As I sit in class, everything just feels… different. No smile seems genuine, no word, authentic. Everything seems like a lie that I cannot trust. I fight my emotions as I stare blindly at the board. The professor is saying something about final exams, but I do not hear a word. I enwrap my mind in my father's world. Somehow,

I feel abandoned. Why did he leave so soon? Allowing trouble to consume… me.

Junior year is rapidly ending, so I must get a grip; but honestly, my grades have been slipping since I lost one of my best friends. How do I cope? How do I surrender? To God's plan, to my life's new renderings? I am grumpy and mean, emotional and wimpy. My mind is an ever-evolving swirl of rainbows, bad things, and cookies. Boarding and teetering the line between reality and my worst fears. How do I know he is still near? I am not sure what to think of this. All I know is I must find a grip. I am slowly losing myself and all that I have worked to become. My mind is slipping, and I do not know how to grasp it.

My mind is slipping, and I don't know how to grasp it…

I sit on the bench in the quad, watching people as they walk by. Afraid to look at my paper, I take it from my shoulder bag, bracing myself for what it entails.

"53%" it reads.

Darn, now I'm a failure.

All my hard work flushed down the toilet at a moment's notice. Sure, I have overslept during class, and have put no energy into… me; but why must I suffer for trying to keep my head above the water?

I am drowning…

I am trying to cope - with the pain, the agony, the mixed emotions. I am slipping and I am not sure anyone knows it. Am I crazy? I am almost sure of it. I paint on a fake smile with lipstick, and place foundation over my dried tears. Wallowing in my anxiety, depression, and fears. How do I breathe? How do I overcome? It is hard to grasp reality, as it shows none. No remorse. No empathy. Not even a streak of sympathy. Just jab after jab, trying to get the best of me.

K.O., knock-out. You win.

First, let me drag myself to the belt and tap out of this round.

My teeth feel bloody, and my face seems swollen with life's swings; but I must continue to fight. I must not let life win.

I am supposed to win in life. That is the purpose, isn't it?

I ask myself, becoming swallowed into this world. To cope, I have taken a mental health break from work. For I could no longer fake a smile as my co-workers got on my nerves. This fight seems harder than I thought; I do not know what I imagined. I guess I imagined life differently: smoother, more rewarding, and with less banter.

I must sweat off the rain…

I head to the gym, ignoring everything and everyone around me. Yes, everyone who knows offers condolences, but nothing quite helps with this sort of agony. I stretch in the mirror, fixing my spandex shorts and fitness crop top. Then I notice my shape is still "shape-ing", as they say, meaning it looks good. Though I must admit, I look a little bloated. For I have been slipping on my diet: eating chips and falling asleep after two burgers.

I must be easy on myself. I will get through this.

I put on my headphones, covering my entire earlobe. I blast my music and go into my zone. Then, here comes Mike, messing with my flow.

"Hey babe, I miss you. Can we meet and talk?" his text reads.

Why is this so familiar? Does he assume he can treat me like trash, then come recycle me for later? Why does he think my love is a bumper car that can take hits, crashes, and bruises? I am not a Styrofoam cup; I am a priceless piece of China. When I was twelve, I learned that from a mentoring program. We were told to treat our bodies like it is fine China, not a disposable item on the shelves. I know that my mind is wandering. Why can I not focus? I must get myself right. I must refocus.

I must refocus. I must keep going…

I ignore Mike's text. Why does he even want a word? He did not come to my father's funeral. He did not even say a word. No condolences. No hugs. No flowers. He needs to leave me alone. He needs to let me live without him.

I must cry with my head up.

I bury my emotions into my usual workout regimen, blasting music and drenching with sweat. Exhaling the weight of this world with each rep. I run on the treadmill and then lift weights. Placing them down, I head to the women's locker room; changing from my gym clothes, I examine my physique before wrapping myself in a towel.

Jumping into the shower, I can feel peace in every water drop that rolls down my back. I scrub as if to wash the pain away; but I cannot. I grab more soap and scrub even harder until my skin turns red; then I realize nothing will help cleanse the wound that overpowers my heart. I sit on the floor of the shower, crying as the water runs down; almost drowning me as the water pours through my scalp, past my eyebrows, and into my vision. Blurring everything I see around me. It feels good to feel missing. Invisible. A small fragment of this world. I cannot stop the rain, but I must find my way through this storm.

I scream, hitting the wall, trying to find peace amid the storm I feel inside. It is then I see my father's smile.

"Don't cry, Mu Baby, and don't sit on that nasty floor!" I hear him say.

I chuckle, coming to reality as my smile fades.

Cry with my head up, I must.
I must make it through this storm.
I must cry with my head up.
Though I do not know how to carry on.

CHAPTER ELEVEN
Can You Hear Me Now?

I WALK INTO my dorm room a little earlier than usual. Yet again I cried in the bathroom, so left class early. As I walk in, I see my mother sitting by the window, holding a beer.

"Really, ma!" I ask, grabbing the beer from her hand.

"We just lost my dad, and almost lost you, and this is what you resort to?" I continue.

"I'm sorry baby, I know I'm not supposed to have another beer," she responds, straightening her clothes and finding more words.

"Ma! You just had a stroke! The doctor told you to stop drinking and smoking!" I scream.

"I know, I just -," my mom continues.

"Just what, ma? Do you also want to go? God saved you from a brain aneurysm. You know this stuff can harm you," I say.

"I know," she says.

"Ok, so why do it?" I ask.

"I just - I'm sorry baby, I'm really trying," she says.

"Aren't you supposed to be in class?" she continues, looking at the clock.

"Yes, ma. But I could not focus. Then again, I guess I can't find peace here either," I say.

"Manz!" she yells as I run out of the door.

Swirling with emotions, I run to Mike's home. I tried calling Damari, but he did not pick up his phone. We are only friends, so what should I expect? He is not exclusive to me, and neither am I to him. So, I figured, why not run back to what feels familiar?

I guess I did not learn my lesson.

I had a fight with Mike again. He stormed out of the house, so I did the same. I exit his apartment building, staggering down the street in lingerie and a trench coat, holding a bottle filled with brown liquor. There is an alleyway.

"I believed in you," says Mike, emerging from the shadows of the alley.

I turn around, almost stumbling to the ground.

"Oh, hey," I say, turning to him.

I stagger again. He catches me.

"You're drunk. This ain't you," he says.

"I'm sorry, baby. I just wanted you to comfort me. I didn't mean for the night to end like this," I say.

Still stumbling in my heels, I wrap my hands around his neck and motion for a kiss on the lips.

"I catch you red-handed, yet you still lie to me," he says, chuckling.

Turned off, I let my arms down, looking him up and down with disgust.

"Ugh, I don't have time for this," I say, walking away and

downing another shot from the liquor bottle.

He follows behind me. "You've been cheating, haven't you, Imani?" he asks.

"Okay, Michael! We're saying governments now?" I exclaim, turning back to him.

"I believed in you," he says.

"Oh, okay! You believed in me! So what? What now? You don't love me no more?" I say, pushing him.

"I never said that," he says.

"So, what do you want from me? Huh?" I exclaim, getting closer to his face.

"I want the truth!" he responds, still calm.

I take another swig from the bottle, getting so close to his face that I step on his shoes.

"Oh, you want the truth? Well! The truth is that I am homeless! Okay! I am fighting to keep my mind together, and make sure my family is okay, all while trying to get my college degree! My mother won't stop drinking despite having an open-skull surgery on her brain! We gotta duck and dodge foster care! My siblings gotta share my two twin-sized beds! My father transitioned while in my arms, and I may have just lost the little sanity I had left! And you know what's worse? I don't have time to get my mind together! No! I must be strong! And courageous! I gotta keep studying for class so I can break that cycle and be the first to graduate from college! Then, I have you… insecure about a friendship. Someone that has been there during times you turned your back on me!" I say, panting.

"There. You happy?" I ask, staring at him.

He does not respond.

"Huh?" I exclaim.

"I'm sorry, Mani. I didn't know," he says, grabbing me.

"Just leave me alone. Okay, Mike? I can't take any more pain from you," I say.

"This ain't you, Mani," he says, yelling at me as I walk away.

I turn back around. "So, what? Huh? You're done with me? You're going to leave me too?" I push him, face squinted and filled with rage.

He looks at me, calm and poised. "Imani, I've loved you more than life itself. It hurts me to see you like this," he says.

"So?" I scream, with tears rolling down my face.

"I'm not finished yet. I see you, okay?" he says. He pulls me closer and looks into my eyes.

"But I don't know what to do anymore," he says.

"How about being there for me, Mike? I just lost my first love, and you come waving your flag of righteousness in my face! Telling me I'm not worthy of you? Well, f—k you!" I exclaim.

I take the engagement ring off, throwing it in his face. "And you can have your stupid a— ring!" I say.

He picks it up off the ground, shaking his head.

"Goodbye, Imani," he says, walking away.

Infuriated, I chase after him, yanking on his shirt and fussing him out.

"Don't walk away from me!" I scream, tugging on him along the way.

He walks faster, trying to escape me. I cannot believe he is making this about him! Why can he not just see my pain and comfort me? Is that even possible for him? Then he runs, losing me. He is lucky I have on heels, or else I would be on him like white on rice!

In my usual "extra" fashion, I take my phone out and send him a text message. "I SAID, DON'T WALK AWAY FROM ME!" it reads.

He reads the text and responds: "LEAVE ME ALONE."

He gets into his car, locking the doors. I bang on the window.

"Imani, leave me alone! You're embarrassing yourself!" he exclaims through the now open window.

"Okay, I got you!" I say, taking off my heels.

"Don't get on my roof!" he says, opening his car door.

I jump on top of his car and lay on the hood, pretending to fall asleep.

"I'm not getting down until you apologize," I say, stretching out and getting comfortable.

"Me? Apologize? You're the one on top of my car!" he says, resisting laughter.

"Oh well, I'll just lay here then!" I say, closing my eyes.

He chuckles a little, softening up a bit, "Your crazy a—!"

He laughs and shakes his head, placing his face into the palm of his hand. I burst into laughter too, reminded of why we stayed together so long. How can something be so toxic yet so soothing, all at once?

I need to catch a grip.

Mike and I are riding in his black Hummer Truck. He is still upset and being stubborn about last night. Nothing new. Though I am tired of his wishy-washy ways, I cannot help but be apologetic. I look at him, contemplating on whether I should comment or not. I clear my throat.

"Thanks for taking care of me last night… Just know that I appreciate you," I say.

He looks at me, then looks away, pulling up in front of my dorm building.

"You're home," he says, looking down at his phone.

I look down in disappointment.

"Nothing to say about anything I confessed to you?" I ask, searching for an answer. He ignores me with his face still plastered to his phone.

I continue, "I'm sorry, I just -"

I choose not to say it. Instead, I gather my belongings to get out of the truck.

"I love you. I'll keep this for memories," I say, kissing his cheek.

He looks away as I exit the truck. Hating to walk away, I stand there with the door open, rotating the ring on my finger. He gave it back this morning. He said he felt bad about taking it away, no matter what difficulties we have faced. It is hurtful to see someone you love so much, be so cold. I muster up the courage to leave.

"Okay, bye," I say as I close the car door.

He looks up as I walk away. How can he turn his back on me when I need him most? This type of pain cuts deeper than what I could ever fix.

If only love could save the day.

We have applied to seven housing programs, visited the mayor's office, and even researched homeless shelters. They keep telling us that our family is too large or there are no males allowed. My brother is only sixteen. Where do they expect him to go? How are we supposed to find a big enough place that we can afford in a gentrified city? It is amazing how people call out for help, scratching and fighting to get out of poverty, only to be pushed down and limited by other people's standards.

Why judge my fight?

All I can do is fight. Thankfully, I made it through exams okay, but I am afraid of knowing the results. I know for a fact that I have not given the best I could in my finals.

Then it hits me: I only have one year left of college, and my father will not be here to watch me walk across the stage. My family does not have a place to call home. I am still struggling to get by. We are still being denied from housing programs.

Why can't they see we are trying?

I walk around in a crowded room, yet no one notices me. They stare and wonder, but they still do not see… me. I was once popular and active on campus. Now I feel like nothing. I am often absent from class. I dropped out of most student organizations. I took a mental health leave from work. Not to mention, I no longer take part in sorority activities.

Since my father passed, it has felt like a slippery slope that I cannot stop myself from sliding down. I am gaining weight, no matter how much I exercise. My brain is foggy, and I cannot think. I am nervous about social situations.

I just don't know who I am anymore.

I feel so broken. I seek to be everything for everyone while trying to be the best version of me for me, as well, only to get hurt in the end. I cannot seem to enjoy good things without consequences or pain. Is it impossible for me to have happiness? Will I always struggle? Is my faith in vain? Why is my heart, my kindness, always taken for granted?

Why can't I be... happy? …

I have been in a wilderness that feels like the darkest space I have ever been. It feels big yet small. Like my surroundings are closing in on me. I can hear a crowd of people beyond the trees, yet I feel so alone. I curl into a ball, waiting for someone to rescue me. Is that possible? Can I only rescue myself?

Yet, I continue to fight. Swinging in thin air, not hitting anything but myself. Taking my rounds throughout my enemy's forest, only to find a mirror that shows my biggest enemy is…

me.

Can you hear me?

Calling
Screaming
Crying
Yelling
Searching

Searching for love, for peace, for healing?

Can you see me?

Faking?
Stumbling?
Hiding?
Wondering?
Doubting
Questioning?
Trying?

Can you see I am trying? Or are my efforts not enough for you? Is it not enough to see my blood, my sweat, my tears - or do you want my soul too? Honestly, you can have it. There is no peace on earth. I cannot stop these thoughts. I cannot stop this hurt.

Can…. you…. hear… me?

My eyes become blurry as tears fill them. There is no one here - my family went somewhere - and I am all alone. I lay in bed, fighting my thoughts. Whispers overcome me, but I attempt to fight them off. Frustrated, I run to the bathroom, slamming the door behind. Turning off the lights, I stand there - so still that I can feel my body wavering back and forth… back and forth.

I grab a bottle of prescription pills from the medicine cabinet, reading the inscription: *"Imani Holley… take only one pill each morning"*. As I close my eyes, I swirl it around and tilt my head backwards. The pills make a rhythmic lap around the container. I rotate my head around and around, tears pouring like rain on a summer's night. Placing one foot in front of the other, I take a few steps forward.

There it is: a mirror. I look myself up and down. I would smile at most parts of me, and frown at others; but this time, nothing looks quite right. Everything seems wrong—my hair, my skin, my eyes, nose, mouth, the mole above my lip, the minor bump by my eyebrow, how one side of my body is bigger than the other. Then I think to myself, everything is just… wrong. I was wrong. I am wrong. I am imperfect. Nothing I do ever makes sense because it never did, and it never will.

At least that is what the mirror shows me.

I read the post-it notes taped on my mirror, ripping each one down.

"I am beautiful. I am smart. I am resilient. That's BS! I am not! I am weak! I am hurt! I am torn! I am nothing!" I scream, my face streaming with tears.

I throw the bottle down, tossing my body to the floor. My arms and legs curve into a circular shape on the bathroom floor as I curl into the fetal position. I cry, sniffling my snot as it escapes along with my tears. It is so loud—the pain, the agony, the unrealized dreams, the dreams deferred. Screaming and crying, I struggle to breathe. Then it stops. No more crying. No more screaming. Just hard breathing. I sit here, my head laying in a puddle of my own tears.

I stand up from the floor, stumbling a little toward the tub. After rebalancing, I position myself in front of the mirror again, opening the medicine cabinet. I pick up my prescription bottle from the floor, then grab two more from the cabinet, staring into the mirror as the whispers overcrowd my mind. I attempt to stop the voices, shaking my head and pulling my hair, only for the voices to become louder. I open one bottle of pills and swallow a handful. Then the next bottle. Then the next. After the third bottle, I choke, coughing up a few pills, tossing the rest of the pills down the drain. Still staring at my reflection, I watch as a tear falls down my cheek. I wipe it, then refocus on the image in the mirror.

Everything freezes.

I drop the pill bottles to the floor and allow my arms to hang limp, hanging below my waist. I look into the mirror one last time, gliding my hand across my cheekbones. First the left, then the right. Next, I put my head down and turn from the mirror. Placing one foot in front of the other, I arrive at my bed.

I lift the covers, plopping down like after a long day of hard labor. Shifting to my right side, I face the wall of my bedroom, closing my eyes. Here I shall fall asleep to a night terror's slumber.

Can you hear me?

My mom enters the dorm room, crossing her legs to stop from using the bathroom. She places her purse and jacket on the couch and runs to the restroom. As she is using it, she notices pill bottles on the floor. She rushes to get up, wiping herself, then washing her hands. She then notices pills in the sink.

"Imani!" she screams as she runs to my bedroom.

There she sees me, deep asleep, lying on my stomach with my arm slouched over the side. She turns me onto my back, slapping my face. She slaps my face harder, and then shoves me. Frantically dialing 911, she continues her attempt to wake me while on the phone.

"Yes, my daughter is not waking up. I think she overdosed on pills—yes, she's still breathing, but she's not opening her eyes. She's not waking up!" she explains to the emergency operator.

She slaps my face again. I open my eyes and then fade away.

Can you hear me?
In the summer's rain,
Knocking on doors
Of the pain of yesterday?
Succumbing to the pressures of today?
And the worries of tomorrow?

Can you see me now?
Filled with a mix of emotions.
Not sure whether to run or lean on your shoulders.
Burdened with the weight of my destiny.
Can't you see…
I am afraid to be me?

Can you understand me now?
For the truth is too painful.
Encapsulated by my purpose.
Discouraged by the world.
I hide and cover the best I know how.

Can you feel me, now?
Crying and apologizing to you?
For it was selfish to end my life so frivolously,
And yet, and still
I call out for you, so…

Can you… hear me… now?

PART THREE

THE REAWAKENING

CHAPTER TWELVE
The Caterpillar

I ENTER A white space filled with a blinding light. Water drenches from my curled and coiled hair as I tip-toe through uncertainty. My blood-stained white dress flows behind me, swiping against my sweaty skin. I rub my eyes with my scarred wrists, attempting to glean past the white light. The sound of a giggle fills the atmosphere. I turn, searching for the root of the laughter. My face is twisted and puzzled. I grow more confused and curious of whom else could be here.

Walking, I am in pain from interior wounds now made manifest into exterior ones; I bear the anguish of greater curiosity about what this could be. Following a young girl, I make it to a dark room that resembles a psychiatrist's office. Sunlight peaks through a set of torn blinds and old wool curtains. Blinded by the light, I cover my eyes with my hand as the sun's rays shine on my arms. I see a woman behind a desk, facing the wall as her hair bun protrudes beyond the top of the chair.

Clearing my throat, I ask, "Excuse me?"

Stopping a few inches from the desk, I stand there, awaiting an answer. The silence stiffens; so stiff one could cut it with a knife. After taking a deep breath, I take two more steps toward the person: right foot, left foot. Still dripping with water and spotted with blood, I reach for a paper towel positioned in the center of the Traditional Mahogany desk. As I attempt to pick it up, I notice a charm bracelet lying behind the napkin. The charms hold pictures of Grammy, as well as butterflies and roses. Puzzled by the unearthing, I decide to pick up the charm bracelet instead.

"You found it," says the woman in the chair.

I jump back, dropping the bracelet to the floor. The woman pivots in her chair to face me.

"You found the bracelet," she says.

At a loss for words, I stumble backwards, falling to my face.

"Do not run, Imani. You are destined for greatness," says the woman.

Still facing the floor, gasping for air, I look to the chair, discovering the silhouette of a woman.

"Who are you? How do you know my name?" I say, sitting up.

The woman gets out of her seat and walks toward me. My heart pounds faster and faster as I hear her heels click toward me. I can feel sweat building in the palms of my hands, and my face flush with warmth and fear. I scoot backwards, breathing harder and panicking, clutching onto the carpet underneath me. Swallowing air, I take a deep breath and debate the very thought of escaping. However, my paralyzed body will not allow any movement. The woman reveals her face as she leaves the shadows.

I gasp.

There she is: African American with honey brown skin, a curvy figure and booty for days. She wears a pencil skirt, button-up shirt, and some fabulous pumps. Her hair is in a messy updo, and she wears glasses without a prescription. Her eyes slant as she smiles with a dimpled cheek; the left dimple being deeper. Why does she look like…

"I am you," proclaims the woman.

I see an older, professional, and more confident version of myself.

In awe. I say, "But how?"

The woman interrupts me, bending down to my level and placing her index finger over my lips.

"Shh… you are right where you are meant to be," she whispers with class and confidence.

I panic, getting off the floor, running toward the door. I try to twist the knob, but it will not turn.

Banging on the door, I scream aloud, "help! Help! Somebody help me!"

Near tears, I try to pick the lock, but I am unsuccessful.

"You cannot run, Imani," says the woman.

Still banging on the door, I lose my zeal. I crumble to my knees, crying into the palms of my hands.

Older Imani kneels to eye level, rubbing my back.

"Imani, you cannot run from your destiny any longer," she says.

I look into her eyes. Then it hits me again… she is me! I am her! In disbelief, I lose my breath, becoming silent and still.

As silence fills the atmosphere, a youthful song erupts, breaking the quietness of the room. Looking over to my left, I see the girl playing with Barbie dolls. She is wearing the same charm bracelet I saw on the desk earlier. The same one I wore as a little girl. So, I approach her, reaching for the charm bracelet.

"How'd you get my bracelet?" I ask her, searching to see her face all at once.

The little girl turns to me. She has almond-shaped eyes, chubby cheeks, and individual braids. The same Colgate smile as me and the older version of me. No, this cannot be possible.

She is the seven-year-old version of me.

Freaked out, I run in the opposite direction, hitting another wall.

"Just believe!" exclaims Younger Imani.

"Let me out of here!" I yell, kicking the door, trying to escape.

"Don't fight it," says Older Imani.

I kick and shout at the door, but it will not open. It feels as if they made it with the best wood possible. I do not know how I can escape. Losing my strength and energy, I squat to the floor, sulking. She walks toward me.

"Just relax," she says.

Slouched over on the floor against the door, I muster up courage.

"What do you want from me?" I ask, still out of breath.

"Greatness," she responds.

I pass out as my life flashes before my eyes.

Playing with my siblings and cousins.
My parents smiling.
Family events.
Graduating from high school.
Hanging with my friends.
The decision to end my life.

Curled into a ball, I remain in a slumber. A white light shines, overwhelming the entire room.

CHAPTER THIRTEEN

The Cocoon

IT IS A standard Intensive Care Unit room: white walls, medical equipment and supplies, a bed, and a dreary atmosphere. My mom and Mike are standing over me as I lie in a coma. I am on life support: breathing tube, IV tubes, and cords connected all over, and several machines around. They rub my hair and squeeze my hands in hopes to awake me. Doctor Waters enters the room. She is an African American woman with long hair and a slim figure.

"Hi, I'm Doctor Waters," she says, extending her hand to my mom.

"Hi, Dr. Waters. I'm Beatrice Holley. Imani's mother," says my mom, shaking her hand.

"It is great to meet you. Would you mind stepping aside for a moment?" asks Doctor Waters.

She motions for her to step outside of the room.

My mom fiddles with her hands, clearing her throat. "Sure," she responds.

They step outside of the door while Mike continues to hover over me.

"I am sure someone has explained Ms. Holley's condition with you?" Doctor Waters asks, placing her hands together in a prayer posture.

"Yes," my mom says, clearing her throat. "Has her condition changed any since yesterday?"

"Ms. Holley, I am sorry to inform you your daughter's condition has not changed. In fact, her condition has seemed to worsen. We are afraid it is best to remove her from the ventilator," Doctor Waters informs her.

"Excuse me?" my mom responds.

"I am afraid your daughter is brain dead. She must have taken too much medicine. We have tried different pathways to keep her organs and essential bodily functions going until she awakes. However, I am afraid her condition is only worsening the longer we keep her here," she explains.

"My Lord," my mom responds, clutching onto her chest. She becomes weak, then regains her strength.

"What proof do you all have that she's brain dead?" she continues.

"Well, we have asked her a series of commands, such as 'wiggle your toes' and she has not responded to any," Doctor Waters answers.

"Isn't she sedated?" my mom asks.

"Yes," Doctor Waters responds. "That is correct."

"Doctor Waters, how can she respond if she's sedated?" my mom asks. She chuckles, attempting to keep her composure.

She continues, "You expect me to kill my daughter based on an assumption? What tests have you all run? What proof do you have?"

Doctor Waters pauses, pushing her hands toward my mom as if to say, "hold on".

"I have been a doctor for twenty years. I am very experienced in patients with your daughter's condition. She will not last any longer than twenty-four hours. Forty-eight hours would be a miracle," she says.

Scooting closer to my mom, she continues, "Listen. I understand, as her mother, you are supposed to keep faith in her recovery," she says. She makes a fist with her right hand, shaking it.

She continues, "But ask yourself, are you only causing her to suffer more? Depending on a breathing machine is no genuine quality of life. Now, I am sorry to say, Ms. Holley, but your daughter's organ and brain function may never be the same. Frankly, her organs are likely to give out at any moment."

My mom takes a moment. She walks in a circle, shaking her head at the familiarity of the situation. It much resembles our experience with my father's health scare a few years ago.

"Doctor Waters is it?" my mom asks.

The doctor nods her head.

"Great. Now. Doctor Waters, with all due respect, I am a firm believer in God. He has the last say... not you. I respect your experience and appreciate your service, but my God made her body. He can heal it. My daughter is strong. He will bring her out of this," my mom affirms to the doctor.

Doctor Waters folds her arms and raises an eyebrow, surprised at her confidence.

A dream too realistic to be true.

The room is dark. Empty. Dark-colored carpet and dusty sunlight shines through the old curtains. I sit in the middle of the floor wearing a bloody white dress and wet hair. I clasp my arms around my folded legs. Here I am... just sitting and staring. No blinking. No crying. Just... sitting.

I have been here for a while. Still, I cannot seem to comprehend why I am here. Now, I recognize I ended my life, but is this what Heaven is like? Or am I somehow stuck in the middle, awaiting judgment? Am I hanging in limber while they decide where my fate lies? I just do not understand.

I sit in silence with my over-analytical thoughts. A rhythmic melody begins, humming to be exact; that of a little girl. It is Younger Imani singing while playing with Barbie dolls. She appears only a few feet away from me.

She sings, "This little light of mine. I'm gonna let it shine. This little light of mine. I'm gonna let it shine."

"Let it shine ... let it shine…" I whisper to myself.

"Let it shine," Older Imani adds, appearing from the back of the room.

I turn back, staring at Older Imani.

"Grammy used to sing that song before every performance. Yet, you still dim your light… Why?" asks Older Imani.

I stare at her, at a loss for words. She looks back at me as Younger Imani continues to hum the rhythm of the song while playing with her Barbie dolls.

Then I hear Mike's voice echo through the door.

"Imani? Squeeze my hand if you hear me," I hear Mike say.

I get up, jetting toward the door. Yanking the knob, I try to escape.

On the other side, Mike is leaning over my hospital bed, awaiting a response. He kisses my hand, fighting tears.

"Beautiful, if you can hear me... I'm sorry. I should have been there for you. Please pull through, baby. I love you," he whispers.

I do not understand where his voice is coming from. Tugging at the door, I try opening it to no prevail.

"Mike!" I yell, banging on the door, "Mike! I can hear you!"

I continue yelling through the door, hoping that somehow,

someway, he can hear me, too.

"He can't hear you," says Older Imani, walking toward me.

"What?" I respond.

"You're in a coma. You can hear them, but they cannot hear you. Your body will not allow you to respond since it is in a sedative space," she explains.

"Well, I'm getting out of here!" I say.

Huffing and puffing, I kick the door, still trying my best to escape.

"I'm afraid you can't leave... yet," says Older Imani.

I stop kicking, looking back at her. "Why not?" I ask.

"You must evolve," she answers with a slight smile on her face.

I hear his voice again.

"Please don't leave me," I hear him say.

I can do nothing but feel hopeless. This is all my fault. All I ever wanted was peace, just like my father now has. Why is everything always so complicated?

Stuck between two worlds, all I can say is… nothing. I lean against the door, swiping my hand down its crease, hoping he will somehow feel my energy. Then I realize he cannot. I take a deep breath and slide down to the floor.

In the meantime, Mike kisses my forehead.

"I miss you," he whispers, laying his head on mine.

Still seated against the door, I whisper, "I miss you, too."

A single tear falls from my eye.

If only it were not too late.

Mike holds my hand, reminiscing about a memory we share.

We are at Mike's apartment, a small one-bedroom with the basics in it: a couch, a small circular dining room table, and a TV with a video game connected to it. It is well-decorated: clean walls, modern furniture; he has a way of making it look like a five-star hotel room. I am about seventeen years old; Mike is nineteen. I model my cap and gown for him.

"Oh, my gosh! I can't believe I will graduate soon!" I say, taking off my cap and gown.

"My baby is so smart," Mike responds.

I tilt my head down. "I'm not your baby," I tease.

"Mm. Still friend zoning me, huh? Heartless," he says, chuckling.

I sit next to him on the couch, picking up a video game controller.

"C'mon and get another whooping," I say, nudging him with my elbow, smiling.

"Ain't you supposed to be studying?" He asks, laughing.

"Mm hmm… You're such a sore loser," I say, smiling and squinting my eyes.

Laughing, I grab my textbook, sitting down at the dining room table.

"Yeah, well, I went easy on you last time," he jokes.

"Um… excuse me, sir? Are you referring to both times that I whooped you?" I say, emphasizing "both," in my usual dramatic banter.

"Yeah… okay," he says, pulling up his pants and scooting to the edge of the couch.

"Yeah, okay," I mock, bursting into laughter.

I pull out my textbook and study, highlighting and taking notes in the margins. In his usual "perfect timing", he pulls out a roll up and lights it, releasing smoke into the air. I cough a little, roll my eyes, then turn back to studying. Distracted by the smoke, I give him a look, shaking my head and smirking.

"Don't let me distract you," he smiles.

I laugh and roll my eyes as he continues to smoke and stare at me. I attempt to focus but keep looking at him.

Blowing out smoke, he says, "You're so beautiful."

A warmth comes over me. Fidgeting, I place my hair behind my ear, blushing extra hard. Tapping the pen on the table, I smile while trying to refocus on reading.

"You know what? I know this stuff anyway!" I say, closing my book.

I walk toward Mike, sitting on his lap.

"Oh no, Ms. Holley. We can't have no dumb babies now," he teases.

"Shh…" I whisper, placing my finger over his lips, then kissing him.

"Such a tease," he smiles.

We continue kissing, enjoying each other's warmth and great energy.

I stop, coughing, "Ew, smoke breath!"

He laughs, "Want some?"

"You know I don't smoke!" I say, rolling my eyes.

He smirks, then blows smoke in my face. I cough hard.

"Virgin lungs," he chuckles.

I punch him in his shoulder. "Shut up!" I laugh.

We resume kissing, holding one another. Mike pulls back, rubbing his shoulder.

"You got a mean hook. You know that?" he says.

I laugh, "Boy, you all late!"

We both laugh and continue kissing. He takes my shirt off and tosses it. I do the same, except I toss his shirt onto the table, knocking over a cup of water. I know, fail. We laugh it off.

"I'm so clumsy," I laugh, placing my palms over my face.

"Yeah, my little clumsy Clums-er," he jokes.

"What? … how does that? … I don't think that's a word," I joke back.

He shakes his head. "I think I just made it one."

We burst into laughter, going back to kissing again.

Mike snaps out of his daydream, smiling while sitting in the chair next to the bed. There is gospel music playing in the background. He holds my hand while reading a poem I wrote in the sixth grade.

"When you've lost your crown and you're all down, never give up; when you've lost your touch and you don't have very much, never give up; when your wheels are flat and you need a pat," he reads.

I listen from the white space while leaning against the door.

"Never give up," I say along with him.

Stuck in the moment, I stop a tear from falling.

"I wrote that poem in sixth grade. It was my first poem," I say, smiling.

"My dad was so cool to me because he could freestyle a poem about any topic. I wanted to be just like him - I wanted to have a way with words as well." I look at Older Imani. "But I guess you know this already."

She smiles and nods.

"He's still around, you know," she says.

Confused by her response, I become at a loss for words.

"Who?" I ask, searching for any answer in her eyes.

"DaddyO," she smiles.

I jump up, standing tall and pouting. Blood boils throughout my body as my jaw and chin clinch together. I walk to the opposite side of the room, trying to ignore everything she is saying.

"He's still here… and he always will be," she repeats.

"Yeah? I can't tell! I could have sworn he left me in pain while dealing with his peace!" I yell.

Emotions overtake me as I fight the thoughts flying through my head. I feel so guilty for being angry with him. Why am I upset? He was the one fighting through his pain. Can I just be happy for him? I do not understand.

"Learn to heal through that pain. It is the only way to grow," Older Imani says in a softer, more comforting tone.

"Just leave me alone," I say, turning from her.

I hear Mike speak again, so I run toward the door.

"Let me leave! Let me leave!" I yell, banging on the door as hard as I can.

"You can't!" she responds.

"I want to let him know I hear him, okay? I promise I learned. I just want peace, that's all. Just let me leave, please," I beg.

"Evolve," she responds.

Irritated, I become louder and louder. She seems unphased and unbothered by my deflected emotional rage. It is almost as if she knows me… oh wait, I guess she does.

"I have evolved! The old me would have cursed you out in

seven languages!" I say.

"That is why you are still here," she says, cleaning her nails and tilting her glasses. "You are a caterpillar who thinks you are a butterfly. Uncertainty will only keep you in the cocoon longer, my dear."

She steps closer to me, grabbing my hand.

"Evolve into me… shine with no apologies," she says, bolstering with confidence.

I search in her eyes, looking for a sign of uncertainty.

"And if I don't?" I ask.

"Then I will never come to exist," she says.

Taken aback, I become quiet. Nothing to say. No quick comeback. No witty retort. Just… silence. In her usual perfect timing, Younger Imani appears on a bike, humming "Let it Shine".

"Just believe!" Younger Imani emphasizes, zooming past, giggling while her braids trail behind her.

Just believe?

I think to myself. How do I believe when I have worked so hard to forget my hopes and dreams? Life seems much too painful to bear. It feels as if I am in a cocoon, twisting and turning as the room closes in on me. I feel alone, no matter who is around.

I know it is all within me. However, I do not think I want to tap into that power.

CHAPTER FOURTEEN
Manifesting Butterfly

TRUE BREAKTHROUGH REQUIRES a refinery process. I have been in a coma for a week. Despite medical advice, my mom has kept me on life support in hopes I will pull through. I am grateful for her faith, as I would do the same. However, I am not sure if I want to pull through. What is there on the other side of life except for uncertainty? Every time my dream comes true, a person or situation snatches it away. It is like I can never be happy. A fear of failure, loss, and rejection always lingers, overpowering my very existence.

I feel like I am in a middle space filled with doubt, uncertainty, and dreams deferred. I cannot help but to ponder - what happens to a dream deferred? Is it much like the Parables of Talent, the biblical scripture where once one buries their dream, they become subject to a life of ruin and mediocrity? Do blessings pour down once one takes a chance to go after their dreams? Is it possible to unbury a dream and share it with the world? I gave up; what if it is too late? They say one can only dream what one is equipped to being. So, why not try?

We miss 100% of the chances we do not take.

As I continue sitting and pondering in the white space, fighting my past and future potential, I cannot help but listen to family speaking to me through the doorway of my psyche. It is amazing to hear the love and support, although I am heartbroken to hear how my downfall affects them.

I sit camped up by the door, eavesdropping on the happenings of the physical realm. My family visits my hospital room - I hear praying, gospel music, and somewhat embarrassing stories being told about me - just as we did for my father. I feel somewhat ashamed, but I must admit I am tired of living for everyone but myself. Giving up is no way to make a point, but I cannot help but consider it as the only option.

My family is in my hospital room: my mom, Pru, Mama, my siblings, a few cousins, and Mike. They are conversing about life when the conversation grows more serious.

"I wonder what caused her to do this. Maybe it was losing Uncle Noah?" says my cousin Tony.

"No, I think she was just carrying a lot," my mom answers, "but losing her dad made it worse."

"She looks like she is in a lot of pain. Maybe we should not keep her hanging on like this," says my little cousin, Amanda. A fifteen-year-old girl with caramel skin and an average build.

"What's wrong with you? Do not say that!" Tracy exclaims to her younger sister.

"I miss Mani too, but I don't think she would want to be on a machine like this," Amanda explains, "plus, doctors say she won't make it, anyway."

"I don't care what the doctors say. My baby is going to make it. Look, it's been past 48 hours, and she is still hanging on," my mom says with a crackling voice. "She gave up for a second, but I believe she will come back."

She squeezes my hand and rubs my hair. "My baby is strong. God got her."

A tear falls from my eye as I listen to what they are saying. How could I do this - to my mom, my siblings, my family? They need me! I am so selfish! Yet my heart feels broken beyond repair, and my soul does not feel it wants to carry on. I can only sit here and ponder on my life choices. How I never seemed to win, no matter how hard I have tried. It is too much pressure on me. Although I am used to being strong, I fear my strength has weakened me.

I fear my strength has weakened me…

The chatter eases, and my family leaves the room. In the meantime, Mike sits by my bed, laughing and describing a memory.

I stood in his bedroom mirror, getting ready for the night. Looking exquisite, I wore a sexy red dress, pumps, and a good red lip. Whenever I look good without him, Mike hates on your girl. Therefore, he was in his feelings. I did not care at all.

"Babe, I told you, it's just me and the girls," I said, puckering my lips.

"You're dressing up for the girls?" he asked, hating on your girl.

"C'mon, babe. You know I gotta look good!" I said with a smirk on my face.

"Yeah, whatever," he pouts.

I put down the makeup and walk toward him, pecking him on the cheek.

"I'll be back by 2," I said, strutting away.

Then, he snatched my wig from my head! Yes! He stood up, walked behind me, and snatched off my beautifully crafted hair unit. One that I paid good money for, might I add? The nerve of haters, sometimes!

"Can't go nowhere without this!" he exclaimed, tossing my wig across the room like a rag doll that owed him money.

I grabbed the top of my head.

"You little!" I yelled, jumping on his back, and straddling him down to the bed.

We tussled on the bed until he pinned me down on the mattress. I then released my arms and gave him a good smack in the face.

"Girl! Stop slapping me," he said in his joking but serious voice.

He pinned me down again, this time gripping my arms much tighter. Looking into my eyes, we both attempted to catch our breath.

"I'm still going out, you know," I said with a sassy tone.

"Yeah, I know," he responded, rolling his eyes.

"Good, now get my wig!" I demanded.

We erupted into laughter, shaking our heads at our own craziness.

I sit against the door, laughing at the hilarious times we shared.

Then, I hear a voice that I have not heard in a while.

"Wassup?" says Damari, greeting Mike while he sits next to my bed.

"Wassup?" Mike responds.

I can feel the tension in the room, and I am not even in the room. Well, I am, but you get what I am saying! I can feel the tension through their words.

"How's she doing?" asks Damari.

"She aight. I've been here with her. Nothing for you to worry about," Mike answers.

"Aight man, I'm just asking how my friend is doing," says Damari.

"Same friend you text in the middle of the night, huh?" Mike says.

"Yeah, the same friend I had to comfort every time you made her cry," Damari responds.

Silence fills the room. This is embarrassing, but there are no lies being told. I am here for the back and forth. I need some sort of entertainment, and two fine men I love fighting over me does not hurt a girl's appetite.

"Comfort! What you mean, slim?" Mike exclaims.

"Yeah, comfort. Every time you did not appreciate her or treat her like the Queen and diamond in the rough that she is," Damari says.

"Oh yeah, so you comforted my girl, huh? I was correct all along. And she lied about it. Okay, I got you slim," says Mike.

"Nah, it wasn't nothing like that. She respected you too much. She a good woman, you just ain't value her. But hey - one man's trash is another man's treasure," says Damari.

"Nah, I ain't gone nowhere... But you better," Mike threatens.

"Nah, playa, she would never admit it, but I know you put your hands on her before. You ain't never hurting her again long as I'm around," Damari responds.

"Oh, yeah?" says Mike.

"Yeah," Damari says.

They step closer to each other. The tension builds.

This time, I am not so entertained. All I can think of is why they cannot behave at my bedside. Them bringing negative vibes to my place of healing only makes them lose points in my book. Yes, I love that they both seem to love and care about me, but I only wish they knew how crazy this makes us all look. I need for them to keep it together.

In her usual perfect timing, my mother enters the room, breaking the tension and filling it with good energy.

"Hey, I know y'all not about to fight while my baby is fighting for her life," my mom says.

Mike sniffles, "No, Ms. Holley, I have too much respect for you and Imani."

"Yeah, ma. I love her too much to see her hurt by my actions," Damari says, still staring down Mike.

"Good. Now come give me a hug, Damari. I haven't seen you in some time," she says, easing the atmosphere.

Damari smiles. "I know, ma. You know we graduate next year, so I've been working to have a job lined up for after graduation. I came to visit the other day, but no one else was here," he says.

"I know, baby. I know you care for her. You don't have to explain anything to me," my mom responds.

Thankfully, the atmosphere lightens and so does my stress. My mom is a saving grace, if only she understood.

Mike and Damari leave the room. My mom sits there, talking to me and continuing to pray, keeping her good faith alive. She has a flashback to my grandmother's journey:

She remembers visiting her mother at the hospital after her open-heart surgery. My grandmother could not talk for some time because of her tracheostomy. So, my mom did her normal activities: wearing the finger pulse detector as a placeholder, straightening any pillows, and any other random requests my grandmother needed. Then Grammy spoke, saying, "Thank you". My mother jumped for joy. "Mommy, you can talk!" she said. My entire family felt lost when my grandmother was sick. So, her healing meant the world to us. She is a true blessing and our queen. This is a memory my mother will cherish forever.

My mother smiles, wiping away a single tear. In walks Grammy, who taps her daughter on the shoulder.

"Tricey," says Grammy.

"Mommy!" my mom exclaims.

I can hear their embrace and the love in the air.

"Mommy, I've missed you! How are you?" my mom asks.

"I'm doing okay, Tricey. I wanted to see how Fé was. How have you been healing since your surgery?" Grammy asks.

"I'm good, mommy, and Manz will be okay. What are you doing here? You should rest! Here, please take a seat," my mom says.

"Thank you," says Grammy, "It feels good to sit."

They both chuckle.

"Did Mama and Uncle Nick bring you here? Where's daddy? Are you okay? You should really be at home resting," my mom babbles, almost panting.

"Yes, they brought me here. And yes, I am okay," Grammy smiles.

My mom sighs, "Okay, Mommy. Well, I'm happy to see you!"

"I'm happy to see you too, Tricey," Grammy says.

I can feel Grammy touching my hands and examining my body. My mom gives her the rundown on my condition, and what the doctors say. Grammy advises her to keep her faith and continue staying strong.

"Mommy, things have been so hard without you," my mom says, fighting tears.

"I feel like I failed you. I try to stand tall, but I keep falling back down again. This is my fault. I know my children are suffering because of my own faults," she continues.

"Tricey, you are strong. It isn't about how many times we fall, but how many times we get up again. Never forget that," says Grammy.

"I know, Mommy. I just cannot seem to get back up this time," says my mom, sulking.

"Look at me," Grammy says, "yes you will. You are my bright little girl. You are smart, beautiful, strong, and capable. Like Mama says, every setback is a setup up for a greater comeback, quoted from Mr. Osteen."

"I know, Mommy, but I'm not strong this time. Look at my baby! Look at me! We're still homeless. I still haven't found a job.

I'm still trying to improve my health. I don't want my kids to hate me when they grow up," my mom sulks, "I'm trying, Mommy. I want you to be proud of me. I want my babies to live better lives," says my mom.

"Beatrice, I am proud of you, and I love you beyond life itself. No mistake can take that away. Regardless of what you do and no matter how you fall. I'll be here to pick you up. If I ever leave, I will be in every song. I will be the cool wind that breezes by you. I will be there in your dreams to remind you I am here. Here I am, Beatrice. Your mother. I'm sorry that happened to you, to us, to all of us…. But things will get better. You are an amazing mother to those kids. Imani's condition is not your fault. You will get back on your feet, and I will be here along the way. No matter what. Do you understand me?" Grammy says, grabbing my mother's hand.

"Yes, Mommy. I understand," my mom cries.

"I love you, Tricey, and I am proud of you. You have been with me when I've needed you, and I don't take that for granted," says Grammy. "I need you to be strong, okay?"

"Yes, Mommy… I'm trying. I'm really, really trying," my mom cries.

"Let it all out, Tricey. Mommy is here and I promise I will never let you go," says Grammy.

"I love you, Mommy. I need you so much!" my mom sulks.

"I know, Tricey, I know. Even after the Lord takes me away, I'll stay with you. I promise," says Grammy, "I am proud of the woman and mother you are, and the one you are becoming. Falling doesn't take away from the beautiful, smart, and loving woman that you are. Get up, honey, get back up again. God got us all."

"Okay, Mommy, I will. I will get back up," says my mom, sniffling.

"You promise?" Grammy smiles.

"Yes, Mommy. I promise," my mom smiles back.

"Okay, honey, I know you will," says Grammy.

They embrace. I cannot help but cry tears of joy and sadness. The strength of the women and men in my family is insurmountable. Resilience runs in the family. Even though we fall, we get back up again.

We get back up again, indeed.

"If only Noah was here to help her. I'm sure she would feel much better with his presence around," says my mom.

"I told Noah this girl wouldn't survive if anything were to happen to him. But I know she'll pull through, Tricey, and so will you," Grammy adds.

They smile. I cannot help but grin from ear to ear. Their faith fills me up, inspiring me to want to be better. However, I cannot help but feel the ever-aching feeling within my heart. It feels like there is an enormous wall blocking me, and no matter how much I dig, nothing can seem to demolish it. Not even my own faith. Not this time.

CHAPTER FIFTEEN
If Only a Butterfly Could See Its Own Wings

ALL BUTTERFLIES MUST experience the cocoon to gain its wings. It has been about ten days since I attempted to gain wings of my own. I have been stuck in this pit of never-ending pain and confusion. It is like I know the answer, but still cannot seem to find it. So, I sit here on the floor, but I have decided to no longer sit near the door. For the conversations became too painful to hear. I need to hear my voice. I need to find my answer. So, I have ignored anything happening on the other side of life.

I must learn to be positive again.

Crying tears like never, I bury my head into my folded arms. It somehow feels safer here. I continue fighting thoughts.

The moment my dad took his last breath.
My mom and grandma's surgeries.
Our eviction.
The struggles we have faced as a family.
My siblings' smiling faces.

Then I remember the moment I took my destiny into my own hands. I cry aloud, screaming and covering my mouth with my hand. My ribs hurt, and my voice goes hoarse. Then I hear a deep voice.

"Don't cry, Mu Baby," says the voice.

I turn around — there he is: dimples as deep as the sea with the smile, charm, and charisma for a million Colgate commercials.

"DaddyO!" I scream, wiping my tears and running into his arms.

There's the "thing": he is standing tall, with both legs! His complexion is back to that smooth, brown sugar-esque skin tone like he always gleamed about. He is radiating with youth, joy, and happiness. He looks healthy and happy. It seems all his scars and wounds are reversed. Every surgery, every cut, every war mark that deemed him miserable at the end of his fight… is… gone. Then, it set in…

He is happy without me.

Emotions overtake me: the best of these are joy; the most minimal, anger; the middleman, pain. How is he joyful when I feel excruciating pain because of him? It is his peace that has brought me misery. It was the stopping of his physical heart that made mine ache with pain. As though someone took a knife and cut it. My heart bleeds with pain, agony, anger, and love all at once; all because I miss him beyond my acceptance. The pain of losing him has made me give up on my life, and I do not think I will be the same again.

I sink into the floor, still holding onto his legs. I cannot believe his legs are back; he is healed again. He pulls me up, grabbing my hands, and wiping my tears.

"Daddy missed you, baby girl," he says to me, smiling.

How can he miss me when he seems so… happy?

"No, you don't. You're happy without me," I respond. My voice cracking like some dry lips in the wintertime.

"I am happy, baby, because I am free," he smiles. "But I am not happy to see you in pain over my freedom. Daddy never left you, baby. I've been next to you when you smile, when you cry, and in each moment that you second guess yourself. I have been there."

He smiles, "I've heard you talking trash about me, too."

"I don't know what you're taking about," I joke.

We both laugh.

He continues, "Mu Baby, daddy experienced a lot of pain while he was on earth. I have relied on dialysis for decades and went through countless surgeries with indescribable pain. So much that my heart grew weak. Baby, daddy fought as hard as he could because I wanted to be here for y'all. But daddy is free now, and it hurts me to see you hurting. I see you are holding a grudge against people who have wronged me."

My face frowns up. *He is right. I want them to suffer the way he did.*

He catches my terrible attempt at a polka face, saying, "I no longer feel any of the pain I felt while on earth. The freedom of this life is rewarding. Nothing they did could ever compare to the peace I feel now. Though I wish I'd been the father I wanted to be for you and your sisters."

He breaks down, tears streaming down his face.

"Mu Baby, Daddy is sorry for every party I missed, graduation I was late to, and each present I couldn't afford to get you. You were always good to daddy. I am sorry for not being there like you needed me to," he says.

My tears stream… again.

"DaddyO, you were the best father I could ever ask for. I wish you stayed around longer to see your life improve. I know you didn't have the money you wanted and didn't always have time. but DaddyO… you did the best you could do," I say.

I continue, "I'll never forget the time we went to the mayor's office after you left rehab. The girls were in foster care, and you were trying your best to get them out. So, you took your medicine just to fight the physical pain you endured while battling the mental wars." I smile. "I remember you nodding off in your wheelchair mid-sentence. Anytime someone asked you a question, your head would pop up, and you'd pretend you were only 'resting your eyes'. When really, you heard nothing we said.

You became harder and harder to wake up. So, after about the tenth time of you dozing off, I let you rest and handled the business for you."

"Yeah, I remember that baby," he responds, chuckling.

"My point is, DaddyO, you may not have been the richest; or not perfect by your own standards, but you were perfect to me. Your strength, heart, and love are worth more than any amount of money in the world. I just wish you'd stuck around long enough to be happy on earth," I say, fighting my trickling tears.

"Mu Baby, I want you to understand that Daddy is still here. I know it's hard on you, and Daddy is sorry for that, but I want you to release that anger you feel, baby. They have as much power as you allow. I'm telling you that every word, ill wish, and action they've ever done against me has washed away, baby. Look," He shows his body, pointing at his legs, "Daddy has his legs back."

Then he shows his abdomen. "No more colostomy bag. No more tubes."

He shows his arms. "No more portals for dialysis. No more surgery scars, stitches, lumps, tears, gangrene."

He cries, "Baby, daddy fought as hard as he could, and never wanted to leave you or your sisters."

"I don't feel the same peace you do!" I exclaim.

"I overdosed Daddy! I wanted to feel at peace - no more pain. But I only feel lost, broken, and confused! I tried to take my life, just so I could feel that same freedom, daddy, and it's not fair." Tears overflow like never.

"Baby girl…" he says in a calm tone.

"No, daddy! You're happier without me and it's not fair. I don't want to feel this pain anymore. I want to feel at peace, just like you. Why did you leave? I know you battled a lot. I don't take that away from you. But - we could've gotten everything fixed. Why, why, why did you leave me, daddy?" I cry.

I collapse into his arms, crying. It feels like every cry I have been afraid to cry is coming out. Like every inch of pain in my body has melted into tears, forming down my face, landing on my father's now-tube-free arms. The cold air hits my cheekbone, and my father's love calms my tears.

"Baby, listen to Daddy," he says while holding me tight in his arms, with my tears soaking up his shoulder.

"I know it felt too soon, but it was daddy's time to go. That's why I feel peace, because I know I did everything I came to do, and God was ready to bring me home with Him. You, baby — you have more life to live; that's why you feel pain. You are supposed to stick life through, and change lives," he says.

I suck up my drool and lift my head to look into his eyes.

"It's too late, DaddyO. I already gave up," I respond.

He shakes his head. "It's not too late, baby. Let daddy show you something."

He grabs my hand and walks over to the corner of the room. There sat a wooden box covered in dust, yet gleaming in the sunlight that peaks through the window. As we approach the corner, DaddyO smiles the biggest smile in the world. He turns me toward him, placing his hands on my shoulders.

"Mu Baby, do you see this box?" he asks.

"Yes, it needs some dusting," I answer, laughing.

He laughs. "You got jokes today, huh? Yes, that is true, it is a little dusty - but its purpose outweighs its exterior appearance," he notes.

"That was kind of poetic," I reply.

We laugh again.

"Where do you think your poetry skills came from? Your daddy!" he boasts with a huge smile on his face.

"Yeah, the coldest to do it!" I add, causing him to smile even bigger.

We both nod and laugh.

"Baby girl, open the box for Daddy," he asks, pointing toward the box that sits on a table near the window seal.

I look at him, then the box. He gestures again for me to open it.

As I open the box, I see a couple of handfuls of golden cards inside. There is a peaceful feeling and ease exuding from its radiant gleaning. I look at DaddyO again, searching for an explanation in his eyes.

"I don't understand," I say.

"Read them. What do they say?" he responds.

I pick up a golden card. The sunlight bounces off it, making it a little hard to read. So, I shift it a little, getting a better glimpse of the black wording imprinted on it.

"Motivate the masses," I read.

He responds, "Okay, read a few more."

I look at him, grabbing a few more cards from the wooden box, and then reading them aloud.

"Mentor the Youth; Love and Heal; Lend A Voice; Blaze a trail." I read aloud, looking at DaddyO.

"Baby girl, what do these cards have in common?" he smiles.

I look down at the cards. Then I shuffle back through them, re-reading each engraving. I shake my head in disbelief.

"These are all my dreams. All the things I have envisioned for my future," I answer.

"Yes, baby. Not only are those your dreams, but they are God's promises to you," he explains.

His hand is on my shoulder.

He continues, "You see Mu Baby, this box is all the things God has purposed for your life. He has given you everything you need to complete what is there."

"But DaddyO, this box is full of cards; and I - well - I don't have time left to finish them." I say.

"You do baby," he says.

"I don't. DaddyO, look at me. I'm stuck in this white space while my body sits in a coma. I can hear mommy and everyone talking to me at the hospital, but I can't respond. Just like the last time I saw you," I say, putting my head down.

A tear streams from my eyes. My father wipes my face and kisses my forehead.

"Look baby, I need you to forgive daddy for leaving you. I am sorry for the pain you experience because of my departure. Mu Baby, you cannot give up, no matter how much you feel like it. You have too much life to live," he says, embracing me.

I burst into tears. "You gave up! So, why can't I?"

"Because you're meant for greatness," says Older Imani.

"And you promised me," says Younger Imani.

The two walk up to me and my dad. Well, our dad. His face lights with joy as he turns to look at them.

"Look at Daddy's baby!" he says.

"Daddy!" Younger Imani exclaims.

He picks up Younger Imani and gives her the biggest, juiciest kiss on the cheek. She wraps her little arms around him, holding him tight. They stand in the joy of reuniting.

"Aww, Daddy's baby girl. My Mu Baby. I am so proud of you! You always make your teachers proud. Keep being smart, okay?"

he says to Younger Imani. She smiles and nods her head. They embrace.

He turns back to me, reminiscing, "I miss you this size! You were stuck to my hip. I used to take you outside with me and spoil you like crazy!"

He looks to Older Imani, "Wow! This is the version I've always seen you becoming."

"DaddyO," Older Imani embraces him, tearing up.

This is the first time I have seen Older Imani break her polka face. It seems she has been trying to keep it together, just like I have. Except she is confident about keeping going. They embrace, then Younger Imani and I join. We surround him in a puddle of tears, joy, laughter, and love. I can feel the rage of emotions swirl as the hug somehow turns to me. I have found what I have searched for. This feels good.

They embrace me as I cry in the middle of the circle. Then, my dad says an original poem he spoke at a family event when I was about sixteen years-old:

"Anything wrong
Or anything less.
Everybody that I involve myself with
Always wish me the best.
Nobody can take
What I know,
What I did,
What I achieve.
And baby, it was because of you,
That your daddy started to believe.
I started to believe in dreams that I had,
That I gave up on.
Because of the girl who God gave me
Special in my life
On May 23rd to Beatrice and Noah
She was born.
Many things come,
And many things go.
But what I really want you to know

Is that everything thing you got,
Is because you deserve it so."

Tears stream down my eyes as he speaks poetically, just as I remembered. I cannot stop the memories swirling in my mind. I see a series of flashbacks.

My dad taking me to school.
Us going shopping.
Him picking me up and lifting me to the ceiling.
Cuddling in his arms as a child when I was afraid.
His warm arms and tight embrace.

Then I remember losing him, and it clicks that this moment will never be real again. Younger Imani and Older Imani fade away as my father continues to hug me. I sulk into his arms, clenching onto his blue t-shirt. His skin feels warm, and his heartbeat is the same. How does this feel so real? I guess the answer is because it is… at least for now.

"Mu Baby, Daddy will always love you. I want you to be strong for your mommy, brothers, and sisters. They still need you. The world still needs your voice," he says, hugging me tighter.

"But DaddyO, I don't want you to leave. Please don't go!" I beg, clutching on.

"Daddy is free now, Mu Baby, and I want you to be at peace, okay?" he asks, lifting my face and staring into my eyes.

He wipes my cheeks as tears stroll down my face like a waterfall.

"DaddyO, I can't take losing you again. Please stay this time. I can't be at peace without you," I cry to him.

"Yes, you can, baby. You are strong, just like your daddy, and just like your mom. You are from a family that is strong. I know life is hard, and sometimes we go through things that seem hard; but baby, Daddy promises you, I will never leave your side. I have seen every tear you cry, question in the mirror, and each smile that brightened your day," he says, smiling.

He continues, "Just know, if you ever hear B2K or New Edition, that is my sign to you I am near. I know how much you love those boys!" he laughs, "And you know Daddy and your Uncle Jimmy… and your mommy and Aunt T… loves some New Edition!"

We both chuckle. Somehow, his usual charisma has gotten to me. He has quieted my tears and soothed my aching heart. How does he cause me pain and happiness at the same time?

"DaddyO, I knew that was you! Especially when you played 'Baby Girl' by B2K when I was crying all alone," I laugh.

He chuckles, "Yes, baby. That was Daddy. I will never leave you, your sisters, or any of our family… okay?"

I nod my head yes; somehow, I know this is the same goodbye as last time: whereas I must be okay with his freedom. He tries to reassure me, but I still do not want my heart to know the truth.

"DaddyO, please don't tell my heart the truth," I beg. "I cannot handle losing you… again."

He hugs me as we bury our heads into each other's shoulders. I can feel his tears soak my white dress, which seems more stained than before.

"Daddy doesn't want to leave, but I have to, baby. I've completed my life on earth," he says.

I cry, "No, no, no!"

"Daddy is sorry, baby girl. Just remember I'll never leave you, and to never give up. How did Daddy used to tell you? You're doing what?" he waits for me to join him.

"Big things in a small world!" we say, laughing.

"That's right. Big things in a small world. Daddy is proud of you, Imani Fé Holley, and I will never stop being proud of my pretty girl. It hurts me to see you hurting," he says.

He cries again, "Just promise daddy one thing."

"Yes?" I ask, still afraid of the impending goodbye to follow.

"Just like your poem in sixth grade, promise me… you'll never give up," he says.

I nod my head, "yes", hiding in his shoulders.

He hums the tune of "This Little Light of mine" as he comforts me in my tears. I let out an ugly cry, still clenching him tighter than ever. My heart must be strong. I must cry with my head up.

"I love you, baby girl," he says.

"I love you too, daddy," I cry.

We embrace in the middle of a somber room that is now filled with sunshine.

"Please daddy, don't go. Please don't tell my heart the truth," I whisper.

"Your heart knows the truth, baby girl. The truth is, I am always with you," he whispers back, landing a big juicy kiss on my cheek, and embracing me in one of his famous bear hugs.

I indulge in my father's embrace. My first love. The man that set the bar high for my future husband. My DaddyO. My warrior. My king. My father. It feels as though we levitate as we remain in each other's arms. Only it is the love that surrounds us, and the peace overall.

"Please don't tell my heart the truth," I whisper.

"I am always with you," he whispers back.

He fades away from my arms, as I keep them in hugging form. Afraid to open my eyes, I decide to face what has transpired. Hoping to see his smiling face again, I reopen them to find he is gone. I drop to my knees, throwing a fit. Flinging my arms and kicking my feet, I destroy everything within my reach. I cry until I cannot cry anymore, though it feels like I have drained my physical form. At this moment, flashbacks come.

Being evicted.
My mom's surgery.
Losing my dad.
My sisters going to foster care.
Struggling for Christmas.
Worried about what to eat.
Being turned down for housing.

I lay in the fetal position in the middle of the dark room, alone. I cry, belching out every utterance of disdain that I feel. I am hurt. I am broken. It feels my heart has shattered into a million pieces.

I am unsure I can be whole again.

At the hospital, my family surrounds my bedside as all my vitals drop. My heart rate drops to zero, causing a long beep. A flat line displays on the screen as my family run into a panic. Doctors rush in to resuscitate me with no luck of bringing my heart rate back. They unplug all machines as my loved ones clinch on to a greater hope.

I cannot help but wonder: what does my new life entail? Why is it worth saving my old one, only for me to feel pain again? I continue to fall asunder, fighting within. I know I have a purpose, but I seem to have more failures than wins. I wish I did not let my family down; but what good am I? All I do is fall shame to my pride. I have fallen so hard; I am not sure how I can get up again. I wish I could somehow be stronger within and dust the humiliation from my chin.

If only a butterfly could see the beauty in its own wings.
If only it saw the beauty in its stride.
Then maybe…
Just maybe…
So could I.

PART FOUR

ALLOW ME TO REINTRODUCE MYSELF

CHAPTER SIXTEEN
Never Give Up

<u>Never Give Up</u>

When you've lost your crown and you're all down,
Never give up.
When you've lost your touch and don't have very much,
Never give up.
When your wheels are flat and you need a pat,
Never give up.
When you've fell on your back and are feeling whack,
Never give up.
When you've been slapped in your face and feel you've been erased,
Never give up.

When you're feeling low, but it never shows,
Never give up.
When you're rusty and dry and want to cry,
Never give up.
When you feel beat and stuck in a seat,
Never give up.
When you only have friends 'cause of the money you spend,
Never give up.
When you've been betrayed and starting to fade,
Never give up.
When you're behind and need to shine,
Never give up.

When you're all alone and barely known,
Never give up.
When you wanna be cool but you look like a fool,

Never give up.
When you've been hurt and feel like dirt,
Never give up.
When you've been teased while trying to please,
Never give up.
When you feel weak and have been called a geek,
Never give up.
Always pray every day and no matter what,
Never give up.

ALL MACHINES ARE unplugged: no oxygen, heart monitor, nothing. Mike leans over my motionless body, sulking. My siblings cry, leaving the room. My mother, mentor, grandmother surround my hospital bed and go into deep prayer. Once they finish, they leave the room.

Mike leans over, kissing my forehead, then wipes his tears away. He pulls out his Bible, reading it to me (Song of Songs 2:16-17):

"My beloved is mine and I am hers.
She browses among the lilies. Until the day breaks
And the shadows flee, turn, my beloved,
And be like a gazelle or like a young stag,
On the rugged hills," he reads.

"I'll never forget you, my love," he says, kissing my lips. "I love you."

He stands over me for a while. Then finally walks away.

"Always pray every day and no matter what,
Never give up," Younger Imani recites.

I lay in the middle of the room, in fetal position as Older Imani and Younger Imani stand around me. My body is motionless, though I am still breathing in this space. Somehow, it feels my existence is vanishing by the moment. Older Imani gets down on her knees, gently touching my shoulder. I slowly open my eyes, which are swollen and burning from all the tears I have cried. I can see in her eyes that she wants me to find the key to leaving this space. There is something holding me back and I do not know what it is.

I can feel myself slipping away.

As I sit bundled up on the floor, my white dress becomes more saturated with my sweat, blood, and tears. A cool breeze sweeps over me, causing goosebumps to appear.

Who am I?

I used to believe in… me.

I used to believe in God's plan for my life.

My purpose. Now, I am this depressed person who feels lazy, unsure, unmotivated - and I doubt the very human existence of Who I am!

I am angry at life. It feels like my soul has shattered into a million pieces, and I am not too sure how to piece it back together again. It almost feels as though I am cursed. Like there is a hex on me that prevents me from breaking through the ceiling into my greatest hopes and dreams. It is almost as if there is a group of people keeping tabs on me, making sure that I only do the bare minimum. I am a good person, right? So why does it feel like everything is crashing down around me? Why does it feel like I am punished for doing right? Why does it feel like I am punished for taking a leap of faith?

It feels like the more effort I put in, and the more I listen to God…. The more I suffer. In the same, it feels like He is still blessing me. So, what is wrong with me? Yes, I am grateful! I am truly grateful for everything God has done for me and my family. However, I am tired of people sidelining and bullying my purpose. Why are they able to snatch what is rightfully mine? Yes, I know what the word says… that no man can take what God gives. Yet, it feels like they take a piece of me every single day. Every job. Every relationship. Every business venture. Even the times where I feel confident in myself… there goes the weapons formed against me. While no weapon formed against me shall prosper, it sure feels like they are getting the best of me. Slicing my heart, my soul, my spirit, and manipulating my mind.

I must be stronger than this.

I must get it together. I know what I heard. I know what God told me, and He did not bring me through the storms just for me to drown in the raindrops. I must dance between the raindrops; just as Mama told me when I was fifteen years old. There must be a bigger blessing here. There must be a destiny so powerful that it took years and tears and tears and years of building and conquering some of the greatest Goliath's.

It is a weird middle ground because I know there is something great within me. I am just angry because it feels as though it will never come to fruition. It feels as though no matter how much I try, and however many tears I cry, I will never touch my dreams.

I must lean into a source greater than myself. For I am not strong enough on my own.

"When you've lost your crown and you're all down.
Never give up," says Younger Imani.

She continues reciting the words to the poem "Never Give Up". A poem I wrote during class in the sixth grade, and later recited at elementary school graduation that year. I still remember my parents, grandparents, mentor, and the rest of my family crying as I tearfully got through the poem myself. My teacher, Mrs. Montgomery, attempted to come to the stage and help me read, only to become overwhelmed with tears as well. We made it through the speech, and those words have rung true to me ever since…

Never. Give. Up.

No matter how hard life gets. No matter how one loses the crown, and feeling down, never give up. Younger Imani is right. I cannot give up. She scoots closer to me, continuing reciting the poem. She leans down next to Older Imani and myself, showing me the bracelet on her wrist.

"When Grammy gave this to us, she told us to be strong. She said we would do great things; and to keep going no matter what," she says.

She touches my arm, triggering a flashback:

I remember being about seven years-old, playing with barbies in my bedroom on Frankie Street. A vision overtakes me. It shows me a spotlight and visions of my purpose. It shows important people in front of my eyes, people who use their platform to speak for the voiceless. The vision paralyzed seven-year-old me by its amazement.

"Motivate the masses. Have a voice for the voiceless," says Older Imani, smiling the biggest I had seen her smile yet.

A single tear strolls from my eyes. A series of flashbacks come to my remembrance:

Christmas as a child.
Getting accepted into Old Meadow High School.
Getting accepted into Bradford Kingsley University.
The face of my mom as she fought through her procedure.
The smile on my dad's face as he embraced me.
My siblings' smiling faces.
The love and support from my friends.

I smile as I remember all the good times through the storm. There was always a rainbow. No matter how dark, there was a sliver of light. It was all a matter of perspective. I believe there is a morning after the night and sunshine after rain. I must believe.

"It was all so simple," I whisper, feeling the tear stroll down my cheek, entering my mouth.

I taste the saltiness of my tear. Then I lift my head up to the ceiling, allowing tears to flow down my cheeks.

"Cry with your head up," I whisper.

I struggle between the possibilities of what could be; and the pains of what has been. Not understanding why there is still a blockage. I feel I am doing everything right, but it still feels so wrong.

"Never give up," I whisper, with my head still lifted to the ceiling.

My dad reappears, bringing the box and sitting it next to me. I smile, hugging him, holding on for dear life.

"It's not your time yet, baby girl. Daddy is with you. Keep doing big things in a small world," says DaddyO, kissing my cheek.

My dad, Younger Imani, and Older Imani surround me.

"There is beauty in the journey. Trust in your purpose, and He will do the rest," says Older Imani.

"Motivate the masses," says Younger Imani.

"Motivate the masses. Do my best and He'll do the rest." I repeat, smiling bigger than I have in some time.

"That's right, Mu Baby. Your brothers and sisters are watching you. Blaze a new trail, no matter how hard it gets. Stay aligned with your purpose, and always remember that what God has for you, no man can put asunder. Trust the process and…" he says, waiting for me to complete it.

"Never give up," I smile, releasing a single tear.

He nods his head in agreement. A tear falls down my cheek.

"I guess all things are possible with God, after all," says Older Imani.

I cry a joyful cry, "I now know so."

All three hum "This Little Light" as they embrace me. I feel my spirit cleanse as my heart becomes lighter and my soul feels more alive. *"Never give up"* echoes as the locked door flies open, filling the room with a bright white light. I stand up, smiling a smile filled with peace, joy, happiness, and fulfillment.

Younger Imani pulls my hand, causing me to look down at her.

"Yes?" I ask.

"I still believe," she says.

I hug my younger self, somehow absorbing the belief in her innocence and the purity of her visions. The same visions that led me to college and inspired me to study law. Somehow, some way, I feel I need to redirect my path.

I look to Older Imani. "So… what got you to this place? What career? Who did you marry? How do you look this fine?" I laugh.

Laugher erupts throughout the white space.

"I cannot tell you all of that! All I can say is, believe what you saw when you were younger, and it shall lead you to me," says Older Imani, embracing me. "Now, hurry and go get it, girl! I'm waiting!" she jokes.

I chuckle. I take a deep breath, turning to my dad. I grab both of his hands, and re-examine his body… no scars, no cuts, no signs of war. He has his original complexion back, from before dialysis made him a few shades darker. His handsome face lights up, causing his deep dimples to form. I smile big (somewhat showing off my dimple too… yes, a bragging moment, I know).

I smile, fighting tears. "DaddyO, how do I live without you?" I ask.

"You won't baby. I'll always be here for you. I promise, baby girl," he says. He kisses my cheek and embraces me.

"I'll never forget you. I'm going to make you proud, I promise," I whisper in our embrace.

"I know, Mu Baby, you already do," he reassures me.

"I love you," we both whisper.

Light overtakes the space, causing my dad, Younger Imani, and Older Imani to disappear. I hear "This Little Light" playing as I walk throughout the white space. My white dress is now clean - no blood, sweat, tears; and my wrist scars are no more. I feel renewed, refreshed. Holding the box in my hand, I am confident I can do this. I place one foot in front of the other as I stroll back to my path.

What does one do with a second chance?
I am not too sure. All I know is to never give up. For, when one

shoots for the moon, and misses, at least one lands amongst the stars. All I can do is try to dance between the raindrops. I come to a last door, extending my hand to turn the knob. I look back once more. There they are: my dad, Younger Imani, and Older Imani. They all smile and wave. I smile back, waving. Then I turn the knob, opening the door. Another light flashes before my eyes, causing me to cover my face with my arm.

I awake in the hospital room. It is bright, yet somber. Still, somehow, the world feels light again. I use slow blinks to look around, as my eyes are heavy. I glance around my bed, seeing decorations posted on the walls: get-well cards, balloons, flowers, stuffed pets.

My mother is in the chairs by the wall. She seems to fight a headache but is still praying. My loved ones - Grammy, Pru, Stoney, my aunts, and Uncle Jimmy - surround me. They are crying and shook, yet still praying. How can my mother and grandmother pray for me when they are healing, too?

How can they still believe?

I attempt to speak, but my throat feels rusted. I eventually get the strength to utter two words, "I'm sorry."

They look up in disbelief, jumping to my bedside, overbearing me with hugs, kisses, and love. They grab my siblings, who run in with huge smiles on their faces. As I look around at everyone, I cannot help but fill a complete sense of gratitude: thankful for the breath in my body, loved ones surrounding me, and a second chance to fulfill each card in the box my dad gave me.

That reminds me, where is my box? I check my bed, but there is no sight of the box. Then I remember it was all metaphorical. I have a task to complete. A mission to fulfill; and I cannot stop until every card in that box has disappeared. I cannot leave here until I have gotten every blessing that has my name on it.

I must push through.
I must survive,
And release
Everything I have inside.
I am filled with purpose.

> *I am filled with strength.*
> *But I must tap into a greater source,*
> *To go the lengths.*
> *So here I am,*
> *Ready to serve.*
> *Through the pain and heartaches,*
> *I promise to never give up.*
> *In life's journey*
> *I promise to go after everything that I deserve.*

I see my dad appear in the room's corner, smiling. His dimples, as deep as the sea, and his smile, bigger than the ocean. My heart flutters as I have finally accepted my heart's truth: my DaddyO, my first love, will always be here in my spirit. He is free; and now, I am free… too. For I had to get rid of my pride to find freedom on earth. This is a new journey, somewhat scary, I must admit. Even though I have fallen many times…

I am proud of myself for getting back up again.

CHAPTER SEVENTEEN
Where Did Time Go?

GET BACK UP again. It is midday. The birds are chirping, and the atmosphere radiates optimism, hope. Mike approaches the automatic doors of the hospital. He goes past the security desk and gets onto the elevators. The light goes from one button to the next as he taps his feet. He fiddles his left hand while clutching onto the bouquet of roses in his right. The elevator arrives on the seventh floor. He rushes off the elevator, hurrying to the hospital room. As he walks by, he sees me through the window. We connect eyes.

I sit on the pillows against the bed. It has been about a week since I awoke from my coma, so medical professionals moved me to a regular room until I am ready to go. My vitals have been steady. After this, I am required to attend a treatment program to be sure everything goes well. My mom is helping with my food and checking lotion and any other needs. Mike enters the room, staring into my eyes as he approaches the bed. My mom stands up to hug him.

"How are you doing, Ms. Holley?" he says to my mom.

"I'm doing ok, baby. I'll give you some time with her," she responds.

"Okay, thank you," says Mike. She kisses my cheek and touches Mike on the shoulders as she leaves the room.

I look down, swallowing air and tucking my hair behind my

ear.

"Hi," he says to me as he stands in front of the bed.

I look up at him. "Hi," I respond, looking away.

Silence fills the room. I look down, turning my head away from him. He taps his leg twice, then walks toward the bed, handing me flowers.

"I bought these for you," he says as I grab the bouquet of pink roses. "I know they're your favorite."

"They are. Thank you," I say, illuminating as I smell the roses and feel each petal.

He nods and then sits in the chair next to me; scooting up to the bed, he grabs my hand.

"I've missed you," he says, looking into my eyes.

I stare back at him, grasping and searching for authenticity in his eyes.

"I've missed you... and was afraid I was going to lose you," he says as a tear falls.

He continues. "My life is not the same without you. I will not question you about why you did it… at least not right now. I just want you to know I miss you. Your smile, how you snort when you laugh too hard. How you burp, then play it off with a laugh. I even miss you getting on my nerves." He chuckles, "but for real, Mani, I miss you. Your presence, your aura… I just miss you, and I'm glad you're still here with us." He kisses my hand and gets closer to the bed.

I look at him, shedding a tear. "I miss you too, Mike," I express, looking into his eyes.

"What happened between us hurt me, and I—" I say.

"Shh..." he puts his finger over my mouth. "All that matters is that you're here. I love you and I promise to never hurt you again."

"But Mike -" I say.

He interrupts me again. "Baby, I love you. Let's forget about the past. I almost lost you and I will not lose you again. Let's start over," he says.

I stare into his eyes, then look down, swallowing air. Going back and forth between his eyes and the floor, I lose the guts to tell him my truth. I take a deep breath in and out.

"Mike, I..." I say.

Something feels different in his eyes. They are sparkling. Sparkling like when we first fell in love. It was before the pain. Before the heartache. Before the confusion and the lonely nights. The same sparkle I have searched for to no prevail. It has been gone for so long.

I have lost the courage to say what I need to say. The time in the white space, in my coma, made me realize life is too short to hold grudges against those you love. For you never know when it is someone's time to leave this earth. Just as important, you never know the battles someone is struggling with; no matter how good of an image they present to the eye. So, I scoot up in the bed. I search for the words to tell him how I feel, but they all seem to slip from me. Everything feels like a blur. Like, I know what to say; but I cannot find the audacity to say it.

He scoots to the edge of his seat, cuddling next to the rails of the bed, holding onto my hand.

"Mike, I experienced a lot while I was in the coma. I discovered things about myself that I never realized were true. I freed a part of myself; one I never want to have control of my life again. A part of me that was broken and had given up," I take a deep breath, "Look, Mike, I love you and have wanted to be with you since we were younger. It's just... I cannot jump into a relationship with you right now. You hurt me, bad. The pain, although now faint, is still there."

"I know, beautiful, and I'm sorry. Let's still work on us,

together," he responds.

"Mike–" I say.

"Mani, I will not lose you again," he says as a single tear falls from his eyes. "I can't lose you again!"

Tears fall down his face; he turns away to face the wall, using his forearm to dry his cheeks. Although I am sure that I want no more pain from Mike, I am hurt that he is hurting. My heart softens up a little, as I see the genuineness of his emotions.

I reach out for a hug. He leans in. As we embrace each other, I cry while another tear falls from his eyes. As we release our hug, he runs his finger along my jawline. He looks into my eyes and then pulls me closer, leaning in for a kiss. I turn my face, forcing him to kiss my cheek instead. He wipes my tears as we embrace one another. I caress his back, almost forgetting how warm his hugs can be.

"Let's just take it slow, okay?" I whisper to him.

"Okay," he answers, kissing my cheek again, then pulling me in close.

We embrace one another, closing our eyes and living in the moment's love. Several memories flood — good and bad — all captured in the blink of an eye. Somehow this moment seems to wash away all the pain of yesterday. However, I am not positively convinced this security will last much longer.

Where did time go?

I finally make it home from the hospital after several weeks. I spent about two weeks in a mental health treatment center where professionals provided me with tools to cope with my difficulties. My time in the center was eye opening. I met others experiencing similar things as me, which helped me not feel alone. I found coping mechanisms for dealing with depression and anxiety; and I plan to use them. Regardless of how tough life gets, I am determined to be that "rose that grew from concrete", as Tupac says. Meaning, I am determined to defy statistics by growing beyond an impoverished and complex environment, blooming into success.

My family will get a home. I will graduate from college. I will fulfill my purpose on earth - and nothing is going to stop me from doing so!

Admittedly, the pathway to getting back on my feet has been a challenge. I have been feeling overwhelmed, though much more optimistic than before my hospitalization. So, to try one of my coping mechanisms, I head to the campus gym. It is summer, so the gym is emptier than usual.

I walk through the doors of the BKU Fitness Center, inhaling the smell of perspiration and exhaling any stress I felt before entering the building. I check out a hand towel and combination lock before heading to the ladies' locker room. After placing my items in a secured locker, I head to the mirror, standing center of the room. Afraid to look at my reflection, I lift my head and examine every inch of my body. As I look a little more refreshed, I can see improvements in my skin and face. Then I notice my back rolls are protruding like buns at a holiday dinner.

Panicking, I run to the nearest weight scale, taking off my shoes and anything I feel will add to unnecessary pounds.

"I've gained ten pounds!" I scream, jumping from the scale.

How did I gain weight when I just got back home? I should have lost weight, right? I do jumping jacks in the bathroom, twisting and turning to hit my obliques. Pondering where my weight gain stems from, I return to the mirror and continue examining what else looks different.

"Well, my booty is getting bigger... that's a bonus!" I joke to myself.

I twist my face as I remember the many nights I overindulged in junk food.

"Oh well! At least the yams, greens, and cornbread are going to the right places!" I say to myself in the mirror.

I poke out my now even-bigger booty and pop it a little.

Making a choice to not over-criticize myself, just as my therapist said, I decide to laugh it off and continue to my workout. I complete an hour at the gym - thirty minutes of cardio, and a circuit of glute, abdominal and upper body exercises. I am trying to pull this hourglass figure back together, honey, and no number of back rolls will stop me from accomplishing my goal!

I arrive back at my dorm room after the gym. Most summers, I apply for summer campus housing, even if it includes working on campus for the break. Thankfully, BKU approved my student housing for this summer through a special housing accommodation application. So, my mom and siblings can continue to stay here with me until we get a home. We have been homeless for almost four years. Although we have tried to keep hope alive, we seem to lose a little more hope each year.

We must continue to believe in the impossible.

We must continue to believe we will someday have a home of our own. Regardless, we will shower each other with love and care. I am still nervous I could get in trouble - or even worse, kicked out of school - for housing my family here. However, my health scare showed me that God is in the business of doing the impossible. I will continue to keep my faith and obey. We are not giving up on Him, just as He has never given up on us. Plus, my mother and siblings make my life so much brighter. I am simply happy to have a place we can all have shelter in.

As I enter my dorm room, I am welcomed by hugs, smiles, and kisses from my family. They have always shown me love but have been more excited than ever to see me since my return home.

"Mani, look at what I drew!" Zoriana exudes, showing me her colorful artwork.

"Nice, Zori! Ooh, I see the sun, and the tree… Oh, is that all of us?" I ask, smiling and kneeling to her eye level.

"Yes, this is mommy... daddy… Kevin… Marcus… me… Quinn… Jasmine… Kayla… Sabrina... and you!" she smiles, pointing at each circle of color on the paper.

Kevin is my brother, who is living on his own. Therefore, the homelessness does not affect him the way it has us. I look at each circle, imagining them to be each person.

"Oh wow, Zori… I see it! Good job, my love!" I say.

I give her a high five, and we hug. Quinn comes up, showing me his toy.

"See, look, Mani… my car goes fast! Vroom!" he says, zooming the mini fast car up my arm.

I chuckle, "Oh ok, Quinny Bear! I see you! Where's your other car?" I ask.

"Right here!" he runs to grab the almost-identical car. "Here it is!"

"Thank you, my love. What color is this car?" I say, pointing to the one in his hand.

"Blue!" he answers with excitement.

"And how about this one?" I ask, smiling.

"Red!" he answers, jumping up and down.

"Good job, Quinny bear!" I say, giving him a high five.

We play with his cars until Jasmine comes up to me. "Mani, come and look at this!"

"Okay, coming," I answer, attempting to get up from the floor.

"Who knew knees give out at such an early age? Is it normal for my knees to crack like this? Mercy! I need to do some leg exercises tomorrow!" I think to myself as I struggle to get up from the floor.

"Ooh! You're getting old!" Jasmine jokes.

She does not know that I am still a beast with my knees. I can outdo any of these young bucks! Sure, my knees are a little rusty; but they just need some oiling. That is all.

"Girl, I am grown and sexy, baby!" I joke.

We all laugh. The twins pounce on me as I am… still… getting up from the floor. They laugh and play, jumping all over my back and head. Jasmine joins in for the fun, pouncing on top of me. We all play and tussle around as my mom instigates from the sideline.

"Get her! Ooh! Don't hurt my babies!" she jokes.

Kayla and Sabrina immerse from the room, laughing and joking. They playfully try to break up the tussle, while throwing in a few licks themselves. We continue laughing and joking with one another, appreciating each other's company. So, yes, a group of kids defeated me, and I blame my knees! Is there a remedy for this?

Someday it will get better.

I awake in the middle of the night, tripping over my brother and sisters as I walk. I grab a glass of water from the kitchen. There I find my mother sitting at the table near the corner of the living room. Only a desk light illuminates her while she highlights through notes jotted down on a paper.

"Ma?" I say, walking up to her.

"Hey, my Gorgeous One. What are you doing up?" my mom asks, forcing a smile.

"Well, one of your kids kicked me in my chin. It was Kayla or Jasmine… I haven't quite figured it out yet. But I will find the suspect!" I joke.

I continue. "But… I also just needed some water. I think they're taking all my oxygen. Their mouths be all open and stuff!" We laugh.

"Don't come for my babies!" she laughs.

"Mm hmm," I say, sitting next to her, "So, can't sleep?"

She places the highlighter down, rubbing the back of her neck.

"Is everything okay, beautiful?" I ask.

"Yes, baby. Everything is okay. I just feel so bad staying in your dorm room with you. We are putting too much pressure on you. I want you to succeed. I don't want to be the reason you're kicked out of school," she says, rubbing her face.

"But ma -" I say.

"Manz. Listen, I don't know what I would have done if we lost you. To know that may have been my fault makes me feel even worse. I must find a way out of this," she says.

"Can I see?" I ask, pointing to the sheet of paper.

I read her hand-written notes. Thankfully, she has nice penmanship, so it is not an arduous task.

"Are these housing programs?" I ask, looking back up at her.

"Yes, baby," she answers, rubbing her neck again.

"Ma, focus on sleeping. You still need to heal. We can look over housing things tomorrow," I say.

"I can't sleep, Manz. I can't stop thinking about seeing you in that coma," she responds.

She stares into space. "I promised God that if he brought you out, I would do my best to get back on my feet again... He did. He brought you through. I must honor that agreement."

"Ma. I did not attempt to take my life because of you or the kids. I was the reason I gave up on me... not you. DaddyO's death shattered me more than I could understand. On top of you getting sick, Grammy having health issues, Nylah Wylah battling cancer, us fighting for housing and never being approved. It was a lot, Ma. My grades slipped; I hated waking up each morning; my skin became dull; I gained an insane amount of weight; I hated being social and disliked seeing other humans. I felt an insurmountable pain; like no amount of words could soothe it. I needed peace... I needed to feel peace, too." I say.

"That isn't how to feel peace. You should have talked to me. I know I haven't been the best, but I always have an ear and shoulder for you," says my mom.

"I know, ma. I did not want to burden you. That's all. You're already battling enough," I say, putting my head down.

She lifts my head up. "Never think I'm so overwhelmed that I cannot talk to my babies. I'm always here for you. Promise me you will always talk to me?"

"Okay, ma," I grab her hands, "but I need you to promise to talk to me, too. I got your back too. I'm sorry for hurting you... for hurting everyone... but I promise I will never give up again; and I need you to promise you won't give up, either."

She smiles, "Never give up."

"Never give up," I smile back.

She lifts her hands to motion a high five. We high five with both hands, cupping our hands together.

"We got it baby," she smiles.

"I know, beautiful, and we're going to get our home soon, too. God got us," I smile.

"Yes, we will! And yes, He does... always!" she smiles. We embrace one another.

Despite our housing and family health challenges, we know God still has bigger plans for our family. There is no way He destines good people for a life of struggle. For God has given us too many visions of rewards for us to become discouraged in the journey. We must press on. We must continue to press forward.

I must get back to myself.

After the entire household is asleep, I head to the bathroom. I stare in the mirror to examine myself. Whispers swirl in my head; however, this time, they do not bring me down. I grab a pack of post-it notes and a permanent marker and write affirmations

down on each sheet.
I AM Beautiful
   I AM Strong
   I AM Intelligent
   I AM at Peace
   I AM Extraordinary
   I AM Talented
   I AM Powerful
   I AM Me

I post the stickers along the bathroom mirror, repeating each one to myself until it has sunken in. Until I believe they are true. As I read each one, a flashback comes:

Me ripping post-it notes off the mirror before taking the pills.

I take a deep breath, fighting the thoughts of my past mistakes.

"All that matters is how you get up," I repeat to myself, inhaling and exhaling.

I grab my journal, shuffling past old journal entries filled with large scribbles of anger and pain. I turn to a new page, dating it. Sitting at the corner of the room, I write the things am believing God for, and how I can show Him I am worthy of receiving it.

I become overwhelmed with emotions. I see flashbacks to the white space. I cannot remember everything verbatim, but still remember my dad's smiling face, and my psyche's desire for me to succeed. So, I place my journal down onto the table. I run to the corner of the room, crouching down to my knees, then sitting on the floor. I tuck into a ball and cry my eyes out.

A cry never felt so good.

I feel clean. Healed. Stronger.

I can.
I will.
I must.

I must persevere toward every gold card with my name on it. No matter how hard it is, I must fulfill my purpose here. It all starts with me. My family will be great. We will break generational cycles. We must go on. I must go on.

It all starts with me.

It feels like time has slipped away from me; like I have been in a vault that catapulted two years into the future. My siblings seem bigger, my mom's surgical wound is much more healed (which is, of course, a great thing), and everything seems to slip from my grasp. I am not even sure if I have friends anymore; I have been so stuck in my world, trying to help my family pull up by our bootstraps, that I have not taken time to check in on anyone else.

It feels good to let out every piece of frustration held within. This cry is cleansing, freeing, and whole. Regardless of my cries, the reconstruction of me is a journey I am dedicated to accomplishing.

CHAPTER EIGHTEEN
The Reconstruction of: Me

THE RECONSTRUCTION OF me begins. I am taking strides to become a greater me. I am determined to become that mature version of myself that I met while in the white space. Some changes I have made include praying every day, journaling more, better nutritious food choices, a consistent fitness schedule, finding time for friends and loved ones, saying positive affirmations every day, and signing up for weekly therapy. Since the hospital, I have been wondering what "Motivate the Masses" means, so I have been evaluating my career path, and deciding how I want to spend my senior year at BKU.

The new school year starts in two weeks, and I have an equal level of excitement and nervousness. I am excited because I will get my four-year bachelor's degree, making me a first-generation college graduate. I do not want to mess this up. The lessons I have learned over the past few months swirl through my head. It is like a beautiful pain, only because most were hard lessons to learn. I have learned to allow my heart to grow strong, cry with my head up, and never give up. Now, I must grow to a greater version of myself so I can grasp every blessing in store for me.

To get back to my social self, I have reluctantly agreed to attend a Brunch Day Party with my best friends Claudia, Chante, and Damari. Three of Damari's friends - named Amir, Amari, and Melvin - join us as well. All seven of us arrive at the hottest lounge in D.C., called The Spot. It has three-finely designed floors, filled with the most luxurious looking greenery and lounge decor. It offers top shelf drinks, gourmet food, and the hottest DJs on the turntable.

Me and my girls strut into The Spot, giving our best catwalks and sexy glances. The guys follow behind us, looking like the kings that they are. My love for "an excuse to wear heels" is back; so, I am dressed to the tee. I am wearing a yellow dress with a slit on both sides, jewelry, cute heels, and a bag. My hair is curled and coiled, with a pair of Hollywood-style sunglasses. Claudia and Chante both wear pant jumpsuits, accessorized with a cute bag and shoes - Claudia opts for pumps while Chante wears wedges. Damari and his friends have on clean-cut fits with just the right amount of jewelry; just enough to shout clean, successful, and fine.

Eyes follow us as we walk through the venue, headed to our own personal VIP table. Damari received a promotion at work, so got the section to celebrate my return home, as well as a celebration for us all for making it to our senior year at BKU. We celebrate, pop champagne bottles, and enjoy endless bottomless mimosas. We dance, sing, laugh, and take on the roles of being the baddest group in The Spot.

It feels good to see friends again. They all stopped by the hospital when I was there, but I refused to let them visit me at the treatment center. I was too embarrassed for them to witness me at my lowest point. Though a little awkward at first, we made up for lost time by catching up and hugging out any differences.

I avoided them for some time because I was much too ashamed to face them. I knew I was not the best friend in the world during junior year. Between my dad being sick, my mom's surgery, hiding my siblings in my dorm, and my personal struggle with mental health, I did not have the mental capacity to check in on anyone. I attempted to call a few times but felt my negative energy would seep through the phone. Therefore, I often texted instead, only to be terrible at responding at a quick pace. None of my friends have yet to find out my siblings and mother have been staying with me at my dorm. Anytime they ask to come over, I just sway the conversation elsewhere, and act busy. I do not hide it from them because I fear they would tell; I hide it because I simply do not want anyone else to know.

Damari and I never talked about the issues we left off with. I assumed he thought the same as me and decided life was too short to hold a grudge. As we are all dancing, I sit down for a quick moment, dazing into space. I swirl my mimosa with my straw, going into deep thought. I see flashes of my family:

My dad's smile.
My mom's healing.
My siblings' playful faces.
Our things evicted from our home.
Us dragging bags through the motel parking lot.

Then, I remember my personal struggles:

Crying on the floor in the motel bathroom.
Walking drunk and barefoot down the sidewalk.
Mike choking me.
Taking pills.
Going through treatment.

I pick my phone up, checking for any text from my mom and siblings. I only have one from my mom asking if I am doing okay. She said she wanted me to get out and have fun with my friends. While stuck in my zone, Damari sits down next to me, touching my leg.

"You good, Fé?" he asks.

No, I am not okay! However, I will be, as usual.

"Yes. I'm good, D," I respond, sipping my drink.

"Alright then, girl. We're here for you, baby. Get up and have fun! We seniors, baby!" he yells, causing all our friends to scream.

He takes the champagne bottle and sprays it across our section, soaking our clothes.

"Yeah, baby!" Chante and Claudia shout, dancing even harder.

Damari grabs my hand, pulling me up to dance. We dance together, laughing and giggling along the way.

Suddenly, Mike appears from the crowd, storming up to our

section. He punches Damari, knocking him against the table.

"I knew you was f--ing him!" Mike yells at me.

Damari stands back up, getting the best of Mike. They break bottles, glasses, and more while causing a commotion in the VIP area. Me, Claudia, Chante, and Damari's friends try to break up the fight.

"Stop, Mike! What are you doing?" I yell, pushing him off Damari.

Mike steps back, huffing, puffing, and drenched in sweat. Mike's lip is busted while Damari appears to be unscathed. Amir, Amari, and Melvin hold Damari back.

"Oh, so you gonna take up for him?" Mike yells at me.

"I'm not taking up for nobody, Mike. It's not cool for you to come punching him like that. You wrong for that!" I scream.

"What you just say?" he says.

He has that look in his eyes. I flinch a little at the thought of him striking me again.

"Nothing, Mike. I'm just saying calm down, that's all. We all are just celebrating Senior Year," I respond, shaking.

Mike breathes harder and harder.

"You lied to me. You ain't nothing but a h-e," he whispers in my ear.

Anger overtakes me. "Just leave!" I scream, no longer afraid of his rage.

He cocks his hand back and slaps me in my face, causing me to fall onto the seats. Damari lunges toward him as they continue fighting. I sit up, holding my face as tears stream down. I can feel how warm my cheeks are, flushed with pain, agony, and humiliation. Claudia and Chante scream at him while coming over to hold me. Damari and his friends force Mike out of the lounge.

"You alright, girl? Oh my gosh baby, how long has he been hitting you?" Chante asks, pulling me to her shoulder.

I cry, too embarrassed to answer.

"It's been a while, huh?" she continues.

I burst into tears, nodding my head "yes".

"Fé, why didn't you tell us?" Claudia asks, rubbing my back.

I just shake my head, still too embarrassed for words.

"We got you, girl. Don't be afraid to tell us anything, okay? You know I was cool with Mike. You should have let me know." Chante says.

"Yeah, I got something for Rico Suave!" Claudia adds. She jumps up and looks around the lounge as if she sees Mike.

We all shake our head at her nickname for him. They surround me with hugs and love as we rock back and forth. I cannot believe he would do this to me, especially in public. I mean, it is not right for him to hit me at all. However, he has always kept his mask on well. He usually waited until we were behind closed doors. While I hated his two-facedness of playing two different parts - a Knight in Shining armor in front of company, and a monster behind closed doors - I somewhat appreciated fighting the battle alone. Now that my secret is out, I must face the concerns of my friends learning what I have wanted to confess to them for so long.

Damari drops me off at my dorm building, walking me up to the door.

"Thanks D, I appreciate you making sure I get in," I say to him.

"Always, Fé. Are you sure you're good from here? You need me to come in and check for you?" he says, breathing hard, face filled with rage.

He pulls his pants up, walking back and forth.

"I'm gonna see him again, watch!" he says, holding his fists.

"D -," I say.

He grows angrier, walking in a circle to calm himself. I try to keep him calm, but he hears nothing.

"Nah, Fé! I knew he was putting his hands on you! You wouldn't admit it, but I knew it!" he yells. "You should've been told me! I would have handled him a long time ago!"

My mom overhears the commotion and opens the door.

"Who put their hands on you?" my mom asks.

At a loss for words, Damari shakes off his rage and gives my mom a hug. He sends his respect and walks off.

"What's going on, Imani?" she asks.

"Nothing, ma," I say, walking into the door.

She closes the door and follows behind me. I am frustrated. I want to be left alone.

"Mani?" she yells.

"Ma! Please! Just leave me be right now. I just want to be left alone," I respond, running to the bathroom.

How do I explain this?

I sit in the bathroom, in the dark, alone. Right now, I am too embarrassed to face my mom and siblings. I do not want them to see me in a low place again. Then someone knocks on the door.

"Mani! Can I please come in?" Sabrina asks through the door, "Please? Pretty, pretty, pretty... please?"

She continues to repeat "pretty please" until I open the door.

"Yes, Sabrina?" I ask, letting her in, rolling my eyes with a slight smile on my face.

I turn on the light and sit back against the tub.

"Are you okay?" she asks, sitting on the floor next to me.

Not sure how to answer. I respond, "why did you ask that?"

"Um… because you've been locked in the bathroom for hours now!" she says.

We both chuckle.

"Well, obviously… there's that," I joke, swallowing air.

I look down, twiddling my finger.

"Not to sound mean, but what happened to you?" she asks.

I look at her, confused by what she means; yet I am clear on her question.

"Can I be honest with you? And I don't want you to get mad at me, or think I'm being disrespectful to you," says Sabrina.

I nod my head. "Sure, be open with me. Wassup?"

Somehow, I am searching for a truth. One that I am discovering but seem to have already buried. Almost holding my breath, I can feel an anticipation build from within. One that clings on to the hope that something she says will somehow unlock my heart's barrier. That something will wake me up and drown out any hesitation, awakening me from my slumber.

"Well," she says, "I want to know what happened to you. You were full of life and faith. I wanted to do things you did. You're in college. You lead groups on campus. And you're graduating soon. I remember when you had big dreams… And I… don't know who you are anymore. We've all been thinking about it, but no one wants to tell you…. Mani, we still look up to you. I know we all have our bad times, but we still look up to you as our big sister."

Her face turns red as tears stream down her face. "I just don't understand what happened? Why are you so different now?

Don't you know you're supposed to do big things? Why are you not acting like it? Why are you settling for less? I don't understand," she cries to me.

Stopping tears, I stare into her eyes. I feel a piece of me opening; like a chain has broken. Like she cracked the code to the once numb and barricaded part of me. It feels there has been a layer of veil removed from my eyesight. Like we have broken a wall down.

"I am still here, okay?" I say, rubbing her back.

I continue, "I just had to go through some rough times. I lost myself for a little, but they say sometimes you must lose yourself to find who you truly are. That's what I did. It took me months to put the puzzle back together after allowing myself to fall into so many pieces. But I am back. And I am better than before."

"I want you to know who you are. You are still our big sister, and we still believe in you," she adds.

"Brina, that means the world. Never forget that I believe in you too… all of you," I say.

"It's just that we've seen you hold yourself back to make sure we're okay, and we don't want you to forget who you are, because of us," she says.

"No, no, no… that could never happen! Y'all don't hold me back. In fact, y'all are my biggest inspiration. You all are my motivation to finish college, have a career, and to dream big! I want you to know you can do it too." I say to her, grabbing her chin.

I continue. "Listen, Brina, I allowed life to knock me down like nobody's business. But here, and today, I promise you I will never give up again. I will always fight for our family."

"But I don't want you to fight for us. I want you to fight for you," she expresses, wiping her tears.

"No one can stop me from fighting for y'all. I love y'all too much to let you struggle, especially if it's in my power to help make it better. If it means risking my college housing so we all have a place to sleep - I'll do it. If it means scraping up change for Christmas gifts or finding a place to go - I'll do it. And if it means trying my best to be the best me I can be, I'll do it. See, Brina, you must see… that fighting for you is my way of fighting for me, too," I confess, smiling.

"But what about when you have kids?" she asks.

"Girl! That's way down the line," I joke, "But when that does happen, you'll still be special to me. By then, we all will be okay. Mommy will have a place. You all will be independent. So, I will focus on my babies… plus, I'll have some of the best free babysitters in the world!"

We laugh.

"Yeah, I like that… so… you're back now? You're going to be our big sister again?" she asks, staring at me, her eyes gleaming with hope.

I chuckle, "Yes, my love. In fact, I've never stopped being her. I just took a little break from being me."

I wink, and she smiles.

"Okay, good! Because I'm tired of seeing you living below your greatness, girl! Do better! We know who you are!" she says with sass.

I laugh, "Oh, okay then!"

We leave out of the bathroom, laughing and playing with one another. My little sister's expression means the world to me. For, I thought they stopped believing in me. Being the eldest of fourteen, I have always prided myself on being an exemplary role model for my younger siblings. However, I have fallen so hard that I thought they were no longer looking up to me as their big sister, their role model. As I did not even look up to myself. Yet, they are still watching. So, I must get back to doing me. I must get back to the Imani I know, who is fierce, smart, and fabulous.

I must be the "me" God destined me to be. An improved version of me.
I go back into the living room with my family. We have a

family meeting where we talk about all our hopes and dreams. Writing our goals on a sheet of paper, we then place it in the middle of the circle. We each voice our concerns and go around the circle, praying over our greatest hopes and desires. This moment fills beautiful. For, I feel more hopeful than ever before that I can still do it. I am sure my mom and siblings feel the same way, too.

I must make some changes.

Mike has been a significant part of my story. He has called me multiple times to apologize; and even shown up at my door - but I never want to speak with him again. While he still has a piece of my heart, I cannot lend it to him anymore. The love we have for one another is special - it feels real, exhilarating, young, refreshing. In the same, it feels toxic, painful, confusing, hurtful. It hurts to let go of the man I love, but it hurts more to hold on. It has been disappointing to see the pain and the hurt in our relationship, knowing we could both do better. I have tried fighting for our love, and to his credit, so has he, but I cannot lose myself hoping to keep him.

I cannot lose myself by fighting to keep him.

I deserve more. I deserve a love that does not hurt. Love that does not leave my pillows soaked with tears, and my heart bleeding with discontent. I do not deserve love that keeps me lonely at night, and always has me questioning why we are no more. Time and patience heal all. However, I can no longer hold myself back by waiting for him to get the picture. He sees me   he sees my value, my beauty, my effort to love him - but there is a disconnect. A disconnect that makes him think it is okay to allow his ego to win. I want a man who loves me through the storm. One who does not allow his ego to trot our love. One who does not take pride in ignoring my phone calls and texts, going days without speaking to me, and throwing other women in my face. Someone who does not diminish my character or put his hands on me.

Does that describe a man who loves me?

He may love me in his own way, but it is not the type of love I need. I need a love that uplifts the very essence of my being. My soul is special. My spirit is radiant. I am sure of this. I deserve a man who will never leave my side. Someone who will not turn his back on me every time I become too emotional for his comfort, or do not play by his playbook. Someone who loves me, for me; and allows my love to flow effortlessly to him. That man will feel our love is Heaven on earth.

He lost me by losing himself.

He got too comfortable. Comfortable leaving me on the shelf only to chuckle and brag about how dusty I have gotten sitting there; sitting on the shelf, waiting for him to see me. Waiting for him to value and appreciate me. Waiting for him to stop taking me for granted, and to show the love he speaks about when he is in a good mood. Then, after waiting for him, he reappears like Prince Charming, expecting me to get reattached to him with a simple dust off of sweet words and a touch of his hands. I am tired. I need more. I deserve more.

Actions speak louder than words.

I am done talking about him. I am done missing him; crying over him; wondering why he has not picked up his phone; questioning his intentions with me; hiding my internal and external bruises. I am done hurting and hoping for him to give me a silver lining in the shadows of this darkness we have called love for the past few years.

I have had his back during times where I did not have my own. I slept in places I have never slept. Dealt with situations I would never deal with - all in the hopes of him loving me. "One day… one day," I imagined. Swinging my feet and pondering the possibilities of our love. The beautiful home surrounded by white picket fences. The traveling and power moves we would make as a couple. The gorgeous children we would reproduce together. The love that would become strengthened by our trials and tribulations.

I am tired of being his flunky. His enemy. His blame. I have worked too hard to be his light, his hope, his peace - only for him to misplace his anger for his own BS onto me. Now, I recognize he can only get peace from God. For I was a mere vessel to get him there, and to remind him of who he is in God, and that His love still prevails. Only God can fill his void, not me.

Therefore, my job here is done. There is no more pain. No more confusion. No more scraping crumbs to make a slice of bread. My new and only job is simply… loving me. I am not choosing him over myself anymore. I choose ME.

I LOVE ME.

If only he had loved me, too. Somehow, I must forget about the hopes and dreams of yesterday. All the time invested. The arguments in a cry to be heard. I wanted to feel loved by him. To feel valued and appreciated. Had he loved me, his actions would have matched his charming words. The pipe dreams and sweet fairytales would have become actionable goals. He would have controlled his anger outbursts. He would have seen me as a treasure worth protecting, securing, and treating with the utmost care. For a woman's value can be a man's greatest asset. If only he found that out.

So yes, it is a struggle to let him go. I cannot help but think of what woman he may end up with… if she will be better than me… if he misses me… does he realize his wrongs? … and so forth.

But… I must move on. I must LET GO.

It hurts to free him from my love's embrace; but I must free myself to gain wings of my own. I must give myself the chance to live a better and more fulfilled life. Then someday, a man will come along to join me in my journey; one, I do not have to settle, cry, beg, and hurt for. A man who will complement me in every sense of the word - protecting me, admiring me, accepting my flaws, and loving me ever so gently. Until then, my only focus is me, not love.

I hope for genuine peace and healing for him. He is a good man and could be so much more if he owned up to his flaws and worked to improve them. However, that is no longer my business. For I have healing to do myself.

I must get my power back.
I approach the Pawn Shop - an older building with a janky

building sign and mysterious fluids flowing along its exterior. I enter, scanning the products cluttered onto countless shelves along the wall. It is an older shop with items as outdated as a black and white televisions. I walk up to the counter, rotating my engagement ring from Mike around on my finger.

"How much for this ring?" I ask the Store Associate.

"May I see?" he asks, extending his hand.

I stick my hand out for observation.

"Can you remove the ring?" he asks.

"Oh... sure," I respond.

As I go to remove the ring, I daze off into space, remembering a memory with Mike:

Mike and I were at his apartment, relaxing on the couch. He sat on one side while I laid in the opposite direction, curled up in a depressive state.

"What's wrong, beautiful?" Mike asks, rubbing my leg.

"Nothing," I say.

"Aww," he smiles, tickling me.

I laugh. "Stop! And why are you saying 'aw'?" I say. I hate being tickled, so I push his hands away.

"You're so cute," he says, trying to annoy me.

"Cute? Cute is for babies and puppies, sir!" I say, trying to keep a serious face.

He scoots closer.

"I'm sorry... Beautiful... gorgeous... stunning." He says, kissing me with each word.

"Is it your grandma?" he asks.

I shake my head "yes".

"She'll be alright," he responds, rubbing my leg back.

"Can I be honest with you?" I ask, sitting up.

"Wassup... Beautiful?" he says.

I take a deep exhale, afraid of how he may respond. Will he judge me?

"I think I'm crazy," I blurt out, closing my eyes of what may be his reply.

"Oh. I knew that already," he jokes.

I punch his shoulder, laughing.

"I'm serious, babe!" I stop laughing. "They diagnosed me with Clinical Depression, and I don't think I can handle it."

He comforts me.

"I get depressed too. Sometimes I want to harm myself," he replies, cuddling me in his arms.

He continues, "But I have too much to live for... like you." He grabs my hand.

"I love you and you got this," he says, "Plus, having depression doesn't make you crazy, your attitude does."

We laugh. I stare into his eyes, pouting.

"So, you don't think I'm crazy?" I laugh, serious at the same time.

He smiles, "Nowhere near it."

He kisses my forehead. A tear flows down my face as I find comfort in his arms. Feeling accepted by the one you love is one of the best feelings in the world.

I can feel warmth overcome my body as I think about the good times Mike and I have shared.

"Ma'am?" says the store associate, snapping me back into reality.

"Yes?" I respond.

"The ring... I need to examine it," he says.

"Oh... right," I say.

 I remove the ring from my finger, handing it to him.

"Hmmm…" he says, examining it.

"Two hundred," he hands the ring back to me.

"Only two hundred?" I ask.

"Yes," he says with a blank stare.

"Oh," I say.

"Do you want to proceed?" he asks.

I take a deep breath, considering whether this man is trying to play me for a fool. Two hundred dollars? I know my ring should be worth more than that.

"Can we do three hundred?" I ask.

He gives me a stern look. "Two-seventy-five."

I give him the "really" look. He clears his throat.

"Alright, three hundred. Fine," he says.

It could be worth more. However, I am ready to cleanse my life of him. If three hundred dollars helps the process, I am all for it.

"Sounds good," I say.

I twirl the finger in my hand, re-examining it. I have flashes of

Mike:

Him staying by my side at the hospital.
Us walking through the park.
Our playful moments.

Then I remember all the times he put his hands on me. I take a deep breath. I give him the ring, then accept my three-hundred-dollar profit.

The breeze whips through my hair as I inhale the flower's scent while walking down the street. This type of peace feels good. Loving myself feels good. In fact, I think I am becoming addicted to the peace that I bring to myself. So, I am off the market until a man loves me the way I deserve.

The reconstruction of me continues…

Before I can offer my love to someone else, I must grow within myself. I must be whole before I become one with another person. I am choosing to focus on me: my dreams, my health, my vision, my purpose. Life has taught me that the rest will follow.

It is well with my soul.

CHAPTER NINETEEN
Just Believe

I AM WEARING a beautiful evening gown on the red carpet, running and dodging flashing lights as they come. I trip and fall, ripping my gown and dragging my fur. Gasping for air, I attempt to get up and catch my breath. I collapse from my weakened legs, attempting to rise again. To escape, I push my body up with my arms and find the strength to crawl. Crawling two steps before growing weak and passing out.

I reopen my eyes as my vision becomes blurry and my surroundings spin around me. There are no more people. The once close and bothersome white light becomes too far to reach. I look up to see a black figure standing over me.

"Motivate the masses," I hear. It echoes seven times.

I jump out of my sleep, breathing hard and gasping for air.

"Motivate the masses," I say to myself, still confused by its meaning.

I look around, noticing all the kids have awakened before me. I lay back down, enjoying the peace and tranquility in the room. My thoughts become too much to bear. I head to the bathroom, showering with my favorite bar soap, body wash, and feminine soap. It feels good to cleanse myself, as showering is one of my coping mechanisms. It helps me to face the day with courage.

The red-carpet dream plays over and over in my head. I keep hearing my older self, urging me to "motivate the masses". What does that mean? Should I use my law degree to motivate people to know their rights? Do I offer work pro bono once I can practice law? How should I motivate others? And how would it impact the masses? I shake off the anxieties and get dressed, heading to the living room with everyone else.

Much to my surprise, Grammy has stopped by to visit us. She and my mom sit at the dining room table, catching up. They both have the hugest smiles on their faces. They are happy to see each other. Grammy does her usual snicker, while covering her beautiful smile.

Wow. I have really missed Grammy: her smile, her beauty, her grace, her elegance. Her unique ability to be a phenomenal and beautiful woman, inside and out. She does everything to perfection: artwork, cooking, hair, handyman work, sewing clothes. She even knows how to make homemade weave tracks! This woman is amazing, and I am proud to call her my Grammy. It feels so good to be around her essence again.

"Grammy!" I scream, running into her arms.

I am careful to be delicate, as she is still fragile from open heart surgery. She seems so frail and quiet-spoken, though still strong. I am so used to her outspoken personality towards us that her quietness makes me a little nervous. She is a different version of my Grammy, so it takes getting used to. Yet her strength and beauty are still incomparable. I am happy she is still here with us.

She smiles and extends her arms for a hug "Hey, Fé! I wanted to come to see how everyone is doing."

We hug. "Smooches!" we say.

We do our traditional smooches, touching cheeks on each side while holding both hands out as if we are sipping the finest of tea.

"I miss you, Grammy! How are you feeling? Are you healing okay? Are you allowed to leave the house right now? How are you? I miss you!" I cheese, jumping up and down like a little kid in the candy store.

She chuckles, "Girl, you sound like your momma."

My mom and I laugh along with her.

She continues, "Yes, I'm okay. I just wanted to see how you're doing since they released you from the hospital. Also, to see how your mom is healing, and to see the kids," she pauses, "I'm sorry what happened to y'all. God got you, and I'm going to help in any way I can."

My mom interjects, "No, mommy, I told you. You have helped us enough! We, in no way, shape, or form, blame you for what happened. I gotta learn to stand on my own two feet... you just focus on healing. You're my mommy, and I'll always love and appreciate you."

"Yeah, Grammy. We need you here. Just focus on healing. Plus, you know we got your back like peanut butter got jelly," I say.

My mom laughs. "Really? Is that what we're doing now?"

I laugh, "What? We do!"

We all laugh. The kids come up loving on Grammy and appreciating her presence.

"My mommy got some housing resources from the social worker. So, we are calling a few programs to see if they have openings. Well, I am. I don't need my momma doing any work!" says my mom, smiling.

I chuckle. "Oh, that's good. Can I help?" I ask.

"Of course, baby," says my mom.

She hands me the second sheet of paper. We each go down the list, calling the programs to inquire if they have any housing available for my mom and siblings. Each program rejects us once we tell them the size of our family. We make it through the list to no prevail of finding any help.

"No one has any housing for me and my babies," says my mom.

Grammy rubs her back, reassuring her, "Everything will work

out, Tricey. You are a good woman and have always been good to me. God got your back. Just ask and believe. It is going to happen for you." She smiles with a calm, yet extreme, sense of confidence.

As we all continue the night, watching movies and conversing with my grandmother, I cannot help but think of the red-carpet dream. I head to the bedroom, sitting on my bed. I open my Bible, feeling the stuffed butterfly my grandmother once gifted me. It is purple with red wings. She said it was a gift from the church. I squeeze the butterfly, pondering what my dream may have meant. Then I hear three light knocks on the already open bedroom door.

"May I come in?" Grammy asks, smiling.

"Of course, Grammy!" I smile with joy.

She walks up to the bed, sitting next to me. She asks for the stuffed butterfly, examining it herself.

"I remember this. It was a gift from the Elders when I had my surgery," she smiles.

"It means so much to me, Grammy," I say.

"I know. That's why I gifted it to you," she says.

"But why? Why did you gift it to me?" I ask, searching for some sort of resolve in her eyes.

"Because you are a butterfly." She leans in and whispers, "you just have to believe you can fly."

She winks, causing me to smile. I become lost in her words. Now I have another layer of confusion.

"Can I ask you something, Grammy?" I say.

She looks at me with a smirk. "You're questioning your wings, aren't you?"

I smile and nod my head as a single tear travels down my

cheek.

"Yes," I confess.

I place my head down, then force it up again. *I must remember to keep my head up, no matter what.*

"Well, you have a powerful destiny ahead of you. It is only natural to be afraid," she smiles.

I swallow air, at a loss for words.

"Grammy, I keep having this dream where I am on a red carpet and gunshots come from the camera lights. I run, but only trip and fall on my dress. I have had this dream since before they evicted us a few years ago. However, now I hear 'motivate the masses' loud and clear. It is almost like the dream is revealing more of itself," I express.

She smiles, fixing her eyeglasses, and shifting herself on the bed.

"Have you ever heard of a household name?" she asks with the kindest smile on her face.

"Yes… kind of," I reply, captured by her beauty and grace.

"Oprah, Beyoncé, Will Smith, Tyler Perry… they are all examples of household names," she explains.

She continues, "That's what you are: a household name. Use your voice to leave a legacy. You will be successful, but you cannot let anyone hold you back."

"Motivate the masses… is that why it's accompanied with a red-carpet dream?" I ask.

"It sounds like you know the answer already. I understand you are studying law. I also know you can do anything you put your mind to. But go back to your original passion," she says.

"Media," we say at the same time.

"Exactly. Make your mark there," she smiles.

"It all makes sense now. 'Motivate the Masses', meaning use my platform to inspire a massive amount of people, all at once," I smile.

"That's it!!! Thank you, Grammy!!" I yell, jumping.

"But wait, I start school on Monday. I'm almost finished my pre-law program. Next, I've planned on taking my LSAT; and then get my Juris Doctor Law Degree; and then pass the MPRE - that's the Multistate Professional Responsibility Examination - then pass the bar!" I say, huffing and puffing at the mouthful.

My grandmother stares at me, smiling.

"Are you finished?" she asks.

I smile, shaking my head, "Yes, Grammy."

"Good! Now, I am proud of you! You would be a phenomenal lawyer. The world needs more like you! I am just letting you know to consider switching to media - it could be a powerful move for you," she says, winking.

I smile. "Thank you, Grammy. I love you!"

"I love you, too, little miss thang," she smiles.

We hug. "As I told you before, don't have no babies before graduating!" she says, poking my arm.

"I know, I know…. Or you'll kill me… and him," I laugh.

"Yes! We've worked too hard to get you here. Education comes first!" she says.

We laugh and continue talking and catching up. Boy, I have really missed my grandmother. She and Mama (her mother) have taught me so much about being a diva: makeup, hair, heels, class, and more. Her impact on my life will always remain. For that, I am always indebted.

I love you, Grammy… always and forever.

My mom, siblings, Joe, and I attend Sunday church service. Bishop preaches a sermon about forgiveness. She talks about how forgiving someone for the pain they have caused us is more for us than for them. That by forgiving the other person, we free ourselves to live our life without holding onto that pain. For that pain only weighs us down.

Bishop's sermons are always right on time, as I have been tussling with forgiving those who, we feel, turned their backs on us during our homelessness. I must also forgive Mike. Although I have kept my distance from him, the pain still lingers inside. I want to be free from his grip on me. I want to be okay with him. Sending a text will re-open the door for communication; I do not want him in my life. So, I wrote a letter to every person I need to forgive, including those that I feel hurt my father in his last days.

Just believe.

To help with my healing process, I go to therapy two times per week. This has helped me to overcome any negative thinking patterns and navigate through life's challenges. The stigma of therapy, especially in some communities, can be discouraging. I have always been an advocate for therapy. I believe one's mental health is important.

My therapist, Ms. Dana Hall, and I comb through the difficulties of my life. We take turns writing letters to every person who I feel I hold a grudge against. I am more confused by the end of the session. So, I take the letters and burn them in a bowl, pouring water on the fire. Being careful in this exercise, I do this outside and away from any trees or things that could catch fire. In an open space, I place the letters in a bowl, light it on fire, and tell myself I am free from its claws. The exercise has helped me to forgive those who have caused harm to me and my family.

I believe in my destiny.

I have given much thought to what my grandmother advised. Admittedly, media was always a passion of mine. However, I was concerned I would not make enough money in that field. The instability and uncertainty of making it in Hollywood scared me.

At least becoming a lawyer has a definite pathway; something, I feel varies per person in media. Media can be rewarding if one meets the mark. I was afraid of the possibilities of not making mine. Despite all its uncertainties, I choose to go after media on the side of my pre-law classes. Somehow, I will merge the two. Therefore, I plan to finish my law degree and pursue opportunities in media. Not living my dreams keeps me up at night, gnawing at the essence of my being. I must live my passion to live life to its fullest.

I must choose FAITH over fear.

Classes began today, so I head over to the administrative building to triple check my scholarship covers tuition for my senior year. I take a deep breath while entering the Financial Aid Office. I am proud of myself for making it this far.

There are two people in front of me. I twiddle my fingers, waiting for my turn in line. I remember standing in this same line at the start of freshman year. How far time has come! Then I have a flashback.

I am in my sixth-grade classroom: the typical classroom setting with about twelve kids, and educational posters plastered on the wall. I stand in front of the class, nervous to read my poem aloud. My teacher, Mrs. Montgomery - a slim Caucasian woman in her early 30s with long, straight, blonde hair - approaches me, squatting down to eye level.

"You can do this, Imani," says Mrs. Montgomery, smiling.

"I can't," I say. I put my head down.

"Yes, you can, Imani. Because you are what?" she asks.

I place my finger in my mouth and twist from side to side. She places her hand on my shoulder.

"Imani, you are what?" she asks again.

"I am smart. I am bold. I am courageous," I say.

"That's right! And someday you will be one of the ones in your family to graduate college," she smiles.

I smile, covering my mouth with my hand.

"Now, let us hear that beautiful poem you wrote!" she exclaims.

Mrs. Montgomery stands and backs up, stepping to the side of the classroom. Still nervous, I place my finger back into my mouth, twisting my body from side to side. I look at my peers around the classroom, then back to my teacher, who gives a "go ahead" nod. Still timid, I read my poem anyway. My hands tremble as I read the handwritten paper in my hand.

At a whisper, I read, "When you've lost your crown and you're all down, never give up. When you've lost your touch and don't have very much, never give up…"

Smiling, I snap back into reality, realizing I am now at the front of the line.

"Next person, please," says the administrator.

I walk up to the service desk.

"Good afternoon! How may I help you?" she says.

"Good afternoon! I am here to verify my scholarship for this academic year," I answer, fiddling my fingers.

"May I have your name and student ID number?" she asks.

"Sure! My name is Imani Fé Holley. My student I.D. number is G5783," I say, smiling.

"Great, thank you! Okay, let's see," she responds, searching for information on the computer.

My heart pounds as I await updates regarding my tuition. My grades slipped last semester. So, I am nervous I may no longer qualify for my scholarship.

"Oh, wow!" says the administrator.

"What? May I see?" I ask, delighted at her reaction.

"Let me print it for you," she responds.

She pulls a page from her printer, handing it to me.

"Wow! That's a lot of money. I don't understand. I thought I would have less money because of my academic performance last semester; but it seems I have more!" I say. "I have more than enough to cover tuition, books, housing, and food."

"That's right," she says, "and it looks like we may owe you a small refund check."

Speechless, I tear up. I promised myself I would not cry as much this year, but happy tears are an exception.

"Congratulations, kiddo. You did it!" she says.

I smile, taking in the moment. "God is good," I express, fighting tears.

"All the time!" she responds, winking.

We smile and shake hands. I head back to my dorm to tell my mom the good news.

… All the time, God is good.

Along the way to my dorm, I decide to sit on the bench. I stare at the sheet of paper from the Financial Aid office, smiling at God's goodness. There is something about obeying one's purpose. It opens doors beyond the human imagination.

I grab my phone from my shoulder bag, going to my visual voicemail inbox. I listen to an archived message.

"Hey, Mu Baby. This is Daddy. Call me when you get this message. I'll probably call you back later. I love you. I was just returning your call. I love you and I'm waiting to hear from you. Alright, bye. Have a good day at school. Have a great day, period. May God bless. Love you," says a past voicemail from my dad.

A tear falls from my eye. "I just wanted to hear your voice. I hope you're proud of me," I whisper to myself, holding my phone to my ear.

I listen to the voicemail multiple times, pressing the speaker against my cheeks so I can feel the air come through the phone. It makes me feel as though he is still here, talking to me.

"So, you don't know how to answer your phone?" someone says.

The voice sounds familiar; there is no way it is who I think. I look up from my phone to find Mike standing over me.

"What are you doing here? Do I need to get a restraining order on you?" I say, grabbing my bag and walking away.

He grabs my arm. "I'm not finished talking to you."

"Don't put your hands on me!" I say, snatching my arm away.

"My bad," he says.

He puts his hands up and looks around to make sure nobody saw him. He grabs my left hand.

"I see you don't wear my ring no more," he continues.

"Yeah, that's because I'm not yours anymore," I say, rolling my eyes and pulling my hand away.

"Oh yeah? It's like that now?" he says.

"Yeah. It's been 'like that' for some time now," I say.

"Oh, so you about to graduate college now, and forget who's been in your corner all along?" he says.

"Wrong! I was there for you. You got brand new on me, sir," I say, looking him up and down. "Be good, Mike."

I extend my hand for a handshake. He pulls me in for a hug instead, pressing his mouth against my ear.

"If I see you with someone else, I will hurt you and him," he whispers.

"Mike. I am no longer afraid of you. If you come one foot close to me or anyone I love, I will come for everything you own," I whisper back, nudging his cheek.

He does a conceited giggle. "Yeah. Well, ain't nobody gonna love you like me. You ain't nothing without me!" he says.

I giggle, taking another step back. "That's the thing. I wanted to be something with you; but you didn't value me. I had to choose me. I see my worth now, and nothing you do can take that away from me. It's dudes like you that try to stop all this Black Girl Magic," I respond.

I smile and strut away, leaving him standing there to stare at all my fabulousness. You never know what you have until it is gone. It is too bad he had to learn about losing me the hard way. My love is too great for him. My essence, too powerful. The man meant for me will embrace all this Black. Girl. Magic. Until then, "Sayonara" to anyone who tries to diminish my light. My little light will shine. Nobody can stop it now, not even me. For I believe in myself.

I believe in ME.

CHAPTER TWENTY
Give Love a Try

EVERYONE DESERVES LOVE. Since my breakup with Mike, I have been pretty closed off to love. Thankfully, he has not popped up on my school campus since I last saw him. As for Damari, he remains just a friend. Our emotions for one another intensified at one period. However, I later realized I may have been looking for the love that Mike failed to give me.

While sitting in the library, I think of moments Damari and I shared: library study sessions, races around campus, and pure intimate moments. I miss my friend. Then I recall a flashback.

Damari and I are sitting in his house, listening to music, and studying, exploring the emotions between us. We lean in for a kiss. Our bodies connect as we explore the exuberance of love. Then we realize it is much too strong. "I love you," he says, looking into my eyes. "I love you more," I reply. We stand there, staring into one another's eyes, now knowing we dare not touch the strength of our bond.

Damari is an amazing person, and a great friend, one I will always cherish; but his love for women would never make me feel secure in a relationship. So, to savor our friendship, we chose not to further explore any romantic feelings. This has not stopped our friendship, as we still have each other's back in everything we do. For that, I remain grateful.

In the meantime, I have reintroduced myself to the world. I have lost ten pounds, toned my midsection, and lifted my booty, honey! I am getting closer and closer to the version of myself I saw in the white space. Though I think about love often. I scroll through social media, living vicariously through the popular influencer couples. The ones who take pictures holding hands while traveling the world. Also, the other types that post cute "every day" videos of one another, with the cute background music to match.

I still believe in love. I am just trusting God's timing.

It has been about two months since school started. After applying for a few jobs, they hired me at the university's hospital. Thankfully, the schedule is flexible so I can work my hours into my school schedule. Although difficult to balance, work, school, family, my social life, and my sanity, I am still grateful to make money. I get paid minimum wage; regardless, I smile at seeing each direct deposit hit my account.

After experiencing so much with hospitals - my grandmother, my mom, my dad, and then my experience - I have grown an interest in the medical field. I work in the Supply area, cleaning medical equipment and delivering supplies to nursing units and patient rooms. It is a relief to be done with work after work hours have ended. This way, I can better balance my schedule. I balance my job with my actual interest in media. Therefore, I am balancing them all: pre-law classes, hobbies in media, and a healthcare job. One day, I will make money doing what I love, so I trust the process.

It feels good to be back.

My mom has gotten better over the past few months. Her head scar has healed, and hair is growing back over the area. She has been better at controlling her cigarette and alcohol intake. It has still been a challenge expressing myself to her about how I feel regarding her decisions. However, we promised each other to always be transparent about our concerns. Since losing my dad, I have become even more worried about my mother. I wish she would realize that we all need her, just as much as she needs us. Maybe then, she will choose her health over her addiction. Regardless, I love her through it all and could not have asked for a better mommy.

Sometimes love comes when you least expect it.

Before each work shift, all staff gather for a team huddle. The supervisor comes and updates us on anything regarding attendance, medical equipment, supplies, as well as hospital and department policies. Some guys at work have inquired about my information. However, I have not been too keen on lending my heart out again. I am not searching for love, though I long for it. I figure it will happen at the right time, with God's blessing.

Myself and about ten other coworkers stand around, waiting for our shift supervisor to arrive. My coworker, Wen - a brown-skinned African American male with a thicker body frame and low cut—smiles and waves at me.

"Hey Imani!" he says, "I have someone I want you to meet."

I smile back saying "hello". He points to a light-skinned African American male. He has a curly mohawk and an athletic build. I look him up and down, fighting a smile escaping my lips. I cannot help but notice his muscular frame and masculine disposition. He exudes the perfect amount of dominance and coolness all at once. I swallow air, telling myself to play it cool.

"Imani, meet Jerome — Jerome, Imani," says Wen.

We shake hands.

"How are you doing, Imani? I'm Jerome," he says.

"Oh my gosh, why is his voice so sexy?" I think to myself.

"Jeroen?" I ask.

"No, Jerome," he responds, placing a little more bass in his voice.

I snicker, "Oh, my bad! It's nice to meet you, Jerome. I'm Imani."

He nods his head. "It's nice to meet you too." He tries to fight a smile, but I see it!

We lock eyes, then hurry and look in opposite directions. I twirl my hair, swaying back and forth. I can feel my eyes light up and my cheeks turn warm. Jerome grabs his Styrofoam cup filled with water, then drinks while looking in my direction. One can cut the chemistry with a knife.

Wen looks back and forth between Jerome and me. "Oop!" he says, chuckling.

The work meeting begins, and we all turn our attention to the Supervisor, Dan—a cool, tall guy with gray hair and an even grayer mustache. I focus on Dan while looking back and forth at Jerome. Attempting not to come across as too interested, I pivot my body toward the supervisor. Jerome focuses on the meeting as well, although he cannot help but admire my beauty, booty, and smile. What can I say? I am a catch! So is he.

Should I give love another try?

Jerome and I have talked several times at work. From the moment I saw him, I have been interested in knowing more. However, I allowed him to show interest first. We spent the first couple of weeks keeping it cordial. Then he grew to start conversations with me, which I welcomed. I love how he makes me feel. We have so much in common, including media and a genuine love for family and spiritual growth. I am intrigued by how intellectual he is, and how we can talk about the deepest topics for hours. We often get enwrapped in one another's charm, causing us to lose track of time. I have not felt this way about a man in a while. In fact, this is the strongest I have ever felt.

I cannot fall too soon.

I try to hold back my like of him, often smiling and allowing him to lead the way. He has an amazing ability to listen and empathize with what I am saying. That intrigues me. After building our bond at work, he invited me to meet him at a bar. I am nervous because we are meeting for the first time outside of work. What will I wear? Will he like me outside of work? I wear scrubs at work. Will he like me in my regular clothes?

A series of thoughts flow through my head as I re-examine myself. I check my body parts, being sure that I scrubbed everything. Body odor is a no-no, honey! I am too fly to go down like that! I put on an extra layer of deodorant and feminine spray, just to be sure my sweat glands do not win the battle tonight! After much self-inspection, I leave out. I am hoping my look presents the right amount of class, beauty, and sexiness.

How does he make me feel this way?

I enter the bar called Dime Nine. It is a dark venue filled with the aroma of liquor, fragrance, and sweat. Forty people fill the smaller venue. It is about 9:30 p.m., so only a few people are dancing; others stand around and talk, busying the bartender with drink requests to get the night started. I straighten my clothes, sucking in my stomach to make sure my waist looks extra snatched. I lift my head and relax my shoulders, gliding across the room. I do not want to appear desperate. So, I look for Jerome while strutting through the crowd in my 5-inch open-toed heels. Might I add, I look good tonight—wearing black leggings with a pink bodysuit that is open at the cleavage area. My hair is out and brushed straight back, showing off my chiseled cheekbones and slanted eyes.

He is looking poised and fine. Like he holds the world at his fingertips and can move it anyway he likes. He is sitting at a table near the wall. Cool and collected, he relaxes against the cushioned bench. I smile and wave at him. He nods, taking a sip of his alcoholic beverage mix of Henny and Pineapple. I try to fight smiling too much. I can feel warmth flow through my body as I get closer and closer to him. He stands up to give me a hug, motioning for me to sit next to him. I cannot help but notice how good he smells. I mean, he always smells good, but goodness - he has a special cologne on tonight. Whatever he is doing is working, and I do not want him to stop.

I sit down. "How are you? I'm so sorry I'm late, my rideshare took forever!" I say, out of breath.

"It's cool. Though I started to think you would stand me up," he jokes.

I laugh, tucking my hair behind my ear. "No, I wouldn't do that."

He nods his head again, taking another sip of his drink. We drink and chat the night away. We can stay out late because neither of us have a commitment tomorrow. He is the perfect gentleman the entire night: opening doors for me, listening to every word I say, considering what I need and want. The best part of it all is that our souls connect like none other. It just feels… right. Could he be the one for me?

I do not want to rush it.

I have been down this road before. Love. Love is…. complicated. It can be hard with someone who makes it that way. I have had my heart shattered, abandoned, and taken for granted. Therefore, I am simply not interested in picking up my heart's pieces again. Jerome should know he has some proving to do before he gets my heart in full.

I want to love him. I want to trust him. There is this one thing, though. He tells me he has a child. While I am excited to meet his son one day and fully intertwine our lives, I cannot help but worry about what the relationship is like between him and his child's mom. I cannot help but tense up my heart at the thought of experiencing betrayal again. I hope his word is as good as his skin. Again, why is this man so fine? Okay, I will focus now. Even beyond that, he has a beautiful soul and a good head on his shoulders. He has his things together: a good job, his own place, a car, a bank account, a nice health regimen, and he has an interest to always improve. Although I am excited at the possibility of our future together, his son included, I cannot help but be on guard. I cannot get hurt again, but maybe I should give love another try.

After a beautiful night with Jerome, I return to my dorm the next morning. Hey, I never said I was perfect. I sneak into the room, tiptoeing, being sure not to awake any of my inquisitive siblings and my mom. Only to hear a cute little voice.

"Did you have fun, Mani?" Zoriana asks.

Startled, I turn to her. How is she up so early? It is six in the morning… on the weekend!

"Well! Good morning, Zori. Yes, I had fun. What are you doing up so early, my love?" I ask.

After dropping everything onto the floor, I approach my baby sister. I stoop down to her eye level.

"Are you okay?" she asks.

"Yes, Zori. I am fine, thank you for asking! How are you, honey bunches of oats?" I ask with a smile.

"Good!" she exclaims with a big smile spread across her face.

"Of course, you are! Because you are what?" I ask, tickling her stomach.

She laughs. "I am smart. I am bold. I am beautiful. I am tw-ourageous," she says, trying to pronounce "courageous."

I smile. "That's right! Yes, you are."

She smiles, twisting her body back and forth.

"Here, I want you to have this!" I say, taking off my bracelet.

"Anytime you feel alone, sad, or like you cannot do something, I want you to look at this bracelet," I say, putting the bracelet onto Zoriana's wrist.

I continue, "Grammy made it for me. I call her 'Isabelle'. Isabelle reminds me I am always smart, bold, beautiful, and…"

"Tw-ourageous!" she smiles, jumping up and down.

"That's right… courageous!" I smile.

I tickle Zoriana's chin, causing her to laugh. We smile and hug. Then I go to make her a bowl of cereal. Kayla and Quinn wake up a short few minutes later, so I make them breakfast as well. I do not understand how these children are up so early on the weekend! I am always determined to sleep in late. Being a morning person must be nice!

I can exhale again.

My life's journey has been one for the books. It feels good to feel love again; or at least, the tingling feeling it can bring. While

I am afraid of giving my heart to Jerome, I am intrigued by the chemistry we have. There is something about him I cannot quite explain.

I have learned to love myself.

I am proud of myself - proud of my success, my failures, my wins, and my losses. I am proud of my journey because it is unique, and it makes me… me. The pain I have experienced has been excruciating, but I cannot help but be thankful for the process. I trust God with the reconstruction of me. For the more I stay aligned with His voice, the more doors fly open for me and my family.

Here I am.
Placing my heart in your hands.
Giving you parts of me
That even I don't understand.
I have been through life,
Torn by its cruelty.
I had given up,
And then stood back up again.
I am giving you me,
In my rawest form.
Will you accept my love?
Or leave it torn?
Allow me to reintroduce myself.
I come unapologetically.
Announcing my presence
And being the truest form of…
Me.

PART FIVE

RISE AND SHINE

CHAPTER TWENTY-ONE
When God Says Jump...

Rise and Shine
The time's divine
To be in line
With all that's mine
With destiny
With purpose
With greatness

I dust off my bootstraps,
Holding on for dear life.
All I can do now…
Is give my journey all that I've got.

Rise and Shine
It's Imani Fé time.
It's time to show everyone…
What I've been keeping inside.

Rise and shine
Rise and shine
Rise and shine…

It's Imani Fé time.

IT IS MY last semester at Bradford Kingsley University! The past few months have been full of bliss and joy. I am excited about a future with Jerome, as I have grown more in love with him. He helps me to open my heart and expand my horizons. My mom and siblings have been getting better. The kids are thriving in school and seem to be happy. As I sit on my bed, figuring out my post-graduation plans, I see a birthday card my Uncle Louie once gave me. Then I remember:

We have stayed with multiple relatives throughout the years (in which we are grateful), but we always remember Uncle Louie's place as feeling as home: the home-cooked meals, good vibes, and a genuine care. It never felt like we were walking on eggshells. Being such a big family, it is easy to feel like an inconvenience. We did not feel that way with him and his family. His essence - his smile, laughter, and full acceptance of us - is something we will always cherish. For that, I am always indebted.

We love you, Uncle Louie… always and forever.

I forgave everyone I feel has hurt me and my family, including myself. Bishop's sermon about forgiveness repeats in my mind, so I had no choice but to listen. I can see why there is a morning after night and sunshine after rain. There is a lesson to be learned during the dark times; and joy comes again. Only, it feels much more worth it since it requires a level of growth to accomplish it. I like to think of it as being on the potter's wheel. Sometimes, God allows us to go through the toughest times: spinning around the wheel, being molded, and then being placed in the fire, which refines us. This happens repeatedly until He sees as us fit to be a masterpiece. Not everything in life makes sense, and some things never will. All we can do is navigate the best we know how by staying aligned with our journey. Despite it all, we must remember there is always something more rewarding waiting on the other side. We just must keep going. We must get back up again.

When God says jump…

Since my decision to follow Grammy's advice, I have taken a renewed interest in media. I started back filming my television show, and I intern at a local news station. This opportunity excites me because it is the news station that I grew up watching. I am one step closer to my dream, and it feels amazing.

… Ask "How High?"

My pre-law classes have helped me to have a more insightful look into my topics in media. I aim to inspire, motivate, and empower via my media platforms. Having a knowledge of the law and its policies helps me to equip my audience with the proper tools to succeed. As I sit in class, I cannot help but think about my college experience. I remember a series of flashbacks:

Dragging a trash bag on move-in day my first year.
Pledging my sorority.
Getting my first check.
Meeting my girls Chante and Claudia.
Good times with Damari.
Campus events I have led.

Besides everything else, I founded a mentoring organization called Positivity Mentoring. We mentor students in D.C. Middle Schools by pairing them with college students. We provide workshops on confidence, academics, health and nutrition, fitness, and more. There are field trips where the youth can experience things they have never experienced before. Because I have so many siblings, I often call on the advice of my younger sisters. They help me survey what programs kids their age would find interest in.

My mentor, Pru, is the biggest inspiration for my mentoring program. She has been a moving force in my life since I was six years old. Without her, I am not sure where I would be. She always taught me valuable lessons about being responsible, no matter how young. She has opened my eyes to things I may have never seen had she not been in my life. In fact, she is one of my biggest motivators! She has read every college essay and helped tour schools. I can go on and on about my mentor's impact in my life, but words will never be enough. I give back, just as she did: by mentoring.

Thank you, Pru. I am forever indebted to you… always and forever.

The doors to the classroom fly open. Students flock out after the professor dismisses the lecture. Me and about seventy other classmates squeeze out the two sets of double doors. Looking around, I notice many familiar faces - ones I have witnessed grow over the past four years. It still has not sunk in that I am close to achieving my dream. I am close to becoming a first-generation college graduate!

The sky is the limit.

My family, Chante, and I are in my dorm room. My friends are still unaware my family stays with me, so Chante assumes everyone is just visiting campus. I sit braiding Kayla's hair, blasting Tupac while drinking a glass of wine and chatting with Chante, who is sitting across the room. We are feeling good, so crack jokes on each other.

"Girl, I think he may be the one for me. He's fine, smart, super protective, and so masculine. I just feel like a delicate little flower when I'm with him," I giggle.

"Girl, I'm glad you found Romey Rome. You already know I couldn't stand Rico Suave!" Chante exclaims, sipping her glass of wine.

"Mm, isn't he your friend, though?" I say.

"Nope. Not after what he did at The Spot," she says, taking yet another sip of wine.

She looks round, remembering that my family does not know about what transpired. We change the subject, continuing to talk and make jokes. Then she pulls out a handheld mirror, checking herself out. She places the mirror closer to her hair, running her fingers along her edges.

"Okay, so first, this edge control has my edges all messed up," she says, rubbing her edges.

"Aw, it's not filling in the missing pieces no more?" I laugh, parting Kayla's hair.

"Girl, no! Got my edges looking like an etcher sketch puzzle!" she yells.

"Shoot, just color it in with some eyeliner like you've been doing," I say, laughing at myself.

She rolls her eyes, swinging her hair. "Well, at least my Brazilian bundles look good."

"But your edges are still from Southeast D.C.," I laugh aloud, slapping my hand on my leg. I am quite the comedian, I know.

"Girl! You're not funny! Using my recycled jokes!" she says, rolling her eyes and sipping more wine.

"Whatever. You ought to slow down on sipping that wine. I don't have time to be escorting you home," I say.

We both laugh. Kayla holds her temples, squirming on the floor while getting her hair braided.

"My brain is exploding!" says Kayla.

She tries to get up. I sit her back down, holding her head in position with my arms.

"Keep your head still or it's going to hurt more," I say, still fighting for her to stay still.

"Ugh!" exclaims Kayla.

My phone rings. I immediately smile and get up.

"Thank you!" Kayla exclaims, running and rubbing her head.

I laugh and shake my head, walking to the kitchen for more privacy.

"Mmmm Hmmm… that must be Romey Rome!" Chante yells.

I place the phone on mute. "Thank goodness it is or else you would've gotten me caught up!" I yell to Chante.

I unmute the phone, conversing with Jerome.

"Hey, my handsome king… yes, we can do that… well, I have to finish my sister's hair, but you can come by… Ok, yes that sounds good… I'll be ready by then… love you too," I say, giggling like a schoolgirl.

"Ooh! Did you say, 'love you'? Y'all dropping the L-bomb now?" Chante yells from the living room, being all loud and nosey.

I hang up, laughing and rolling my eyes at her usual nosiness. Chante and I continue talking about everything from senior year and graduation to love and adulting. It feels good to spend time with her. She always knows how to make me laugh. For laughter is good for the soul.

There is hope in homelessness.

For an episode of my campus television show, my siblings and I shoot a video regarding the effects of homelessness. We lease a loaner camera from the campus media department to film the segment. Through it, we all become empowered that there is still hope in homelessness. Meaning, although tough times may last a while, they can end eventually. It has been close to four years since we lost our six-bedroom home. We have applied to multiple housing programs, contacted the mayor's office, and even applied to family shelters. Each one rejected us. Despite all the rejection, we know our God is bigger.

Taking a leap of faith.

While at my news internship, I sit and talk with my supervisor, MB. She is a gorgeous African American woman with brown-skin and a tall, slim, yet curvy build. Her personality exudes before she utters a single word. Since day one, I've been in awe of her, so I go to her for advice often.

I approach her desk, chatting about the usual updates: how life is going, how I like the internship, and her life tidbits. The conversation becomes so exciting that I begin to babble.

"Yeah, because my family and I have been homeless for four years," I say, continuing to chat.

"Wait a minute," says MB, "did you just say your family is homeless?"

"Oh, yes. We have been homeless for about four years now," I respond, almost dismissing it.

"Wow. You say that so casually!" she responds, amazed at my

demeanor.

"Well, it's just that we've been homeless for so long that it's become normal. I usually don't mention it," I respond.

I no longer have the same hope because I am used to rejection.

"So, wait. You run a mentoring program for the youth and come in every day smiling and being nice. And this entire time, your family is homeless?" she asks.

I nod my head, "Yes. Well, my mentor is a huge inspiration for my mentoring program."

"Wow. That is remarkable. Would you mind if we do a story on you and your family?" she asks.

"On me? Really?" I ask, taken aback.

"Yes! You are amazing! I think your story could inspire others," she says.

"Oh wow, sure! It sounds good to me, but I'm not sure how my mom would feel about it. Do you mind if I check with her first?" I ask, still shaken.

"Sure! No problem. Talk to your mom and let me know!" she says.

"Okay, I will! Thank you! I'll let you know what my mom says," I smile.

Somewhat nervous, I tell my mom the news and ask her thoughts. Much to my surprise, she agrees with no hesitation. Therefore, my family and I meet with the news station staff to give details about our story. It is amazing what happens when you jump when God tells you to. This leaves room so He can work wonders.

All one must do is take that leap of faith.

CHAPTER TWENTY-TWO
You Go First

THE TIME HAS come. My family, mentor, and I film our news segment about our lives. It highlights our battle with homelessness, my mentor's amazing impact in our lives, and my leadership on campus, including my mentoring program. They follow me around campus and have an intimate interview with my mentor. The news reporter, Ms. Parker, does an amazing job capturing our story. She scans every detail and layers it in a true storytelling format. We are happy with how she narrates our story.

To celebrate the news story, and in her usual kind gesture, my mentor Pru takes me, my mom, and siblings out to a dining restaurant. The news story replays on television as we sit in the back room. Waiters from the restaurant come into the room. They watch the television, then look at us. Doing this a few more times, they soon realize we are the same family from the news story. They cry.

"Oh, my gosh! That's y'all. That is so amazing!" a woman cries.

She goes and gets her manager, who offers us all free ice cream. We cry and thank them for their kind gesture as we sit there basking in the moment's beauty. I have a flashback to how I got my internship with the news station.

Determined to get the internship, I would take a forty-five-minute Metro bus ride to the news station multiple times per week. Attempting to gain entry each time to no prevail. Until one day, He opened the door. I put on my best suit, reformatted my resume, and took it to the station. I scheduled an interview with the right personnel after the security guard granted me access. The rest is history. It is remarkable what can happen with a little faith, action, and perseverance.

I smile, thinking about the goodness of God. To go from watching the news to interning with some of my favorite newscasters to having a story on the channel is… mind-blowing.

I must go first.

I must blaze a new trail. I must decide which path to follow, finding a new way to create a different destiny. No one promised it would be easy or fun. Still, I am determined to blaze a new one. Since our news story aired, countless viewers have called up to the station. They inquire about updates on our story, and offer a variety of resources: food, mentorship, and more. I have received multiple offers for speaking engagements, including speaking in front of churches, teachers, students, and social workers. They also invited me to a youth retreat where I held workshops for young girls. The beautiful part is, five of my younger sisters - Sabrina, Jasmine, Neb, Kayla and Zan - traveled with me, free of cost. So many of our needs are being met with just one touch of God's grace. Had I given up, there would be no sunshine after the rain. I am grateful for a second chance.

So do not throw away your confidence; it will be richly rewarded.
(Hebrews 10:35, NIV)

My mom, siblings, and I are in my dorm room. My mom is helping the kids to complete their homework. I prepare for an upcoming presentation while also prepping for my mentoring banquet. We have six girls in our Positivity Mentoring program - all from a cheerleading squad - so we plan to use their dance skills to create a memorable show. While I am deep into work, my phone rings. It is Ms. Parker, the amazing reporter who covered our story.

"Hi, Ms. Parker!" I answer, excited to hear from her.

"Hey, Imani! How are ya?" she asks, in her usual laid-back manner.

"I am great! It's great to hear from you!" I say, waiting to hear any updates.

"I have some exciting news for you and your family!" she exclaims.

"Okay?" I ask with the hugest smile on my face.

"Many viewers have called the station asking for updates. One viewer named James S. has offered you all his 4-bedroom home for a discounted price! His home is a two-story home in Maryland. We have already checked it out, and he is legit!" she exclaims.

"Oh, wow!" I jump for joy, screaming and running all over the room.

My mother and siblings look at me, curious about what the good news is.

"That's not all!" Ms. Parker continues, "there are also charities that have offered to give you all furniture, household items, coats, clothes, and to help with money donations! How awesome is that?"

"That's so awesome! Thank you so much, Ms. Parker. We could not have asked for a better person to tell our story. You are so amazing. I cannot wait to tell my family the good news!" I exclaim, oozing with joy through the phone.

"Alright! I will call you back once I have more details. The viewer, James, wants to meet with you and your mom so you all can look at the home. If all goes well, you all will sign the lease to your new 4-bedroom home! Congratulations! You all deserve it!" she exclaims.

"Yes! Thank you again, Ms. Parker! Please tell him and everyone else we say thank you from the bottom of our hearts. We appreciate it!" I say.

"Okay, will do! We will talk soon!" says Ms. Parker.

"Talk soon!" I yell, hanging up the phone.

I jump around, screaming.

"Guess what, y'all?" I yell to everyone.

"What?" the kids yell.

"What's going on, baby?" my mom asks.

"Someone offered us a 4-bedroom home… for less than the original price! The guy, named James, wants to meet with you and me, ma, so we can go over any details!" I scream.

My mom bursts into happy tears, amazed by God's goodness through others.

"Look at God. My God!" she rejoices.

My siblings shout and celebrate. We jump for joy as one of our greatest wishes has finally come true.

Thank you, Mr. James, and all viewers who have offered your kindness to us in our time of need.

Patience is a virtue.

My mother and I meet with the new landlord, James. After touring the house, we decide to meet in a public place to sign the rental lease to our new home! I observe my mom's face as she fights tears while signing what seemed like an impossible feat. After many housing rejections, motels, relatives' houses, and nights of crying and praying, God came through for us once again. He is always on time, and this moment is no different. It is nothing short of his miracle-working power.

With God, all things are possible. (Matthew 19:26, NIV)

My grandfather, Stoney, rented a large U-Haul truck, picking us up to go to storage. As he pulls in front of us, I read the "U-Haul" name, signaling a flashback:

Stoney pulls up with the moving truck, parallel parking it along the front of our home. He gets out, stares into our faces, becoming lost in our worry. He shakes it off, hugs my mom, and begins moving our items into the truck.

I snap out of it, jumping into the truck. Excitement fills the air as we arrive at our four-year storage room. A storage room that we have struggled to pay for all this time. One that holds items we have not seen in years. As we open the door, dead rodents, insects, and foul odors greet us. Due to us being evicted, they tossed all our items into miscellaneous bags. Therefore, everything is mixed with no particular order. There is old food mixed in with clothes, photographs spilling from the bags, and broken valuables that were shattered during transport. We smile as we reminisce about old photos and keepsakes, stopping tears as the occasion overwhelms us.

It is okay to smile again.

At last, we arrive at our brand-new four-bedroom, two-story home! It has a spacious backyard, updated central air-conditioning, and sits next to an extensive field. My siblings' faces are priceless as we carry bags into what is now our new address. They immediately comment on the freedom we now have.

"This is our home? Wow!" Jasmine exclaims.

"I know right, it's so beautiful!" Sabrina adds.

"Yeah. Now we don't have to ask for nobody's permission to have company," Kayla adds.

The twins run around, playing tag. They jump for joy as they find adventure in our new home.

My mother, Stoney, and Joe enter, taken aback by our new blessing.

"Wow, I'm so happy for you, Tricey," says Stoney, wiping his eye and hugging her.

"Thank you, Daddy! God is so good!" she exclaims.

They continue hugging as we all smile and tour the home. We designate bedrooms and decide where each child will sleep.

Stoney orders pizza to celebrate. We are all filled with joy and gratitude as we live in a manifested dream come true. Moments like these make the bumps in the road worth it. I cannot help but remember all the tears cried. All the times I did not have an address to put on an application. All the sleepless nights filled with hope. There is no stepping on eggshells anymore. No more uncertainty about where we will stay. No more rejection from housing programs. Thank God we did not give up. Thank God for never giving up on us.

We are grateful to have our own.

"Just Believe" rings in my head as I remember the white space. Though my memory is much fainter than before. How is my younger self so wise? I guess there is something about life that strips us of our beliefs and our pure hopes. Thank God for a second chance.

CHAPTER TWENTY-THREE
Bea-YOU-tiful

KEEP RISING. IT is official… I graduate college in a few days! This moment has felt like an eternity away. I have learned many lessons. Best of all, I have learned that all the bad things - doubt, insecurities, hesitations, and failures - have prepared me and my family for the blessings we now receive. I can only imagine if I had succeeded that day. What if I did not get a second chance? Would my family be experiencing the bliss they are now? I am certain they would one day. For sure, I would not be.

The closer one gets, the harder it becomes.

There is a famous illustration of a caveman axing his way through a tunnel. Right before he is near the end - right before he is successful at getting out of the cave - he gives up. If only he knew he was so close to his breakthrough; I am sure he would have kept going. In the same, that is what life has felt like for me. At my darkest times, I wanted to give up; I tried giving up. It felt like it would never end; like I would never make it from the cave. It was at that very place that I put my axe down, that I was the closest to my breakthrough. A few more swings - a few more weeks - and I would have made it.

I remain forever grateful for the white space. It taught me I could heal through my pain and showed me how to turn my test into a testimony. Since the talk with Grammy, the red-carpet dream has subsided. I guess my psyche is pleased that I am pursuing my path of "Motivating the Masses". I have been the most beautiful version of myself, flaws and all.

Bea-YOU-tiful… Be you to the fullest.

After applying for several jobs, they offered me a position at a top entertainment company. It is an entry level role in the legal department. I plan to use my knowledge to build an on-camera presence, informing viewers of a variety of topics. I continue to merge my knowledge in law with my passion to inspire via media.

And so, the blessings continue…

My mother and siblings rush me from campus to our new home. I grow worried thinking something is wrong. As we leave the car, I notice decorations in the backyard. So, I give them the side-eye. I am almost sure they have something up their sleeves. Yet, I am impressed, so I dare not utter a word. As we walk through the front door, everyone jumps out.

"Surprise!" they scream.

I jump back, smiling from ear to ear.

"All of this for me?" I yell, cheesing hard.

My face turns red from an over-explosion of emotion. Friends and relatives approach me, congratulating me on my upcoming college graduation. So many loved ones are here: Mama, Grammy, Stoney, Pru, Joe, Uncle Jimmy, Nylah, all my siblings, my cousins, my cousin's mentor Win, Chante, Claudia, Damari, Amir, Amari, Melvin, Uncle Louie, Aunt Tonya, Aunt May, Aunt Eva, other aunts, uncles, and more. Yes, I have a vast family! Phew! It feels good to have parties in our own home again. I see the joy all over my mom's face as she experiences welcoming her family into her home. She can now throw her own celebrations, as she takes pride in doing.

Uncle Jimmy pulls me aside.

"Hey Unc!" I shout, giving him a hug.

"Hey, little one! I am so, so proud. Congratulations, young buckaroo! My brother, I mean your father, would be so proud right now. I just know he's crying tears of joy in Heaven. Have I ever lied to you? I told you this day would come, and I would be right here with you. God bless you, little one," says Uncle Jimmy.

There is something about Uncle Jimmy that, no matter what he says, always makes me giggle. He has a way of lightening any dull moment with his encouragement, euphemisms, and life lessons. My cousin Tracy and her husband David, who is also as close as family could get, approach us. We all hug and catch up, laughing about random stories and family drama.

I look toward the corner of the room to see Grammy crying, something I have rarely seen her do. I head to comfort her, but my mom, Stoney, and Aunt Eva beat me to it. So, I turn and enjoy the party. Everyone continues approaching me with gifts and positive energy. Damari, Chante, and Claudia hand me their gifts.

"We did it!" Damari exclaims, getting the entire party hyped.

"Yes, D!" I celebrate with him, jumping up and down.

Us four celebrate with a group hug. It feels good to see my friends again. From freshman year to senior year, we have only grown stronger in who we are to one another. I hope our bond transcends beyond college, and that we always support each other's losses and wins.

"See, y'all trying to have me crying!" I say, waving my makeup to be sure not to mess it up.

In walks a beautiful surprise - it is Jerome with his son, Jerome the third, in whom I have nicknamed J3. He is the cutest little thing - two years old and filled with questions, curiosity, and lots of personality. My mother calls him her "Happy Baby". I become overwhelmed with emotion as they walk through the door. I hug J3, then give his dad a big kiss, embracing his warmth. To have their support at a time like this is indescribable.

Although my mom and siblings have met them, it is their first time meeting my entire family at once. I become more in love with Jerome as I watch him interact with everyone. Family means the world to me, so it is beautiful to see how well he blends in with my loved ones.

We all head to the backyard where Stoney, Uncle Jimmy, and Tony are taking turns on the grill. Hip-hop and Go-go are playing while everyone gets down on the dance floor. Fabo, Mindy, Walter, Keisha, Tracy, David, and Kevin start a dance battle. I do not know who made them a dancing team, but I am entertained. We beat our feet, erupting in laughter.

I walk Jerome and J3 to the grilling area to make proper introductions.

"Hey y'all, this is my future hubby, Jerome, and his miniature, Jerome the third. I call him J3," I say with the biggest smile on my face.

"It's nice to meet you, young man. Take care of my Pebbles, okay?" says Stoney, extending his hand.

"Always. I got her 1000%," Jerome responds, giving a solid handshake.

They all make proper introductions.

Then here comes Uncle Jimmy. "Alright, young buckaroo, I don't want to hurt nobody, alright? I'm an old man now, but I will still protect my Niecy."

"I got you. She protected on this end," Jerome responds.

I laugh to myself, shaking my head. We all try not to laugh as Uncle Jimmy continues his usual tangent.

"Where's my Bible? Aye, Tony! Go get my Bible for me... I gotta give this Champion and Championette a word. Have I ever lied to you, little one?" he asks me.

I chuckle. He asks me this every time we talk, and I love it.

"No, Unc. Not that I know of!" I respond.

He motions for Tony to grab his Bible; he runs instead.

Uncle Jimmy shakes his head in utter displeasure. "That's the problem with y'all young people nowadays, always running from the truth," he fixes his glasses. "Alright then. Let me play a song for you."

He grabs his drink from the table.

"No!" we all scream at once.

"Oh, y'all going to do me like that? I may be drunk, but I'm not a fool!" he says.

We all burst into laughter, shaking our heads. He laughs along with us as we continue to celebrate together as one. The party turns into an Oldie but Goodie vibe, as the back-in-the-day songs begin. Stoney hand dances with Grammy; and Joe dances with my mom. Me, Jerome, and J3 dance together as well. This is a beautiful moment in my family, and I am grateful to have them experience it with me.

It is nearing the end of the cookout when my four-women tribe approach me: my mother, Grammy, Mama, and Pru. They say it takes a village to raise a child. These ladies are the true definition of a just that. Together, they have taught me strength, poise, beauty, grace, perseverance, logic, and being an overall extraordinary woman. We are all talking while Jerome and J3 are chatting with the guys.

"So, sweetie. How does it feel to be an almost-college grad?" asks Pru.

I smile, overtaken with joy and excitement, "It feels so great, Pru! I can't believe that I made it to the finish line!"

"We are so proud of you, sweetie. Even though things have been difficult, you persevered. We could not have asked for a smarter and more loving girl," she says, pinching my arm.

I smile like I do with Pru. She always boosts my spirit with her sweet and genuine energy. She has a way with people that I cannot explain.

"Yes, we are, Missy Gorgeous. You keep being great out there! And what did I tell you?" Mama asks.

"Never let anyone put their junk in my trunk," I answer, snickering.

We all laugh.

"Correct, Missy. Don't you do it, and you will go far!" she says, patting me.

"I see you followed your calling and changed your path back to media," Grammy says, smiling.

"Yes, Grammy. Your advice meant the world to me and was right on time, per usual. It's like doors have been flying open since then. Thank you so much," I respond.

She gives me a hug, rubbing my back, "Oh, and remember… I want you to strut across that stage like you own it, honey!" She snaps her fingers in a z-formation.

"Yeah, go up there and show them who's boss!" Mama adds.

"That's right! I want you to go on that stage and show them who you are. Shine bright, my Gorgeous One!" my mom adds.

We all giggle as they agree.

"Thank you all for sticking by me. I know I scared you some months ago. You could have listened to medical advice and removed me from life support. But you did not. You gave me a chance. For that, and more, I owe you the world. You're my village, and I could not have asked for a better four-women tribe," I express, near tears.

"I love you," I continue, wiping tears from my eyes.

"Aww," they say, pulling me into the center of a group hug.

"We got you, always, Gorg. Keep shining, baby," my mom whispers.

We continue hugging, then disperse as they give me more diva tips, and future notes for succeeding in the adulting world. In this moment, every part of my journey has been worth it. I have everyone here that matters to me. Well, except for one.

There is one other person I need to visit.

The day before my graduation, Jerome comes with me to visit my father's gravesite. We place flowers near his headstone as I voice all my concerns to him. I tell him about the good news and how I wish he were here to experience it. I reminisce about my cherished moments with him.

"Thank you for telling my heart the truth, DaddyO. If it were not for you, I do not know how I would have made it out of my coma. Maybe I would be on the other side, experiencing the milk and honey of the promise land with you. Then again, maybe not. I am not sure what happens when you give up. Like, would I still have access to Heaven's gates? All I know is, had it not been for you, I would have given up a long time ago. I would have chosen my false sense of peace over the true peace I experience now. And for that, I thank you," I say.

Tears pour down my face. Jerome pulls me in closer for comfort.

I continue, "For so long, I held anger in my heart. I was so angry at them for hurting you. For wishing ill on you! I was angry at the nurses. Angry at the doctors. I was angry at every person who I felt had ever harmed you. I was ready to go to war with everyone who I felt caused me to lose you! Then I realized… I was angry with you, too. But I was the angriest with myself. I felt your passing was my fault. Like, somehow, I could have saved you from your own transition. It took me almost losing my life to realize that your transition was just that - it was yours."

I wipe tears from my eyes.

"I'm proud of you, My Warrior. My First Love. My DaddyO. You showed us all that unconditional love is possible, down to your very last breath…. I wish you were here with me. You can't walk me down the aisle. I'll have your grand babies without hearing the excitement in your voice; telling me 'About time!'" I laugh.

I take a pause, wiping tears from my eyes. Taking deep breaths.

"I hate being without you, DaddyO. I just want to make you proud," I cry.

I giggle, exhaling all the emotions I feel. I wipe my face, grabbing onto Jerome's arm.

"I brought my man along with me. This is the man I hope to marry and give him some more babies someday," I say, giggling and looking at Jerome. He grins, kissing me.

He clears his throat, touching my dad's headstone. "Mr. Jones, I want to say thank you for raising such a beautiful woman. She is the true epitome of beauty, grace, class, and essence. Sorry I did not get the chance to meet you in the natural realm. I want you to know that your baby girl is safe with me. I promise to protect her heart, her love, and her future. I will never let her fall or spend one night alone. And I promise to protect our children - your grandchildren - and show them the value of a good man in the house, just as you did. Thank you, Mr. Jones. I hope you rest in peace," says Jerome.

Tears stroll down my face as I lean on Jerome, laying my head on his shoulder. He rubs my back and pulls me in closer for a hug.

"You okay, beautiful?" he asks, kissing my forehead.

"Yes, love. I'm okay," I answer.

I wipe my eyes, then squat down, touching my first love's headstone.

"It took me a while to accept your peace, but now I know you live forever in my heart. Please tell me you're here. I need to know you will be with me when I walk across that stage," I say, wiping tears.

My tears stream like never before. It feels as if a river is coming out, cleansing every wound in my soul. I remember flashes of my first love, my warrior, my DaddyO:

His charming smile.
His famous two-step.
How he listened to slow music while cleaning and singing out of tune.

His amazing, warm hugs that melted all my worries away.
His big juicy kisses that made me squeal, though I loved them.

Then I think of all the things my father will not be here for:

My college graduation.
To walk me down the aisle.
To hold my babies when I have them.
The smile on his face at the news that I'm pregnant.
Him enjoying the pleasures of life.
Him becoming whole again.

I grow quiet, listening to the breeze of the wind. Suddenly, I feel goosebumps and a cool breeze overtake my body. I hear, ever so faintly in the wind, *"I am always with you."* A tear falls from my eyes as I feel peace and harmony overtake my heart and soul.

As a river streams down my face, I whisper back, *"I will never stop loving you, DaddyO. I miss you."*

I hold my hand close to my heart, inhaling all love I have for my dad and exhaling any pain and regrets. With the wind, I let go of dreams unrealized, accepting the fact that he will be here in his own way. It pierces my soul to accept his departure. I curl up; then I remember… *I must cry with my head up.* So, I lift my face to the sky, allowing each tear to become cold as the wind blows on my chilled cheeks. It feels I have a million more words to say, so many more emotions to feel; but none will ever be quite enough. My father is no longer here to wrap me in his arms, so I must stay in tune with his spirit. With his essence.

If Heaven were a mile away, I would go to be in your embrace.

You will forever be in my heart,
My Warrior. My First Love. My DaddyO.
I love you… always, forever, and beyond that.

The day has come! The day in which I have traveled the most tiresome journey to achieve. A day I had given up on. Here we are, celebrating our commencement on D.C.'s monumental National Mall. The mall is full of hundreds of graduates decked in caps and gowns; and three times the family and friends here to support. It is a beautiful day, as the sun shines with just enough ray of light. The birds are chirping, and the atmosphere feels peaceful.

I am a designated speaker for today's ceremony, so I am walking to the stage with the honorees. The news channel is here to capture the moment I graduate from school. I stand in line, prepared to walk to the stage, looking into the crowd. The camera man smiles and waves at me, signaling for me to wave at the camera as I walk by. I walk down the aisle in my navy blue BKU cap and gown, passing hundreds of people and waving at the camera along the way. This is truly a God-sized moment! Something I would have never imagined.

The ceremony begins. When it is my turn to speak, I strut to the center of the stage, just as Grammy directed. I look around at the crowd, which looks like tiny specs because of the amount of people in attendance.

I begin my speech.

"Bradford Kingsley University. The late, great Tupac Shakur once spoke about the rose that grew from concrete. One who blossoms no matter the circumstance they stem from. How dare the baby who fed from government cheese grow up to aspire to be more? I'll tell you how—it is the audacity to believe and persevere toward one's dreams.

When a baby learns to walk, it secures its feet onto the floor and attempts to step forward. With repetition, error, and courage, the baby will progress to walk on its own. Similarly, you have secured your education and have advanced to your next step: graduation. You may encounter obstacles, nervousness, and fear along the way, but you must remain courageous in your journey to guarantee achievement.

You are amazing. Your story is powerful. You have a prominent education. Your drive is unparalleled. We are a diverse group of individuals united, stemming from various backgrounds. This moment is proof that you are capable of greatness. However, do not become complacent in this victory. There is more work to be done.

On August 28, 1963, citizens from all over the nation rallied in the March on Washington for Jobs and Freedom. Civil Right leaders such as Martin Luther King Jr. marched for equality on this very land. Fifty years later, President Barack Obama spoke to a crowd of all ethnic backgrounds — some of whom were BKU students. Do you see? We are standing in history, but we also fervently write it.

Here at BKU, we are members and leaders of organizations; we march for human rights and petition for the better good. Our intellectual drive and curiosity help to propel this nation forward and make a mark no one can erase. From BKU Inauguration to graduation, BKU never fails to remind us to give back to our communities and to prepare for our future. Every moment spent at BKU has been fundamental to the happenings of today. Every moment is a stepping-stone to something greater.

So, raise high, Kingsters! Bleed the buff and blue. Hold your head high. Despite the unforeseen circumstances that may have occurred during your time at BKU, you will thrive! Class of 2023, we are world changers! We will take a stand for succeeding generations, speak up for the speechless, and pave a path for the disabled. We will make our presence known, going beyond the call of duty to guarantee that the job is done… at least for now.

Fellow graduates—Congratulations! We did it! Smile, laugh, cry, or maybe jump for joy. Regardless of what you do, never forget that you can do anything you put your mind to! Thank you!"

The crowd stands and applauds. I glance into the audience, spotting my family in the front row: my mom, Pru, Grammy, Mama, Stoney, Uncle Jimmy, Jerome, and, of course, my siblings. I look to the other side, noticing Damari, Claudia, and Chante jumping and shouting. We turn our tassels, later throwing them in the air.

As we embrace the moment of a dream come true - an accomplishment that we have all aimed for - I turn to see my DaddyO standing next to my loved ones. His Colgate smile stretches from ear to ear, as his dimples deepen like the sea. I smile back, shedding a single tear.

He kept his promise. He made it here.

Throughout life's journey, I found my way through the storm. Although, it sometimes felt like those around me were the ones causing me to drown; in all reality, they help me stay afloat. Some may consider it an unhealthy co-dependency. However, I consider it as us helping one another out. What is the purpose of succeeding if no one makes it to the top with you? What is the use of making it through the storm if everyone else in the boat washes away with the tides?

The word "crazy" has various definitions. One can perceive it as negative or positive, depending on its connotation. For example, when I am joking around, one of my friends may laugh and say "girl, you crazy!", meaning silly.

Today, the word "crazy" is most viewed as something negative. It is sometimes used to label someone with a scarlet letter of instability, untrustworthiness, and isolation. However, may I propose a different narrative? What if one can be "crazy" because they think outside of the box? Maybe they are more passionate than most, or simply out of the ordinary. Sure, there are different spectrums to the word. I will step out even further to say we all have a little "crazy" in us. Meaning, we all have the potential to step outside of the box. We all can become more passionate than most.

Embarking on a new chapter of my life, I take a moment to remember each time I have fallen and gotten back up again:

The struggle through homelessness while in college.
The battle with clinical depression and anxiety while fighting for my wildest dreams.
Healing through the grieving process.
Navigating through domestic abuse and finding freedom to let go.

Reconstructing myself to a more improved version.
And most of all… trusting God when He says to jump.

As the graduation ceremony ends, I embrace my family. They shower me with smiles, love, and gifts. I still cannot believe we made it this far. I am excited to become the older version of myself I saw in the white space. The younger me feels free. Here is to being a rose that grew from concrete, conquering all battles that came to destroy me. I hope my thorns do not frighten. It is how I have survived the storm.

No matter what, never give up.

During life's storms, just buckle up.

Lift your shoulders and hold your head high.

Keep your faith and don't push your dreams aside.

Things can get better; for it is still possible.

And if you need a reminder…I believe in you.

You will smile again; you will find joy. Just believe.

I promise you, warrior… it is within you to succeed.

Thank you for traveling this journey with me.

I am Imani Fé Holley, and these are my Crazy Girl Chronicles.

Summary

Faith-based and inspired by a true story, *Crazy Girl Chronicles: A Vanished Hope* details the journey of a homeless first-generation college student and her many battles in the fight to succeed. Outlined with raw storytelling and poetry, it divulges the challenges of homelessness, mental health, love, and the determination to exceed beyond expectations. Based in Washington, D.C.

It follows the life of Imani Fé Holley, a homeless first-generation college student who attends an Ivy League school on a full scholarship. The odds rise against her when family conflict arises, deeming her responsible for her five younger siblings. Can she balance academics, love, her job, and raising children all while trying to keep her sanity? Will this sweet, resilient girl become bitter and cold?

We get a glimpse into the life of an extraordinary young woman who is unique, yet relatable to many. Stuck in between two worlds, she attempts to battle depression, grief, poverty, and the fear of success with a happy polka face - rarely letting even those closest to her see her sweat. Ultimately leaning onto her faith in God to get through, she is determined to never give up, no matter the odds stacked against her.

Asianna "Imani Fé" Joyce

Asianna Joyce, professionally known as Imani Fé, is the author of the new faith-based fictional novel, *Crazy Girl Chronicles: A Vanished Hope*. She is also a poet, public speaker, real estate agent, entrepreneur, actress, and purpose coach who lives in Los Angeles, California. She speaks on the issues of poverty, homelessness, the stigma of mental health and more. Through her platforms, she aims to empower, inspire, and enlighten, as she believes everyone has the potential to succeed. Born and raised in Washington, D.C., she is the eldest of fourteen children. Stemming from a large, close-knit family, she takes pride in blazing new pathways for others. She is determined to defy statistics by rising above an impoverished background, pushing toward success - just as a rose grown from concrete. Her goals are to lend a voice for the voiceless, and to motivate the masses.

So do not throw away your confidence; it will be richly rewarded.
Hebrews 10:35 (NIV)